THE ULTIMATE LOVE

A SPIRITUAL ROMANCE

CARLA VICTORIA WALLACE

To: Madelyn
~ Great co-worker & friend ~
Love & Blessings!
CVW

Peace in the Storm Publishing
Giving Your Soul a Rise, One Page at a Time

PUBLISHER'S NOTE

The Ultimate Love a Spiritual Romance
Copyright © 2015 Carla Victoria Wallace

ISBN: 978-0692722541

Although the author and publisher have made every effort to ensure the accuracy and completeness of information contained in this book, we assume no responsibility for errors, inaccuracies, omissions, or any inconsistency herein.

PEACE IN THE STORM PUBLISHING, LLC.

P.O. Box 1152
Pocono Summit, PA 18346
Visit our Web site at
www.PeaceInTheStormPublishing.com

Acknowledgements

To my Lord and Savior, Jesus Christ, without You, none of this would be possible. You are the reason why I write. Thank You for blessing me with the gift of the pen.

To my husband, Dave. You've been supportive and understanding while I pursued this new direction in my life. Thank you for believing that I could do this before it was even done. I love you.

To my parents, Carl and Deborah Caulley, I am eternally grateful to you for your unconditional love and support. I learned so much from you. I love you and I thank you. To my in-laws, Ivor and Iolene Wallace, thank you for loving me and accepting me as your own. To my sister-in-law, Marcia, your kindness is refreshing. I hope we will grow closer as the years go on. To my brother-in-law, Ivor, thanks for being someone that we can always count on. To my grandmother, Daisy Caulley, and the memory of my grandmother Lillian Edwards who both gave me love and wisdom over the years, I am grateful. To my very large extended family of aunts, uncles, and cousins. If I listed you all by name, I would have to add another chapter to this book. But you all know who you are, and I love you all. Thanks for all of your prayers. A special thanks goes to Elisha and Norelle who read this book before it was published and gave me immediate feedback. I appreciate your support.

To Elissa Gabrielle, the founder of Peace In The Storm Publishing, thank you for helping me take my dream to the next level. To the many authors from each imprint of the Peace In The Storm Publishing umbrella, I sincerely appreciate the mutual support we show one another.

To the friends, acquaintances, and co-workers who have supported me over the years, though I haven't listed you each by name, you all hold a special place in my heart. To the students who I have taught, seek God for your purpose and calling, and don't give up on your dreams.

To all the readers, just to know that you are reading this book is humbling. I hope you enjoy it.

From the heart,

Carla Victoria Wallace

A note to the readers: Some of you who are reading this may consider yourself a spiritual person, while others may not. Regardless of your beliefs, my request as you read this novel is that you read it with an open mind, but most of all an open heart.

CHAPTER 1

"I'll take you up on that"

"I'M SO GLAD YOU COULD COME!" Jada said as she hugged Tonya in the lobby of Consecration Christian Church.

After warmly ending their embrace, Jada and Tonya began to follow the rest of the congregation out of the church exit doors. Someone seemed to follow behind them. In the corner of her eye Jada saw a tall, slightly-tanned, muscular white man trailing their steps. She had to keep herself from staring at this handsome, cleanly shaven man who still seemed to be closely following their lead.

"I really enjoyed Pastor John's message on hearing from God," Tonya began. "I never really heard anyone break it down that way…"

Jada was trying to listen to Tonya share her thoughts, but the man that seemed to be increasing his proximity to them made Jada have to interrupt.

"Tonya, either you've forgotten to introduce me to your friend or somebody is trying to get your attention," Jada whispered in Tonya's ear.

Tonya stopped and turned around. "Oh!" she exclaimed. "I'm sorry, Pete! I thought you went to the car already." Tonya apologized. "Jada, this is my brother Pete. Pete, this is my friend and co-worker, Jada."

Pete extended his hand and looked at Jada with light brown eyes. "It's nice to meet you."

Jada shook his hand, "It's nice to meet you too," she greeted through a polite smile. Jada gently released Pete's hand and looked at Tonya thoughtfully, "Why didn't you call me to tell me you were coming?"

"I called you this morning," Tonya answered, "but it went straight to voicemail. So I figured I'd just wait for you in the lobby." Tonya glanced at her brother, "Where'd you go Pete?" she inquired. "You said you were going to warm up the car."

Pete smiled, "Yeah I got sidetracked when I saw the media stand. I went to pick up a CD of the message."

"Well, you both will have to come to my mother's house for dinner," Jada beamed at the thought of getting together with her extended family for their traditional Sunday meal. "Tonya, I mentioned to my mother that you might be visiting my church today, and she invited you to join us for dinner. I'm sure Pete is welcome too. The whole family will be there."

Tonya looked at Pete inquisitively, "You want to go?"

Pete stuck his hand into his pocket and jingled his keys a little, "Sure. We can follow you Jada. My car's right over here," he pointed to a cranberry Maxima a few steps away from them. They all proceeded to walk toward his car.

"That's my car right there," Jada pointed to the silver Honda Civic parked three spaces away. "We should be there in like ten minutes."

Jada started her car and pulled out of the church parking lot with Pete and Tonya following behind her. Piles of dirty white snow lined the sides of the road from the latest snowfall. As she drove under the cloudy February sky, she began to wonder what it would feel like to have Tonya and Pete join her family for a soulful meal. Sometimes Jada's grandmother would have a craving for chitterlings, and the smell would hit her nose before she even walked through the door. How awkward would it be to explain to them that today pig intestines was on the menu? The rancid smell of chitterlings made Jada sick to her stomach. She couldn't look at them, let alone try them. However, according to her grandmother, they tasted much better than they smelled. Even so, Jada hoped that today the meal would be something a little more aromatically friendly.

Having arrived at her parents' house, Jada parked her car in the driveway. Pete pulled his car up to the curb. They exited their vehicles and simultaneously walked toward the front door. As Jada turned her key to unlock the door, two other cars arrived. Jada recognized her cousins Gene, Joe and Tyrese in one vehicle. The three brothers often traveled together. The other vehicle was occupied by her mother's sister Linda, and her husband Bob. They were the parents of Gene, Joe and Tyrese. Aunt

Linda and Uncle Bob had brought Jada's grandmother and Great Aunt Ira along with them.

Jada, Pete and Tonya entered the home of Jada's parents, Dana and Charles Calloway. Jada's other family members followed behind. They all stood in the large foyer and began to remove their winter gear. Jada began to collect the coats and hang them in the closet.

"It's a lot of white folks over here today isn't it?" Aunt Ira said as Jada took her coat.

"Aunt Ira. There's two white people here," Gene chimed in.

"That's what I said. It's a lot of white folks here today," Aunt Ira repeated as she sat in a chair and rested her cane beside her.

Jada assumed that Tonya must have heard Aunt Ira's comment, because she had now turned bright red. Pete was running his fingers through his hair. Jada looked at Gene and they both shook their heads. It was just like Aunt Ira to say whatever was on her mind. Coming from the south, back in the 1950s, two white people over for Sunday dinner was a lot of white people.

"Hello, everyone!" Dana emerged from the kitchen with her hair tied back, and a potholder in her hand. "I'm glad you all could join us," she said with a bright smile.

Tonya and Pete smiled politely as Jada went around the foyer introducing each of her relatives. One by one the family members began to migrate to the family room after they were introduced.

"It smells good, Mrs. Calloway," Pete announced. "You must be doing your thing in that kitchen."

"Yeah, thanks for inviting us," added Tonya.

"Oh, you're welcome," Dana waved her hand toward the family room. "Ya'll have a seat and make yourselves comfortable."

Jada, Tonya, and Pete joined everyone in the large seating area. Aunt Ira was staring out the window, and Grandma was already getting herself an afternoon nap in a chair. Uncle Jack, the brother of Jada's mother, had arrived earlier and was watching a basketball game on T.V.

"So you visited Jada's church today?" Uncle Jack asked looking over to the couch where Tonya and Pete were sitting. Uncle Jack was one of the coolest uncles one could have. He was thirty-seven years old, but due to his fit body and high energy, he could fit in with any college crowd.

"Yes," Tonya said cheerfully.

Pete nodded, "We were a little late, though."

"What did you think?" Uncle Jack asked.

Tonya paused for a moment, "I grew up Catholic, so it's different than what I'm used to, but I enjoyed it. Everyone seemed so…happy!" she smiled.

A thoughtful look appeared on Pete's face. "It's a lot like the church I was going to out in California," he said.

"Oh, you're from California?" Gene looked at Pete with raised brows.

"Well I moved there after college, but now I'm back in Connecticut," Pete explained. "I just got hired to teach math at the high school."

"Good for you," encouraged Uncle Jack.

Suddenly, the smells of barbecued chicken and macaroni and cheese began to travel throughout the room. While everyone sat patiently watching the athletes run back and forth on the court, Jada began to think as she sat on the chair across from Tonya and Pete. Pete seemed so comfortable around her family. He had already begun to engage in a conversation about sports with Gene and Uncle Jack. The masculine adrenaline was running high as they commented passionately about the televised basketball game. If it weren't for Pete's tanned ivory complexion, one would have thought he was one of the family. The sound of her mother's voice interrupted Jada's thoughts.

"The food is ready," Dana announced.

Everyone gathered in the kitchen. The counter was filled with chicken smothered in barbecue sauce, cheesy macaroni, dark collard greens, fluffy mashed potatoes with gravy, and golden corn bread. Jada's father blessed the food. He thanked God for providing them with food, having a loving family, for meeting all of their needs, and for the presence of friends. Everyone said, "Amen," and went off to fill their plates.

Throughout dinner, Jada found herself drifting from conversation to thoughts of Pete. He seemed to fit in so well as he engaged in the various side conversations that took place around the dinner table.

"I was stationed in Long Beach, California back in my navy days," Charles lifted his glass and looked at Pete. "Did you live in that area when you were out there?"

Pete finished chewing and wiped his mouth. "No, I lived in San Francisco."

"Did you teach there?" Charles inquired.

"I had an engineering job there," Pete explained. "But after working at a desk for five years, I got kind of bored. I started looking on-line for high-school mathematics teacher openings, because I really enjoy math. I did some tutoring in college, so I figured I have some experience. I saw an opening right here in Connecticut. I took a flight out in December on vacation, visited the school, and substituted there for three days. On the third day, they asked me if I'd be interested in the position permanently, and I took it."

"Isn't it strange to get hired in December?" Charles asked.

"Well the teacher was pregnant, and she decided to leave teaching to raise her family," Pete explained.

Charles nodded, "That makes sense. So how do you like being back in Connecticut?"

"It's great!" Pete smiled. "I tell you, when I was out in California, one of the things I missed the most was getting soul food combos from Mama's Place and beef patties from GoldenKrust."

Jada immediately looked up from her plate to glance at Pete. All the times Jada had gone to Mama's Place, the popular soul food restaurant, she'd never seen anyone white in there.

"But if you want the best beef patties, you have to go to New York," Uncle Jack suggested.

"I'll have to remember that," Pete replied. He shifted his eyes to Dana. "Mrs. Calloway, I have to tell you that the food is excellent."

Dana beamed, "Well, thank you!" You and Tonya are both welcome here anytime." She stood up and pushed in her chair. "Excuse me, I'm just going to get started on clearing up the food."

Jada looked at her empty plate, "I'll help you, Mom," she offered. She picked up her plate and followed her mother into the kitchen.

"Pete seems really nice," Dana said to Jada. "Are they from around here?"

"Well Tonya has an apartment in this area now, but they grew up near the Massachusetts line."

"I didn't think many blacks lived up that way, but the two of them seem like their black in white people's bodies," Dana chuckled. "I was floored when Pete said he missed Mama's Place and beef patties. And the way Tonya cleared her hefty plate, I know she loves soul food."

"Yeah." Jada pulled a large plastic container out of the cabinet. "Tonya says that when she grew up, a lot of her closest friends were black."

As she silently piled leftover food into the container, memories of her own past began to flood Jada's thoughts. Although she was now twenty-seven, the events from her days as a child were still vivid in her mind. Throughout elementary and middle school, Jada had been the only black person in her class. She even remembered a time in childhood when she had wished that she were white. She had gotten teased because her hair didn't look like the little white girls' hair, and her butt was bigger than all of the other kids butts. That was when her parents told her to be proud of who God had made her. Jada's mother had said the children were probably just mimicking the ignorant behaviors of their parents. Her father had told her about how he had also been teased when he was in school. He was one of the first generations to go to an integrated school in the south. He knew how it was to be made to feel inferior because of the color of his skin.

Jada remembered that in the eighth grade, her history teacher had the class do oral presentations on a historical United States leader. Jada had done her presentation on Martin Luther King, Jr. She wondered if that was why the white girls gradually became nice to her. However, the boys were relentless. For a while, Jada wondered if she were attractive at all. As she matured, Jada started to find clothes that fit and complemented her lower curves. She began to appreciate the uniqueness of her figure. Although she was becoming more confident, she had developed resentment to the way white boys had treated her. She didn't care much for white guys after that. She focused all her wishes on finding a black man that would appreciate her for the beautiful black woman that she had become.

When the counters had been cleared and the last dish placed in the dishwasher, Jada wandered into the family room, and sat on the couch next to Tonya who was watching the conclusion of the televised basketball game.

"Hey!" Gene announced. "Tyrese, Joe and I are going bowling this Friday night. You guys should come," his eyes lit up as he looked from Jada to Tonya and then Pete.

"I haven't been bowling in a minute," Jada said. "I'm down," she smiled.

"I'll go too," Tonya added enthusiastically.

Gene looked at Pete. Pete was looking at the last domino in his hand. Then Pete put his last domino down winning the game. "I'll take you up on that," he said with a dimpled grin.

Jada watched Pete begin to remix the dominoes. He was moving his hands in an even circular motion when suddenly his eyes lifted and met hers. It caught her off guard. A hint of his dimples reappeared, and it seemed as if he had no intentions of removing his eyes from her face. Jada simpered uncomfortably until Pete finally refocused his attention to the beginning of their new game. Relieved that she had escaped the awkward eye contact, Jada decided to turn her line of vision to the TV.

She didn't want to read too much into anything, but to Jada it seemed that Pete had let his eyes linger on her face a little too long to call the look friendly. She sure hoped she was wrong about the way he was looking at her, because he was definitely not her type.

CHAPTER 2

Lewis Lanes

JADA WAS WASHING THE CHALKBOARD INSIDE her classroom when Tonya walked in, and sat down at the kidney shaped reading table.

"So you're definitely going to the bowling alley tonight?" Tonya asked.

"Yeah, I'm just going to go home and eat first," Jada replied. She walked to the sink and squeezed out the chalk-filled sponge. Then she sat down next to Tonya.

"I'll just go with Pete then," Tonya began absentmindedly stroking the flipped ends of her short, auburn hair.

Jada looked at Tonya. All week, she'd been looking like her thoughts were miles away. "What's got you down these days?" Jada's voice was full of concern.

Tonya sighed deeply, "I'm just really bummed out about Pete moving in with me." She rolled her eyes in frustration. "With him getting hired so last minute, he begged me to let him stay at my place until he finds a condo that he can buy."

"What's so bad about him living you?" Jada asked with a furrowed brow.

"I lived with that boy for seventeen years, sharing a bathroom with him and all that. I was so happy when I started my senior year of high school and he finally went away to college." Tonya shook her head. "I just thought the next person I'd be sharing my place with would be my man." She chuckled, "That is when I get one. I'm so tired of being single."

Jada's eyes grew wide. "I feel you, girl. I'm still waiting for my black prince to come. Where are all the good men these days?"

"I know, right?" Tonya agreed. "Well until I have a man in my life, I wanted to continue enjoying my own space." She placed her right arm on the table and began to massage her forehead. "I'm just not enjoying living with my brother again."

"You're splitting rent, though, right? Jada inquired.

Tonya released a sarcastic laugh, "Definitely!"

"Then count it a blessing." Jada also chuckled with sarcasm. "Cause we know how easy it is to live on a teacher's salary."

The tension on Tonya's face began to fade. "You're right. I should be looking on the bright side of things." She stood up and clutched her bag to her shoulder.

Jada rose to her feet, "I know what you need," she smiled at Tonya. "Some retail therapy." Jada's smile grew as she thought of the fun she and Tonya always had when they went shopping together. "We've got to plan another bargain spree."

Jada turned out her classroom light and closed the door behind them. The sound of her heals echoed down the hallway as she walked with Tonya to the exit doors.

Jada could hear the loud crash of bowling balls knocking down pins as she entered Lewis Lanes. Hip-hop music cranked over the sound system. Jada found herself walking to the beat as she headed to the front counter to rent her bowling shoes. She scanned the Friday night crowd that occupied the lanes. She saw young teenagers and rowdy college students. Then there were the bowlers who looked about her age, as well as a few older sophisticated groups here and there. As Jada looked around the alley, she could see Gene practicing at one of the far end lanes. Reaching the front counter, she handed the attendant a few folded bills in exchange for her size nine bowling shoes. Then she proceeded to join her family and friends.

As Jada approached the last two lanes, she saw Tonya sitting next to Gene and Joe. Tyrese stood aiming his ball at the pins. Pete was sitting on a step, changing his shoes. Even in the dim lighting, Jada could see the color of Pete's closely shaven hair. It was brownish-red, a trait that he and Tonya shared. The glow of Pete's copper hair complemented his complexion. Jada couldn't deny that he was a good looking man. He definitely stood out in a crowd. From her angle, she could see the dimple in Pete's cheek, indicating that he was smiling. He was talking to two brown-skinned young women seated next to him.

Jada recognized one of the women as Nicole, who she knew well. They had known each other since church youth group. Nicole had been giving Jada her Dominican blow-outs since their freshman year in college. Jada knew the other woman as Sasha. She had seen her in church every now and then. Sasha's eyes squinted as she threw her head back and laughed at something being said. Nicole grinned slightly.

Jada also recognized Fernando, Nicole's brother. He would always whip up a good plate of rice and beans when she was over their house getting her blow-out. Fernando was preparing for his practice throw.

"What's up, guys?" Jada said sitting down next to Gene.

"What's up J?" Gene said with his usual friendly tone. He rarely greeted Jada by her full name. "We're just doing some practice throws. You should go next."

"Man, do I have to?" Jada replied looking for sympathy. "I told you, I haven't been bowling in a minute! It's probably been like five years." She pleaded .

"Too bad. You're going," Joe said with his famous teasing smirk on his face.

Jada laced her shoes and waited for Fernando to complete his throw. Pete was still chatting with Sasha and Nicole. Sasha's eyes were fixed on Pete, as Nicole watched Fernando's ball coast down the alley and scatter every pin.

"All right!" Nicole shouted as she and Fernando smacked hands to celebrate his strike.

That was going to make her look real good, Jada thought sarcastically as she stood up to get her ball.

"Come on, Jada!" Nicole said in her sweet, cheerful voice.

"Once a cheerleader, always a cheerleader," Jada said looking back and smiling.

"You know it!" Nicole replied. "Now throw the ball. We ain't got all night."

Jada swung her right arm, and released the ball. She stood there frozen and watched her ball hit the wooden floor and roll straight into the gutter.

"That's all right, girl. Try it again," Nicole shouted.

Jada picked up another ball and stood in the center of the lane. She focused her eyes on the middle pin and slowly swung her arm. Her ball hit the center of the lane and slowly picked up momentum. She got a little excited, until the ball took a detour and entered the gutter for the second time.

"You'll get it next time," Nicole cheered.

Jada turned around feeling very embarrassed. She could see Pete looking directly at her. She had hoped everyone was too busy talking to notice her poor bowling skills.

"Jada," Pete called from his seated position.

"Yeah?" She stopped next to him.

Pete stood up and grabbed a ball. "When you throw your ball, it always goes to the left. Try standing more to the right when you throw the ball, and it probably won't go into the gutter."

"Oh, okay. Thanks," Jada smiled somewhat timidly. She was surprised that Pete had been watching her closely enough to see what she may be doing wrong.

Pete's dimples appeared as he smiled back at Jada before turning to practice his throw.

Jada sat down and watched as Pete aimed the ball. He took three giant lunges forward, and threw one of the fastest curved balls she had ever seen. His ball hit the pins sending them flying in each direction before both the ball and all ten pins disappeared. Then it was Tonya's turn. Tonya did a ball between the legs throw, managing to get seven pins down. Sasha and Nicole knocked down nine pins each. Gene, Joe, Tyrese, and Fernando threw strikes. Then it was back to Jada.

Taking Pete's advice, Jada began her throw from the right side of the lane. To her surprise, she knocked down seven pins on her first throw. Then she clipped two more pins on her second throw for a total of nine pins.

"You go, girl!" shouted Nicole.

Jada flashed a cheesy smile and danced back to her seat. As she neared her chair, she caught sight of a tall, slender man with almond brown skin, walking toward them. He was wearing tan Timberlands, light blue relaxed fit jeans, and a loosely fitting tan sweater. A brown leather jacket fell just below his waste. He held a cell phone to his left ear. A crease appeared above his brow as he stopped in his tracks to respond to the person on the other end of his phone.

Jada studied his face. Where did she know him from? Before she could begin her trip down memory lane, the subject of her attention closed his phone and walked straight to Gene.

"Mike, you made it, man," Gene said as they clasped hands to greet each other.

Mike Jenkins, from Jordan Baptist? Jada had attended Sunday school with him until her family started going to Consecration Christian Church. It had been over ten years since she'd last seen him. Time sure had been good to him! He was looking good! Jada decided to wait and see if he remembered her.

Mike greeted Joe, Fernando and Tyrese with the same friendly gesture he used to greet Gene. He gave a quick nod to acknowledge Sasha and Nicole. Then Gene introduced Mike to Pete before turning to face Tonya.

"Mike, this is Tonya, Pete's sister," Gene announced.

Mike shook Tonya's hand and flashed a bright, flawless smile.

Gene continued his introductions, "And this is"

"Jada?" Mike interrupted with a widening smile. "Little, Jada Calloway?"

"That's me," Jada replied. "Just not so little anymore."

Still smiling, Mike stepped back and looked at Jada. "You look good, girl," He said stroking the thin line of hair that ran from his sideburns to his chin.

"Thanks," Jada replied with a nervous grin. She lowered herself into the seat she had occupied throughout the night.

Mike sat right next to Jada, and placed his bowling shoes on the floor. Then he leaned over, and slipped the shoes onto his feet. "So how long has it been, Jada?

"We left Jordan Baptist when I was twelve. I'm twenty-seven now."
Jada looked at Mike thoughtfully. "That would make it fifteen years."

"That's right. "I was a freshman in high school when your family left."

"So that means you're going to be thirty this year!" Jada said with a
teasing smirk on her face.

"Don't remind me," Mike groaned. "So, what have you been up to
lately?" he asked, glancing at Jada.

"I've been teaching. That's about it," replied Jada. "How do you know
Gene?"

"I work with him," Mike said leaning to the side in his chair to look
at Jada.

"For real?" Jada's voice rose in curiosity, "Doing what?"

"I teach physical education at the high school," A proud grin appeared
on Mike's face. "I just started coaching varsity basketball this year too.
Some of my students said Gene is their favorite teacher. They said they
never liked History until they took his class."

Jada squinted in thought. "How long have you been teaching there?"

"This is my first year. I was teaching at the middle school before. I love
coaching, though. It's been my dream." Mike looked around the bowling
alley, and then looked back at Jada. "So what grade do you teach?"

"First," Jada said, nodding her head. "They're cute, but they're a
handful, too."

Mike smiled, and kept his eyes fixed on Jada. Then Gene walked up to
them, clapping his hands.

"All right, Mike," Gene said. "I'm not trying to break you guys up or
anything since it looks like you two are having some kind of moment, but
we gotta get this show on the road. Practice is over, you're up."

Mike stood up, and grabbed a ball. With two swift steps and a swing
of his right arm, he whipped the ball down the lane. Both the ball and the
pins performed a disappearing act as they instantly vanished from site.

Mike let out a bass filled, "Yeah!" as he pimped back to his seat.

Jada was up again. She grabbed her ball and took her position. She
made sure she was standing slightly to the right as she prepared to take

her throw. For some reason, she found herself even more nervous about keeping her ball out of the gutter. She released her ball and watched it coast from the right side of the lane to the center. The ball hit the center of the pins giving her a split. She had two pins to knock down on opposite sides of the lane.

As Jada turned around to get her second ball, she was surprised at what she saw. Sasha was picking at her shoulder length hair while talking to Nicole and Tonya. Fernando seemed to be entertaining the guys. Rather than looking at Fernando, both Pete and Mike had their eyes on her.

Not liking to be the center of attention, Jada quickly stuck her fingers into a red ball, and turned toward the pins. How was she going to get these pins down?

"Stay to the right!" She heard Pete shout.

Jada repositioned herself to the right of the lane, walked forward, and swung her arm. The ball hit the wood and began to pick up speed as it rolled to the left side of the lane. Jada slapped her hands to her face thinking for sure that the ball was going straight for the gutter. The ball continued to drift left. As it picked up speed, it managed to hit the left pin before it could reach the gutter. The pin fiercely slid to the right, and knocked the last pin out of sight.

"What?" Mike shouted. "Jada, you got skills!"

"Yeah right." Jada rolled her eyes. "You should have seen me twenty minutes ago."

That throw seemed to set the tone for Jada. She began to consistently knock down nine to ten pins each time. She also rolled two strikes in the last frame.

When the final frame was completed, the scores were pretty close. Mike was the top bowler with a score of 297. Pete came in at a close second scoring 292. Gene and Fernando tied for third with a score of 280. Sasha was hot on their trail all night, ending her game with a 278. Nicole had also shown her competitive edge with her score of 251. Jada surprised herself when she managed to finish with a score of 225. Tyrese, Joe and Tonya ended up having the lowest scores.

While everyone began to grab their belongings, Tyrese and Joe sat staring at the scoreboard. They seemed to be in shock over the bad night they both had. Each of them barely beat Tonya, who was the true amateur of the group. Joe threw a 130, and Tyrese finished with 119 which made Tonya's 101 look pretty good.

"I'm just happy I bowled over 100!" Tonya announced.

Tyrese and Joe let out a low groan as they sat shaking their heads.

"With scores like that," Tyrese threw his hand up toward the scoreboard in frustration, "it's a good thing I'm not going to be bowling with you guys in the league anymore."

"You're leaving the league?" Fernando asked.

"Yeah. Gene didn't tell you?" Tyrese picked up his bowling ball. "Business has been booming at the barbershop, and we got to go with the flow. Thursday's becoming a popular day for guys to come in and get their hair cut, so we don't finish our last heads 'til like 7:00. By then everyone's already started bowling."

Nicole looked at Joe. He and Tyrese were co-owners of J.T.'s Barbershop. "So you're leaving the league, too?" she asked.

"Yeah. Things are going well for us, so we got to make that money!" Joe winked at Nicole. "Now it's down to just you, Fernando, Gene, and Mike."

"Who's going to take your spots?" Nicole's face had a look of concern.

"You want to bowl on the league, Pete?" Gene asked with a pleading look in his eye.

Pete shrugged. "Sure, if you need me to,"

"Great," Gene smiled contently.

"I'll join if you think I'm good enough," Sasha offered. She stared at Gene waiting for a response.

Gene looked up at the scoreboard. "Yeah, girl. You got some fire in you. We could use that. We'll catch opponents off guard with you."

"Yeah. They'll be like, 'What's that girl gonna do?'" Fernando added jokingly.

"You'll be our secret weapon," Gene teased.

By now Sasha was grinning from ear to ear with all the praise she was receiving.

"That reminds me," Mike suddenly remarked. "We've got basketball tournaments coming up, and I might have to miss a lot of games. I want to still bowl with you guys, but I don't know how committed I'm going to be able to be."

Gene and Fernando both looked at the scoreboard in silence for a minute.

"Why don't we let Jada be the substitute?" Fernando suggested. "That's if you want to, Jada." He looked at her hopefully.

"What's that mean?" Jada asked, obviously clueless.

"It means, if I can't bowl, I'll call you, and you can fill in for me," Mike explained.

"Does that mean I'll have to be here every Thursday" Jada wanted to know.

"Only if you want to," Fernando said with a toothy grin.

Jada stood there staring at the pins for a moment. "All right. I guess it's the least I could do for an old friend."

"Thanks, Jada," Mike smiled gratefully.

"I'll put Pete and Sasha's names in as the new bowlers, and Jada as the substitute," Gene said.

With the game and conversation complete, they all began to walk to the front desk to return their bowling shoes.

"Any of you guys going to the comedy show tomorrow?" Joe asked.

"What comedy show?" Mike inquired.

"They're having a Christian comic come to our church tomorrow at 7:30 p.m.," Gene said. "Advanced tickets were ten dollars, but they're fifteen dollars at the door."

"Me and Jada already got our tickets," Nicole announced excitedly. "We 'bout to get our laugh on," she said breaking out in the old school cabbage patch dance.

"Nicole, it's not that serious," Jada said chuckling at her friend. She felt a tap on her arm and turned to see Mike looking at her.

"What's your number, so I can call you if I need you to bowl for me?" Mike took out his cell phone.

Jada gave Mike the numbers to her cell phone as he keyed them into his phonebook. She looked up at his face, admiring his full lips, and almond shaped eyes. He was no longer the skinny little kid who always needed a haircut. Now he had a little more meat on his bones and his hair was shaped up nicely. She couldn't believe it was the same Mike.

Pete stood watching Mike enter Jada's telephone number into his phone. Tonight Jada looked even more attractive than she had on Sunday. At one point during the night, Pete found himself wanting to get to know Jada better. Only Mike showed up and began dominating her time.

Pete wasn't sure he was ready to get involved with another woman yet. His ex-girlfriend, Stephanie had unexpectedly dumped him just when he thought things were going well. Memories about the way things had ended with Stephanie made him hesitant to the idea of beginning a new relationship. However, he was finding it hard to keep from staring at Jada's bright smile, and petite, curvy figure.

Looking at Jada smile made Pete want to smile too. Instantly, the urge was gone when he noticed the grin Mike had on his face as he closed his phone. Pete was beginning to wonder if Mike would use the phone number exchange as an opportunity to pursue Jada. The thought of it gave him an unpleasant feeling. If Mike was in the picture, he wouldn't stand a chance.

CHAPTER 3

The Show; The Afterparty

JADA AND NICOLE WALKED THROUGH THE church lobby toward the ladies room. Jada could hear the crowd roaring with laughter at the completion of the comedian's latest joke. She hadn't wanted to leave so close to the end of the show, but nature had called. Nicole, being the busy body that she was, offered to come along.

The ladies room was empty when Jada and Nicole walked in. The scent of Lysol hung around in the air.

"I didn't know Mike was going to be here," Jada said quietly as she searched in her purse for her lipstick.

"Girl, Mike is fine isn't he? And what's it to you that he's here?" Nicole asked with a smile and a raised brow.

Jada capped her lipstick and dropped it back into her purse. "It's nothing to me. You're the one talking about how fine he is."

"I just wish a man who looked that good would approach me for once." Nicole scrunched up her face. "The men who've been asking me out lately haven't exactly been easy on the eyes."

Jada laughed heartily. "There's someone for everyone. They'll find the right woman, and the right man will find you."

They continued to talk as they each entered a stall.

"Why didn't Tonya come tonight?" Nicole asked.

"She said she needed to cook some things for her aunt's surprise party tomorrow."

"Pete's cute, too. He seems like such a sweetheart."

"Yeah, but did you see the way he was talking to Sasha at the bowling alley last night? I think they might be into each other. I have to ask Tonya if he likes black women."

Jada exited the stall and washed her hands. She dried her hands on a paper towel and walked back over to the sink to wait for Nicole. She began repositioning her black bang with her French-tipped nails. "I need you to hook my bang up the next time you do my hair."

"No doubt," Nicole said approaching the sink.

Jada watched Nicole's thick, long black hair fall over her shoulders and around her honey-brown face as she leaned over the sink to wash her hands. Jada didn't realize that she was staring at Nicole's bouncy, smooth mane with a wishful look in her eye.

Nicole looked at Jada as she reached for a paper towel and smiled. "Your hair looks fabulous too, girl."

Jada smiled back at her friend as they exited the bathroom. Nicole knew her so well. They'd known each other since they were twelve.

Reaching the sanctuary door, Jada slowly opened it. She and Nicole tiptoed back to their seats. Jada lowered herself into her chair. Pete was sitting directly next to her on her right, and Nicole occupied the aisle seat on her left. Mike was sitting directly in front of them. Uncle Jack and Aunt Tina were also seated nearby, as well as Gene, Joe, Tyrese, and Fernando.

The comedian was in the middle of his latest joke. "...an old lady who's so loud in church, she spits in your face when she gets close to you to talk. She's so loud that if you sit in front of her, she spits on the back of your neck." The comedian began blurting out a loud, "Bbblesss the Lord! Ohhhh my Sssoul!" as the crowd continued to throw their heads back and double over in laughter.

Suddenly the comedian turned serious and said, "Take the hand of the person next to you as I minister to you for a moment. Some of you have been laughing here tonight, but you're going to go home crying, because you're hurting on the inside. I've been there. I used to perform at comedy clubs across the east coast smiling on the outside and making people laugh, but I was a mess on the inside. I had a filthy mind, filthy mouth, and a filthy heart. I wasn't saved, and I had no joy on the inside. Telling jokes gave me a temporary joy; a temporary escape from the memories of my past mistakes and pain. I was a once-a-year Christian. I only went to church on

Easter Sunday to make my momma proud. Then one Easter Sunday, the Lord said, 'Use your gift for me. I'll give you unspeakable joy.' I gave my life to Christ that Sunday, and I've been smiling on the inside ever since. God loves you, and he heals and forgives. If you want to give your life to him, right where you're standing you can pray with me..."

As the comedian prayed, Jada closed her eyes, lost in her own memories of past mistakes. She remembered her mistakes of fooling around with any cute black guy who gave her compliments and attention. Her self-esteem was so low. Then came her high-school sweetheart, Tony. The popular honey brown athlete who told her she was the finest thing in their school. He was extremely cute and very charming, and she fell for him hard. They went to the same college, where he said she would always be his woman. Jada made the mistake of becoming sexually intimate with him. Everyone is doing it, and they were going to get married anyway, she had told herself. Then she found out that there were three other girls on campus that felt the same way. Seeing that her sinful lifestyle was causing nothing but pain, Jada decided to leave Tony alone. She made the decision to rededicate her life to God. She would not be intimate with another man until wedding vows were exchanged.

As the comedian brought the prayer to a close, Jada felt a single tear trickle down her right cheek as she said, "Amen."

Then she felt a gentle squeeze on her right hand. She opened her eyes to see Pete looking at her with a concerned look in his eye. Jada quickly wiped the tear from her cheek and plastered a smile on her face.

"I'll be up here to minister to anyone else who wants to speak to me personally after the service. The pastors will be up here, too," the comedian continued. "Thank you so much for supporting me. I have some DVDs on sale in the lobby. Also check my website for the exact date of my next show. I'll be at Laugh Attack Comedy Club. I promise there'll be new jokes, and new laughs. God bless."

The crowd rose to their feet in applause as the comedian walked off the stage. Then everyone began to disperse in different directions of the sanctuary.

"That was good!" Uncle Jack said, turning to face the row where Jada was seated. "Afterparty at my house for anyone that can make it. There'll be plenty of food, if you're hungry."

"I heard that!" Fernando said. "I have a tin of rice and beans in the car."

"That'll go great with the barbecued meatballs and pasta salad I made," added Aunt Tina.

Jada's mouth began to water when she heard meatballs and pasta salad. Aunt Tina's meatballs were tangy and sweet, and her pasta salad was the best she'd ever tasted.

"I'm in," she said quickly.

After a chorus of agreement from Gene, Tyrese, Joe, and Nicole, the only people who hadn't responded were Mike and Pete.

"Man, I'd love to hang out with you guys, but I'd better get going," Pete said. "I have to get up early tomorrow to go help my dad set up for my aunt's surprise party."

"Oh, I understand," Uncle Jack replied.

"I had a nice time with you guys, though" said Pete. "I'll catch up with you next time."

Pete clasped hands with the guys before giving gentle hugs to the ladies. Then he disappeared into the crowd.

"Nice guy," Uncle Jack said with a brief nod.

"I'm hungry!" Mike announced excitedly. "Show me where to go, and I'm there."

Jada, Nicole, and Fernando followed Uncle Jack and Aunt Tina into their home. They owned a neatly maintained two-story duplex style house. The first floor had an open floor plan. When entering, the living room extended into a dining space, and then a half wall separated the kitchen. Uncle Jack was into the idea of renting out a space to help pay off their mortgage, so he purchased the duplex and rented the other side to a young couple. Then the couple began to have kids and needed more space. They moved out, and Grandma moved in.

Aunt Tina and Fernando went straight into the kitchen to arrange the food. Jada and Nicole followed to see what help they could give. Uncle Jack turned on the mounted plasma TV. The sweat on the basketball players' brows stood out through the high definition screen.

Gene walked in with a deck of cards in his hand. "You got the card table, Uncle Jack?" he asked.

"You're lookin' at it." Uncle Jack pointed to the dining room table.

Joe and Tyrese walked in and plopped themselves on the couch in front of the TV. Then, in walked Mike. From her spot in the kitchen, Jada saw him flash his flawless smile before sitting down next to Tyrese.

As Jada was taking the paper plates out of the pantry, the doorbell rang. Uncle Jack opened the door, and Grandma walked in.

"I brought your chicken," she looked over her glasses across the room.

"Thanks, Mom," Uncle Jack took the tin out of her hands.

Grandma placed one hand on her round hips, and continued to scan the room. Her salt and pepper hair was pulled into a low ponytail. Her black-rimmed glasses sat halfway down her nose. She looked from the couch to the kitchen, and back at the couch again. Finally, she said, "Where's my little boy?"

Uncle Jack just stood there with the chicken in his hands. The ladies in the kitchen were frozen in place looking at Grandma with confused looks on their faces.

Grandma's lids lowered over her eyes, and her other hand went on her hip. "I said, 'where's my little boy?'"

"Who are you talking about Grandma?" Joe asked with his eyes still fixed on the TV.

"Yeah, because last time I checked, I didn't have any kids," Uncle Jack sounded somewhat confused.

"Pete!" Grandma replied with frustration in her voice. "Where is he?"

Uncle Jack sighed. "Mom, I thought you had lost your mind for a minute there. Whew! Anyway, he has to set up for his aunt's surprise party, so he couldn't come."

Jada was still confused. She didn't understand why Grandma was so concerned about where Pete was. She'd only met him once.

Grandma dropped one of the hands from her hip. "I really liked that boy, Pete." I hope to see him around next time." She fixed her gaze on Mike. "Now, you look familiar. I'm sure I know you."

Jada walked over to her grandmother, "Grandma, that's Mike Jenkins."

Grandma smiled, "That's right. You're my friend Myrtle's grandson."

Mike stood and reached out to give Jada's grandmother a brief hug. "Nice to see you again Mrs. Benson."

Grandma's smile faded, "I haven't talked to Myrtle since she moved back to Virginia." Concern laced her face. "How's she doing?"

"She's doing good," Mike answered reassuringly.

A look of contentment replaced the concern on Grandma's face. "Well, it's getting late for an old lady like me," she said finally opening the front door to return to her adjoining home, "but ya'll have fun. Enjoy the chicken now."

A chorus of 'Good-bye's' filled the room as they watched Grandma exit the front door.

"Food's ready when you guys are," announced Aunt Tina.

Jada filled her plate with a spoonful of rice and beans, four meatballs, and pasta salad. She sat at the dining room table with Nicole and tried to watch the basketball game. She actually found herself staring at Mike more than the TV. If he weren't just a childhood friend, she could see herself being attracted to him.

Gene threw his plate away and sat back down at the dining room table. He took his playing cards out of the box and began to rapidly shuffle them. "Who's up for spades?" he asked.

Jada saw Mike look around the room as if he were waiting for someone else to respond. "What's the matter with you guys?" Mike asked. "You can't watch TV and play a game at the same time? I'll play." He pushed himself up off the couch and sat across from Jada.

Fernando came over and began to nudge Nicole out of her chair. "Move over, lil' sis," he said. "You know you're no good at spades."

Mike looked at Jada. "Do you play?"

"Yeah, I'm all right." Jada replied.

"Let's be partners then."

Jada gave a slight smile. "If you say so."

Gene dealt the cards. The four players picked up their cards and spread them in their hands. Fernando picked up a pen to write down the books each player would bid.

"I say I have five," Gene announced.

"Then I'll bid three," Fernando said while jotting the numbers down.

Just as Jada was about to make her bid, a musical tone began to fill the air.

"That you?" Fernando asked, looking at Mike.

Mike patted himself down and pulled out his cell phone as the ringing increased in volume. "Yeah," he sighed. He looked at his phone and put it to his ear.

"I'm going to go to the bathroom real quick," Gene said.

Fernando turned around and focused his attention on the basketball game. Jada only pretended to do the same. She was having a hard time keeping herself from listening to the conversation Mike was having with the person on the other end of his phone.

Mike shifted his body in his seat and turned his face to the half wall as he quietly answered the person on his phone. "I told you I wasn't going to be able to come today because I had plans…Well, I'm sorry it was last minute," his tone was abrupt. "I'll be there tomorrow…I know, I'm sorry…Just tell him I'll be there tomorrow…Ugh…" Mike closed his eyes and shook his head. "Hey!" The shortness in Mike's voice was now gone. "What are you doing up?…I'm sorry. I'll see you tomorrow, though…Me too…" Mike sighed heavily. "Really, I got to go," his tone had suddenly become sharp again. "All right."

Jada watched Mike close his phone and sit staring at it for a minute. His face was fixed in a blank stare. Jada was feeling perplexed by the conversation she had just heard. She was now very curious about who had been on Mike's phone.

CHAPTER 4

Reminiscing

JADA SAT LISTENING TO THE PRESIDENT of the PTA give her closing remarks. It was the first Wednesday in March. PTA meetings were held on the first Wednesday of each month, and Jada always made an effort to attend.

"Is there any further business?" The president stood scanning the cafeteria.

Tonya raised her hand.

"Go ahead, Miss McKnight," the president smiled and sat down.

"Thank you," Tonya smiled. "We will be finishing up our before school tutoring program in May. This year was the first year that Miss Calloway and I have run the program, and we noticed that teachers are using books from the regular curriculum to tutor the kids. For the next PTA meeting, I move that we discuss a possible financial contribution from the PTA for the purchasing of books next school year."

The president rose from her seat, "It has been moved that at our next meeting we discuss a financial contribution to the tutoring program."

"I second the motion," a voice announced.

Jada glanced in the direction of the voice. It was the mother of Desiree Martin, one of the third grade girls that she tutored. Mrs. Martin made eye contact with Jada and they exchanged a brief smile.

"All in favor?" the president inquired.

All hands across the cafeteria went up.

The president leaned over and began jotting on a piece of paper. "Financial contribution to the tutoring program has been added to the agenda for next meeting." She put her pen down and pleasantly looked at the members. "This meeting is adjourned."

Jada watched as black, white and Hispanic parents began to leave the PTA meeting. Unlike the elementary school she had attended as a child, this school was racially diverse. Jada loved teaching here. She waved to a few familiar faces and walked with Tonya out of the cafeteria.

"I'm going to head home," Tonya said. "Pete and I decided to take turns cooking, and it's my night tonight."

"Pete can cook?" Jada sounded surprised.

"Yeah," Tonya smirked. "He cooks better than me. You should come have dinner with us sometime."

"Maybe I will one of these days," Jada smiled.

Tonya looked at her watch. "I'd better go. Have a good night!"

"You, too!" Jada headed down the hall toward her classroom. She planned to finish correcting some of her students' work before leaving for the night.

Jada had just sat at her desk and picked up her pen when her purse began to ring. She sighed, walked over to her purse, and took out her ringing cell phone. She didn't recognize the number displayed on the screen, but she answered it anyway.

"Hello?" she said with uncertainty in her voice.

"Jada?" a smooth voice replied.

"Yes?" Jada was still unsure.

"It's Mike." His voice was calm.

"Hey, Mike! What's up?" she asked cheerfully. "You need me to bowl for you tomorrow already?"

"Not exactly," Mike paused. "I wanted to ask if you'd like to have dinner with me tomorrow night. Then maybe you could come to the bowling alley to hang out with us."

Jada felt a quick flutter in her stomach. She couldn't believe she was getting butterflies. Finally she said, "Sure, that'd be nice."

"Okay," Mike crooned with a smile in his voice. "Where would you like to go eat?"

Jada was still too surprised to think of a single restaurant. "It doesn't matter to me. You decide."

"How about Honeybee's?" Mike suggested. "They're pretty quick with their service, and the food is pretty good."

"I like Honeybee's," Jada grinned. "That's fine with me. Do you want me to meet you there?"

"I can pick you up if you like," Mike chuckled. "I'm sure those first graders ware you out."

By now the flutter in Jada's stomach had turned into a tsunami. She stood there speechless and unable to respond.

"Is five o' clock okay?"

Finally managing to find her voice, Jada said, "That's fine." Through massively smiling lips, she gave Mike her address and hung up the phone. This was unbelievable. She had a date with her childhood friend.

Mike parked his fairly new black Honda accord next to the curb. He turned off his engine and stepped out of the car. He quickly adjusted his jeans to make sure they fell over his navy blue Timberlands just right. Then he walked up to the front door of the Calloway home and rang the doorbell. After a few seconds, Jada's father, opened the door.

"Hello, Mr. Calloway. I'm not sure you remember me. I'm Mike Jenkins."

Charles stood at the door with a thoughtful look on his face.

"I went to Sunday School with Jada at Jordan Baptist Church."

"Oh." Charles replied. "I'm sorry, I didn't recognize you." He opened the door wider. "Come in and have a seat. "I'll let Jada know you're here."

Before Mike could reach the couch, he saw Jada enter the room. She was wearing a black, fitted long sleeved shirt that accentuated her upper body curves, with dark blue jeans. She walked over to him on short, black boots.

"I'm ready." She smiled.

Mike felt himself returning Jada's smile with a big cheesy grin of his own.

"Have a nice time," Charles said.

"It was nice seeing you again," Mike said as he waved goodbye.

Mike escorted Jada to the passenger side of his vehicle. He opened the door and closed it when she was seated. Then he rushed to his side and got in.

"So," he said as he started the engine and drove away. "I see that you still live at home with your parents."

"Yeah. I moved back in with them after college five years ago to save some money. I'm actually looking for my own place now. I'm currently looking to buy a condo."

"That's smart. I bought a condo four years ago, and I love it."

Mike looked over at Jada as he pulled up to a stoplight. Her hands were resting on her handbag. He was enjoying looking at her smooth light brown skin. Her fingers looked so delicate, and her nails had a shiny glow to them. He glanced at her from head to toe. She looked as if she put a lot of time into her appearance.

"Are you high maintenance, Jada?" he asked curiously.

"High maintenance?" Jada sounded surprised. "What do you mean?"

"Do you shop a lot?" Mike prodded. "Have to wear a new outfit like everyday?"

"No, that's not me." she chuckled. "I mean I like to look nice, and I do like to shop, but I'm also kind of cheap."

Mike laughed. "Well, for someone who's kind of cheap, you look real good."

Jada smiled and looked over at him, "Thanks," she said.

When they arrived at Honeybee's, Mike parked his car and escorted Jada to the door. The hostess seated them at a booth toward the back of the restaurant. They quickly looked over the menu, and were ready to order by the time the waiter came to ask what they'd like to drink.

"I'll have a Coke, and the Honey Glazed Chicken," Jada said.

"I'll have a Coke, and the Bacon Cheeseburger," said Mike.

The young waiter jotted down their orders, took their menus, and walked away. Mike and Jada were left looking at each other underneath the dim table lighting.

"So how's your family doing?" Jada rested her hands on top of the table.

Mike looked at Jada's hands. Something about her hands was so sexy to him. He slowly moved his eyes from her hands to her face. She was looking at him intently. "They're good," he finally said. "My brother's still in the Army. He's stationed in New York now. My mom and my grandmother have been living in Virginia for almost ten years."

Jada's eyes widened. "I didn't know your mom moved down there."

Mike's face grew serious. "I think the change of scenery has been really good for her. After my dad died she started saying that she wanted to leave Connecticut."

Mike looked down uncomfortably. It still pained him to remember how his dad had died in combat while serving as a soldier in the United States Army. As a child, he was used to his dad being gone for long periods of time on various military assignments. As a military wife, his mother had been the sole parent for most of his childhood. However, the day they found out that his father wouldn't return, it had hit his whole family hard. Mike had only been twelve years old when it happened.

He felt relieved when he saw the waiter returning with their drinks. Talking about his family was making him uneasy. The waiter informed them that their food would be out in a few minutes. Mike was glad for the interruption.

Jada pinched her straw between two fingers as she began to sip her soda. "So do you still go to Jordan Baptist?" she asked between sips.

"I don't really get to go much. I'm usually visiting family in New York."

A thoughtful look came over Jada's face. "When's the last time you've been?"

Mike shrugged. "I couldn't even tell you to be honest."

"That would explain why my grandmother didn't recognize you at first. She still goes there."

Mike tried to think of something else to talk about, because he was starting to feel like Jada was asking too many questions. She'd already asked about his family and now she was asking about church. Both were uncomfortable subjects for him. Mike hadn't gone to church regularly since high school. He had let himself get distracted by the young ladies in his life. He was so busy playing the field that he didn't have time for church. Now Mike was trying to get away from his playing days, but some habits are hard to break. He thought carefully about how he could change the focus of the conversation. As he was thinking, the waiter came, placed their food on the table, and told them to enjoy.

Before Mike could voice his next thought, he heard the sound of Jada's voice.

"Why aren't you settled down with a family by now like your brother?" Jada placed a bite of food into her mouth and waited for a response.

Mike's eyes grew wide. "Me?" He cleared his throat. "I wasn't trying to settle down early like him."

Mike let out a deep breath. He knew he wasn't being honest with Jada. The truth was that he could have had a family, but he hadn't been man enough to handle it at the time. What would Jada think if she knew he had a four year old son? Mike wasn't ready to find out, so he decided to change the subject.

"That was a good spades game you played the other night. Gene and Fernando couldn't believe we beat them."

"I couldn't either."

"I don't know, Jada Calloway. Good at spades, good at bowling. I think we might end up getting real close to each other. So far we make a good team."

Mike saw the teasing smile return to Jada's face. "You sound mighty confident."

As they were finishing their food, the waiter came over and brought their check. Mike looked at the bill, and stood up to reach in his pocket for his wallet. As he searched for the right bills, he glanced at Jada. He saw her glance at his wallet with an inquisitive look in her eye.

Mike took his eyes off Jada to look down at the object of her attention. His hands froze when he caught sight of the image that was in her view.

Jada thought she saw a picture of a young woman and little boy tucked in one of the credit card slots of Mike's wallet. She did a quick mental inventory to figure out who it could be. Right when she left Jordan Baptist, Mike's older brother, John had gotten married and joined the Army like his father. Was it John's wife and son? Why wasn't John in the picture? Was he stationed oversees at the time of the photo? Was that the family Mike goes to visit in New York?

Mike quickly closed his wallet and gently took Jada's hand. "You don't mind if I hold your hand, do you?" he asked. "We used to hold hands all the time when we went on church trips back in the day. You know how our grandmothers didn't want us getting lost."

Jada thought a first date was a little soon to be holding hands, but she didn't pull away. Mike's not a stranger, she thought.

They walked hand in hand out of the restaurant back to Mike's car. Then Mike began to drive toward the bowling alley.

"Remember the trip to Playland?" Mike glanced at Jada.

Jada nodded. "I must have been like seven," she smiled slightly. "That was fun."

"We got partnered up, as usual." A grin appeared on Mike's face.

"Our grandmothers were real tight back then." Jada gazed at Mike thoughtfully. "They thought you were so protective of me."

"I remember you almost didn't get to go on the Himalaya because you were too short," Mike laughed.

"I'm pretty sure my ponytail is what really got me on." She smirked. "Then you were crushing me the whole ride!"

Jada looked at Mike and saw him begin to laugh as he leaned to the side to glance at her.

"Sorry about that." He smiled. "Guess I wasn't as protective as my grandmother thought I was."

Still laughing, Jada walked with Mike into the bowling alley. She waited for Mike to get his shoes, and then they walked to the lanes where the rest of the team was seated. Jada could see the puzzled looks on everyone's face when she came over with Mike.

"Jada?" began Gene. "You decided to come watch?"

"Yeah," Jada answered sitting down in an empty seat. She didn't offer any information as to why she had decided to come watch.

Mike didn't say anything either. They seemed to have an unspoken agreement to not mention their dinner date.

For a moment, everyone still had their eyes on Jada and Mike. Finally Gene got up to bowl. Fernando finished lacing his shoes. Sasha and Nicole went back to searching for the right balls. Pete, however, continued to look at Jada. He was still looking when Mike sat down next to her to lace his shoes. Jada was unsure of why Pete was staring at her. She avoided eye contact with him as she took her lip gloss out of her purse.

Gene was able to rescue Jada from Pete's interrogating gaze. "You're up, Pete," he said.

"All right," Pete answered as he rose to his feet with his ball in hand.

Jada noticed that Mike was turning his back to her as he took out his cell phone. She found herself straining her ears to hear what he said.

"…Yes, I'll be there tomorrow," Mike told the person on the other end of his phone. "…all right…Bye."

Jada watched Mike close his cell phone with a familiar blank stare. That must be the same person he was talking to at Uncle Jack's, Jada thought. She was beginning to wonder if Mike could be hiding something.

CHAPTER 5

Deja Vu

JADA WAS PAINTING BLACK MASCARA ON her already thick, long lashes when Mary J. Blige's Just Fine ring tone began to play from her cell phone. That meant it was Nicole calling her. She was tempted not to answer the call, because she was in a rush.

Jada had seen Nicole in church on Sunday and asked her when she could do her hair. Nicole had said she'd call her. Four days later, Jada was just now getting that call. Desperate to get her hair done, Jada picked up her phone.

"Hey, Nicole," she said flatly.

"I'm sorry for taking so long to get back to you, girl. I've been so busy at work. We just hired a bunch of new associates, and they have me training all of them," Nicole explained.

Nicole was a store manager at Marcell's, a retail chain store that sold name brand clothing at discount prices. Jada had tried to tell her that with her management skills, and her talent for doing hair, she should open her own salon. Nicole said that if she was going to do that, she wanted to do it right. That meant paying for hairdressing classes so that she could get a license. She wasn't ready to take that step of faith, yet.

"I can do your hair today before I go to the bowling alley," Nicole continued.

"I'm not going to be able to do that." Jada capped her mascara.

"Why?" Curiosity crept into Nicole's voice. "What are you about to do?"

Jada hesitated before answering, "I'm going to dinner."

"With who?" Nicole sounded surprised.

Jada hadn't had a chance to tell Nicole about her previous date with Mike. Early in the week he had called and told her that he wanted to get together again. After a lot of convincing on his part, Jada had accepted Mike's invitation to let him cook for her before bowling tonight. He had insisted that he could throw down in the kitchen. Jada wasn't sure about going to his place so soon, but she figured it would only be an hour before they would have to leave for the bowling alley. By the time they finished eating it would be time to leave. She still wasn't sure about giving all the details to Nicole just yet. Jada knew that Nicole had a tendency to jump to conclusions, so she chose her words carefully.

"I'm going to dinner with Mike," Jada cautiously said.

"Jada I'm gonna get you for not telling me this." Nicole was relentless. "Where are ya'll going?"

"Nicole," Jada added a humorous tone to her voice, "If I don't hurry up my behind won't be going anywhere. I'll tell you about it later."

Nicole sighed in retreat. "You'd better."

"Can you do my hair tomorrow afternoon?" Jada added quickly.

"Yeah, I get off at five."

"That'll work. I'll talk to you later."

Jada hung up the phone and took out her comb. She felt a little bad about hurrying Nicole off the phone and being so sketchy with her details. But she didn't have time to get into a conversation about her going to Mike's place for dinner. She had already decided to go, and she didn't want to be late.

Jada combed down her dry black bang and finger combed the rest of her hair down over her shoulders. Then she sprayed a mist of oil sheen around her hair before giving it one last rake with the comb. She stepped in front of her full- length mirror and checked out her outfit. The brown boots she wore matched her brown cropped fitted zip-up sweater, which layered over a tan cotton shirt. She clipped in her gold hoop earrings, and clasped her gold Xs & Os bracelet. Then she grabbed her brown designer handbag, and headed for her car.

Minutes later, Jada parked her silver Honda Civic across from Unit 33. She walked up five steps to Mike's front door and rang the bell. In no time, the door opened, and Mike's tall, lean body appeared. He was dressed in loose fitting gray jeans. He wore a black plaid button down, cuffed to his elbows, over a white tee shirt.

"Hey, girl!" he said with a smile. Mike stepped back and stretched out his arm for Jada to pass through.

"Hey," Jada replied as she brushed past Mike.

Mike closed the door. He took her coat and hung it on a hook beside the door. Then he turned around to look at Jada. "Can I get a hug?" he asked.

"Sure." Jada felt Mike's arms wrap around her waist as she put her arms around his back.

Mike released her, and then stood back looking at her. "Umph! You look good. A little nervous, but good."

Jada didn't realize that she looked as nervous as she was feeling at the moment. Mike was looking good to her too. She was starting to feel things she hadn't felt in quite some time. Having his arms around her had given her a warm feeling inside. Jada still felt flushed.

"I'm fine." Her hands clutched her purse draped over her shoulder.

"Give me a few minutes to set things up for our dinner. You can have a seat in the living room, if you want," Mike said with a smile before taking a right into a long, narrow kitchen.

Jada left the small foyer to reach the large living room. A brown couch and matching love seat lined the walls. Jada walked over to the love seat, and sat down. She then began to take in her new surroundings.

She saw a few African inspired paintings hanging on the white walls. Straight ahead on the far side of the living room was a sliding glass door leading to a small deck. To the left of the sliding door was a fireplace. To the right was a large flat screen TV. The TV was playing the news on mute. A laptop was hooked up to a stereo shuffling various songs. Jada listened to the low beat of John Legend's Heaven Only Knows, as it vibrated through the speakers. Just then Mike walked out of the kitchen with a plate in hand.

"Ladies first," he said.

Jada took the plate and smiled. She walked into the kitchen toward the stove. She helped herself to a piece of fried chicken, some yellow rice, and string beans.

"Let me," Mike said, taking the plate from Jada's hand and placing it on a small glass table in front of a bay window at the end of the kitchen.

"Thank you." Jada was trying unsuccessfully to tone down her enormous smile. She sat down at the table as Mike fixed his plate. She was amazed by the view from Mike's kitchen window. She gazed at the sun setting behind the mountains that outlined the town.

"What do you want to drink?" Mike asked.

"Water's fine."

Mike filled two glasses with bottled water and placed them on the table. Then he brought his plate over and sat down.

"Do you want to bless the food?" Jada asked.

Mike's head lifted quickly. He looked somewhat surprised by the question. "Sure." Mike said grace. When he finished, he leaned back with wide eyes. He rubbed his hand across his face as if to relax himself. "What are you scared to try my food?" he asked.

"No," Jada said with a wavering voice. Well just a little, she thought to herself. The food looked sort of bland.

Jada picked up her fork and knife and cut off a tiny piece of chicken as Mike used his hand to pick his up and bite it. Jada brought the chicken to her mouth and chewed it carefully. It was actually pretty good. Not greasy, and gently seasoned.

"Do you like it?" Mike wiped his mouth with his napkin.

"Not bad, for a guy."

He laughed. "Hey, don't you know men have made some of the greatest chefs?"

"You're right," Jada looked up at Mike's flirtatious smile.

"You must be spoiled, Jada living in that big house your parents have." Mike looked at her curiously. "Your dad's a doctor or somethin', right?"

"An ophthalmologist." Jada took sip of water.

"What does your mom do?" Mike scooped up some rice and put it into his mouth.

Jada put her glass down. "She does all of the administrative work at his office downtown."

Mike leaned back in his chair. "So, are you spoiled?"

"Absolutely not," Jada replied with surprising attitude in her voice. She did get tired of people assuming that she was spoiled just because her dad was a doctor, and she was an only child. "I had mad chores growing up. I dusted, vacuumed, and washed dishes to earn money. I've been working since I was sixteen. I was running track and working at Marcell's. Nicole and I worked there together actually. I had to pay half the cost of my first car." Jada thought for a moment. "What about you? You're the baby in your family. Were you spoiled?"

"I can't even lie. My parents spoiled the mess out of me. They spoiled both of us, just me more than my brother." Mike paused before changing the subject. "So, Jada, I already know you can bowl. Can you hoop?"

Mike's question sent Jada into a series of her own thoughts. He had reminded her of someone she had decided long ago to forget. The last person she played hoops with had been Tony—her three timing ex-boyfriend. She didn't want to remember Tony at all.

"It's been a while," she said.

"Maybe we can shoot hoops sometime." Mike stood up and took their plates. "Right now it's time for some dessert."

"Dessert?"

"Yeah. Why don't you relax in the living room, and I'll bring it out to you."

Jada stood up wide-eyed and returned to the love seat. The TV was still muted and the stereo was now playing Alicia Keys' Fallen. She rubbed her hands down her jeans and leaned back against the sofa. Mike walked in and sat next to her holding two bowls of fudge swirl ice cream.

"I didn't know if you like chocolate or vanilla, so I banked on this one," he said.

"This is fine." Jada took a bowl from his hand.

They each leaned back eating the ice cream and watching the muted TV. As the voice of Alicia Keys faded out, the smooth beat of Mario's Let Me Love You began to play.

As Jada leaned forward to put her empty bowl down on the glass coffee table, she felt Mike's hand touch hers. He placed his bowl down next to hers, and raised her hand to his lips. Jada felt Mike's soft lips rub against her hand as he placed kisses on the palm of her hand. Then he clasped his hand around hers as he wrapped his right arm around her waist. Jada could feel him pull her close as he began to kiss her lips. Jada was caught up in the moment and allowed herself to be seduced by Mike's kisses. As his hand began to caress her back, she stiffened. A familiar memory crossed her mind. Jada remembered what happened when she allowed Tony to raise desire in her. She suddenly realized that this scene was the same. She didn't want to go too far with Mike like she did with Tony, and she was getting the feeling that Mike was taking her down that similar road.

"What's wrong?" Mike asked before placing another kiss near Jada's lips.

Jada backed away. "We should stop. It's getting a little too hot up in here."

Mike removed his hand from Jada's back. "I'm sorry, Jada. I didn't mean to make you uncomfortable."

"It's okay. We were both getting carried away," Jada nervously rubbed her fingers through her hair.

"We should get going, anyway," Mike said, standing up. He picked up the bowls and went into the kitchen.

Jada walked toward the front door, put on her coat, and waited for Mike to turn off the TV and stereo.

"Thank you for cooking for me," she said.

"No problem. Anytime," Mike answered as he opened the door and stepped to the side to let Jada through.

Jada walked to her car as Mike walked to his. She waited for Mike to pull off so she could follow him to the bowling alley. As she began to drive, Jada had an uneasy feeling inside of her and she wasn't quite sure why. She figured she was probably just worried about what everybody would think when she and Mike walked into the bowling alley together again. Since leaving college, Jada had become private about her personal life. She had been so embarrassed about the way Tony had played her that she now often delayed telling her friends when she started dating someone new. Jada was afraid of getting involved with a guy who would embarrass her all over again. She purposely took things slow with guys now to avoid making the same mistake twice. Jada had almost moved too quickly with Mike tonight. Thankfully, she'd come to her senses. So why was she trippin' like she had something to hide?

Mike pulled his car into his garage and dragged his heavy legs up the stairs. His body gravitated toward the couch where he could finally relax after a hectic day. He felt good about his bowling score of 300. It had been a while since he'd bowled that well. It had also taken every last ounce of energy out of him. He took off his boots, stretched out on the couch, and grabbed the remote. He turned to BET to watch the end of Comicview.

The voice of the comedian began to fade into the background as Mike's eyes grew heavy. As he began to doze off, the remote control slipped out of his hand. His eyes opened at the sound of the remote hitting the floor. Bending over to pick it up, Mike saw a gold bracelet lying on the gray, carpeted floor. It was the same bracelet he remembered seeing on Jada's wrist after dinner earlier. He put the bracelet on the coffee table, and looked at the clock. It was just 9:50 p.m.. He figured she'd probably just gotten home. He picked up his cell phone, searched for her number, and pressed okay.

"Hello?" he heard Jada say.

Mike grinned at the sound of her voice. "Did you make it home safely?"

"Yes, I just got home actually. Thanks for asking," she added cheerfully.

Mike's grin widened. "Is your wrist missing something?"

"My wrist?" she paused for a moment. "My bracelet!"

"Don't worry." Mike said drowsily. "It's here at my house." He stretched and looked at the bracelet. "How about I return it to you over dinner tomorrow?" He slowly perked up.

"Dinner again?" Jada sounded surprised.

"Yeah. We can go out to eat this time," The energy in Mike's voice began to increase. "Then maybe we can catch a movie after or something. Maybe that Tyler Perry movie that's out."

Mike waited anxiously for Jada to respond. He was really attracted to her and hoped she was open to seeing him again. However, he couldn't help but wonder if he had already scared her away. She had tensed so quickly when things got physical between them today. He could tell Jada was attracted to him by the way she had kissed him. However, the way she had pulled away let him know that she was being cautious about getting involved with him too quickly.

"We can do that," Jada finally said.

"What time should I pick you up?" he asked eagerly.

"Seven would be good." Her voice was calm.

Mike beamed contently, "I'll see you at seven."

He pushed end on his phone and smiled to himself. Closing his eyes to relax, a quick image came to mind, causing his lids to flip open and his smile to fade. Sighing heavily, he reluctantly looked at his cell phone. There was one more call he needed to make.

CHAPTER 6

A Moment Of Truth

"PLEASE TELL ME YOU'RE NOT GOING to his house again," Nicole said as she took a roller out of Jada's hair.

"No. We're going out to eat, and then to a movie," Jada replied.

"I can't believe you didn't tell me you were going to his house yesterday!" Nicole said while one hand shook a roller in Jada's face, and the other rested on her hip. A hint of humor crept into Nicole's voice. "Rushing me off the phone so you can go to his house."

Though Nicole was now in back of her, Jada could just imagine the swerve that was in Nicole's neck with that last statement.

"I thought we were tight." Nicole sounded somewhat disappointed.

"We are tight," Jada said reassuringly.

Nicole unraveled the last roller from Jada's hair. "Then next time give me the details. All you had to do was keep it short and sweet."

Jada sighed. "You're right."

"I know I'm right." Nicole picked up the blow dryer and stepped in front of Jada to look at her. "With me being a virgin, and you a born again virgin, we have to look out for each other."

Jada smiled at Nicole. "For sure." She couldn't help, but be slightly amused at how worked up Nicole had gotten. Still, she really appreciated Nicole's genuine concern for her, as well as her input.

Jada kept her head straight as Nicole turned on the blow dryer and began to blow out her hair. She sat thinking about how much she admired Nicole for her commitment to her beliefs. Nicole was saving herself until marriage to have sex. She believed that having sex before marriage was against God's will. As teenagers, both Jada and Nicole had faithfully attended youth group sessions. The youth pastors had used Bible scriptures and discussions to teach them about sex. Jada and Nicole had learned that God created sex to be beautiful, but His will was that it take place between a married man and woman. The youth pastors had even gone into detail about the diseases that can result from going against God's will. Nicole had dated guys in her past, but once they started pressuring her to have sex, she would break things off with them. Jada had wanted to wait until marriage as well, but she'd given into temptation when she met Tony. When Jada made the decision to wait until marriage before having sex again, Nicole had been the supportive friend that she needed. They had both agreed that it was never too late to recommit to one's beliefs.

Nicole turned off the blow dryer suddenly. "I'm glad you didn't let yourself get carried away, but you don't even know Mike like that to be chillin' at his house. You need to find out more about him. A lot can happen in fifteen years."

As the blow dryer cranked up again, Jada began to think about what Nicole had just said. Conversation always flowed effortlessly between her and Mike when they talked about the fun they had as kids. However, they hadn't really talked about the things they had each been through during adulthood. She realized she didn't know anything about the details of Mike's adult life. Jada decided she should take Nicole's advice before her feelings got too deep.

With her hair straight and lightly bouncing over her shoulders, Jada left Nicole's apartment to go home and get ready for Mike to pick her up for their date. She changed into a blue long-sleeved shirt, dark blue jeans, and black boots. Thirty minutes later she was on her way to Rib Eye's Grill with Mike.

Jada looked at the crowded parking lot from the passenger side of Mike's vehicle. Mike circled the lot before pulling into a parking space and escorting Jada to the front door. He held the door open for her, as they walked up to the smiling young hostess.

"Hello!" the hostess said enthusiastically. "Two?"

"Yes," replied Mike.

"Okay, it should be about a five minute wait or so," the hostess said, handing Mike a flat electronic device.

Mike turned to Jada. "You want to sit down?"

"Sure," answered Jada.

They sat down on a bench across from a couple with a small boy and girl. A buzz of conversation flowed from the restaurant tables out to the small waiting area. Mike leaned forward, resting his elbows on his legs as Jada watched the two children snuggle with the young couple.

Jada alternated between watching the children and Mike. He appeared to be nervous sitting there. That was unusual for him. He was usually so calm and collected. She detected uneasiness about him. He kept looking around at the busboys and waitresses that would quickly pass through. He was stretching his neck to see into the dining area. It seemed to Jada that he wanted to get out of that waiting area fast. Jada couldn't understand why when he was the one who offered to sit down.

"You hungry?" Jada asked.

"No, I'm all right." Mike said.

"You sure? You seem kind of anxious."

"Do I?" Mike turned to look at Jada for a quick moment. A waitress floated by, and Mike snapped his neck in the direction she was headed.

Suddenly, Jada heard the sound of a musical ring tone. She watched Mike take his phone out of his pocket, and look at the screen.

He glanced at Jada, "Excuse me. I have to take this call." He stood up and placed the electronic device on the seat.

Jada watched Mike step outside the exit doors. She wondered what could be so important that he had to answer the phone right now. She could see him pacing back and forth with an agitated look on his face. Just then, Jada heard the device next to her begin to buzz and shake. Mike was still outside on his phone. She picked up the device and stood up to go tell him that it was their turn to be seated. As soon as Jada opened the door, she heard Mike talking.

"...'ove you, too," he said before closing his phone.

Jada felt her body stiffen. Did he really just say what she thought he said? Jada felt a mechanical shield begin to go up around her heart. She was beginning to feel like there was going to be a war tonight.

Mike looked at the flashing electronic buzzer. "That's us," he said.

He opened the door and waited for Jada to pass through. They followed the hostess to a small table for two. She placed the menus down and told them to enjoy their meal.

Jada immediately held her menu up to her face and began to read the selections. Peeking over the top of the menu, she saw Mike lean back and let out a deep breath. Then he opened his menu and looked down to read. His anxious behavior seemed to be non-existent. Now Jada was the one who was anxious—anxious to find out who was on the other line of Mike's cell phone.

When the waitress came over, Jada ordered Chicken Fajita's, and Mike ordered Glazed Ribs. They both ordered ginger ale, which the waitress brought over promptly.

"I still can't believe you're a teacher, Jada," Mike said, smiling at her.

"Yep," Jada replied in a flat tone.

"Sometimes I can't believe I'm a teacher either," continued Mike. "Now that I'm teaching high school, I feel even older. They remind me of how long it's been since I've been in high school myself."

The waitress came and placed their plates and extra napkins on the table. For the first time since they'd been dating, Jada was more focused on her food than she was on Mike. Throughout dinner, he told teaching and coaching stories, and Jada only half listened. Tonight she didn't want to hear about what was going on with his students. The only thing Jada wanted to hear was the name of the person who had called Mike's cell phone a few minutes ago. She couldn't stop thinking about that phone call.

With their plates empty, Jada and Mike waited for the waitress to bring their bill.

"I almost forgot," Mike said.

"What?"

He reached across the table and pulled Jada's right hand toward him. With his other hand, Mike reached into his pocket. His hand reappeared holding Jada's bracelet. He draped it over her wrist and secured the clasp.

Jada felt herself wanting to smile. Mike's sweet gesture was distracting her from her thoughts.

"Thanks," she said, smiling faintly.

Finally, the waitress arrived with their tab. Mike looked at the bill and pulled out his wallet. He opened it to retrieve his money revealing the same picture of a woman and a little boy that Jada had previously seen. Mike repositioned his wallet, but not quick enough for Jada's sharp eyes.

"Who's that in the picture?" she asked.

Mike's hands froze on his wallet. He had meant to cover the picture with a credit card the last time he knew Jada had seen it, but he forgot. Now she had asked the dreaded question. Asking about the picture would force him into discussing his complicated past.

Mike gulped. "It's my son," he sighed.

Mike saw Jada's eyes widen and her lips tighten. "And who's the woman?" she asked.

"His mother." Mike answered softly.

Jada glared at Mike, "Are ya'll together?"

"No, we're not together," he said exhaling deeply.

"So why do you have a picture of her and him in your wallet?" Jada demanded to know.

He shrugged. "It's the only picture she gave me."

Mike rubbed his hand back and forth over his closely shaven head as Jada stared at him. She had a scolding, disapproving look in her eye. Suddenly he felt like a suspect at a police station. He knew the interrogation wasn't over.

"Why are you just now telling me about your son?" Jada asked slowly.

Mike looked down shamefully. "I was going to tell you, Jada."

"When?" Her tone was short.

"When I felt like the time was right," he pleaded.

Jada shook her head. "You know I asked you if you had a family."

"You asked me if I was settled down." Mike's tone was defensive. "My son's mother and I have never been married and we're not together. I only talk to her because of my son."

Jada's lids came down over her eyes as she stared at Mike, indicating that she was still thinking. Mike knew that whatever she was thinking was just going to lead to more questions that he wasn't exactly excited about answering.

"Is that the family you go visit in New York?" she asked tilting her head to the side.

Mike took a deep breath while rubbing his head. "Yes," he replied.

Jada leaned back in her seat and folded her arms across her chest. "Mike, what's going on? How often do you go down there?"

Mike felt his leg rapidly shake up and down. Each one of Jada's questions was becoming more and more uncomfortable for him to answer. "I usually go down there on Fridays. We have joint custody, and I usually see him on weekends."

"So why aren't you down there tonight?"

"I called Brenda and told her I couldn't see Mike Jr. because I had plans tonight. "She's always blowing me up, acting like she's clueless about why I'm not there."

"I don't know about this, Mike. I don't like the idea of you canceling on your son to be out here with me." Jada rolled her eyes. "Yeah, that's real noble."

Ouch! Mike thought. Jada's last comment had really hurt. He did have to admit that she had a point. For years, Mike had told himself that it didn't matter if his son only saw him every once in a while. Now that Mike Jr. was getting older, Mike could see that his son really looked forward to spending time with him. He quickly thought of a comeback to retrieve his dignity.

"I'm going down there tomorrow, though, and I'll stay with him until Sunday." Mike said proudly.

"What do you mean, 'stay with him'?" Jada repeated.

Mike felt his leg begin to shake again. "Well, I stay with him in New York."

"Stay with him where?" Jada asked with a raised brow.

Mike rubbed his hand up and down his face before finally saying, "I stay at Brenda's, but it's not what you might think."

Jada folded her arms across her chest. "Mike, I don't know what kind of game you're trying to play by acting like your son and his mother, Brenda don't exist, but I do not want to be involved.

Mike rested his chin on his hand and looked at the seriousness on Jada's face. He felt completely embarrassed about how the truth about his son had come out. As he began to search his mind for a way to rectify this situation, he realized that Jada wasn't done.

"Running from your feelings and responsibilities is only going to push you into a dead end." Jada said. "Eventually, you're going to have to deal with them."

The waitress must have noticed the tension at their table, because she returned for the bill appearing shy and almost afraid. "Do you need change?" she asked in a timid voice.

"No, thanks. We're all set," Mike replied, trying to smile. After the waitress took the bill and quickly walked away, Mike reluctantly returned his eyes to Jada's. "Do you want me to take you home?"

"I'd appreciate it," Jada replied, grabbing her purse and standing up.

Only the sound of cars driving by could be heard as Jada walked with Mike to his car. The awkward silence continued as Mike drove and Jada simply stared straight ahead, lost in her thoughts. Jada decided that she would not go out with Mike again, because she didn't have any tolerance for dishonest men. Right now she was too upset to be around Mike. She would not hang out at the bowling alley anymore, unless she was called ahead of time to substitute for him. She could forgive Mike for deceiving her, but she wasn't ready to forget.

When they arrived at Jada's house, Mike pulled up to the curb. Jada turned to look at him.

"Thank you for bringing me home," she said.

"You're welcome. Will I see you again?" He asked in a timid voice.

Jada shook her head. "I don't think so."

Mike sighed. "Okay. Take care."

Jada left the car and walked to the front door. She turned the key without looking back. Then she heard Mike drive away.

CHAPTER 7

Moving On

JADA WOKE UP SUNDAY MORNING AND decided to pray for Mike. She knew that he must be confused to be behaving the way he was, so she asked that his heart would be open to receive God's guidance. Then she dressed comfortably, as it was her Sunday to work in the children's ministry. She grabbed a Nutrigrain Bar and headed off to church.

Working with the children that morning quickly raised Jada's spirits. She enjoyed seeing their smiling faces as they worked on their morning craft. She helped the children make noisemakers using popcorn, small plastic cups, coffee filters, and rubber bands. Then the children used the noisemakers to act out a Palm Sunday skit. When the craft and skit were complete, Jada and Greg, the lead teacher that Jada worked with, walked the third grade children to their classroom for Question and Answer time until their parents picked them up. When the children were gone, Jada and Greg began to clean up the classroom.

"So how are your kids?" Greg asked.

Usually when Greg asked about her kids, Jada would give him details about what was going on with her first graders. He always appreciated her stories. He worked with kids too as a social worker for the Department of Children and Families.

"They're fine," Jada replied.

Most of the time, after listening to Jada talk about her first graders, Greg would tell her about the foster kids he monitored. But today, rather than bringing up thoughts of her students, Greg's question had reminded Jada of Mike and his son. Jada could see Greg looking at her with curiosity, as if he were waiting for more of a response. He put the paper towel and bottle of white board cleaner down. He folded his dark, muscular arms across his chest.

"What's wrong?" he asked.

"What do you mean?" Jada continued to push in chairs while Greg watched her.

"I've been working with you long enough, Jada to know when something's wrong."

Jada paused thoughtfully. She knew Greg was a genuinely nice person so she decided to open up. "About two weeks ago I started dating this guy that I know, and I just found out that he has a son."

Greg looked at Jada questionably. "So you're bothered by the fact that he has a son?"

"That's not really what's bothering me." Jada sat down in one of the chairs. "He keeps a picture of his son and the mother in his wallet. Then he told me that when he visits his son on weekends, he stays at the mother's house." She paused. "What do you think about that?"

Greg lowered himself into the chair across from Jada. "From what you told me, it sounds like a man who doesn't know what he wants."

Jada's shoulders slouched. "That's what I thought."

"Are you going to keep seeing him?" Greg's eyes were filled with sympathy.

Jada shook her head, "No."

"I think you're making the right decision," Greg reassured her. "That situation just sounds weird."

She smiled faintly. "Thanks for the male opinion."

"No problem." Greg stood up and went back to cleaning the white board. "Go on home. We're done here. Get something to eat."

"What are you doing for the rest of the afternoon?" Jada asked, gathering her Bible and purse.

"I'll probably stop by my mom's house to eat."

"Okay, well have fun," she said as she left the classroom.

Jada walked upstairs to purchase a CD of the morning message. As she stood in line, she looked around the church lobby. Her eyes drifted to a familiar face sitting outside of the congregation reading the church newspaper. As she looked closer, she recognized that it was Pete. Is he here by himself? She silently wondered. She decided she should go say hello. Jada turned around to pay for her CD, and stuffed it into her purse. Then she walked over to where Pete was seated.

"Hi, Pete," she said, looking down at him.

Pete looked up from his newspaper. When his eyes met Jada, his signature dimples immediately appeared. "Hey, Jada" he replied, closing the newspaper and rising to his feet. "It's good to see you."

Jada looked at Pete's smiling face. He always looked so peaceful and happy. "Are you here by yourself?"

"No, Tonya's in the bathroom." His light brown eyes continued to look at her.

"Oh." Jada nodded.

"I was looking at the church newspaper." Pete's voice filled with enthusiasm. "This church has so much to offer. There are so many different ministries and activities. Youth ministry, children's ministry, home fellowship, men's fellowship, concerts, softball. You name it, they've got it."

Jada grinned. "Yeah, it's great here. I work in the children's ministry."

"So that's probably why I haven't seen you." Pete sounded as if he'd just had a revelation. "I haven't seen you here since the first time I came, and today makes the fourth Sunday in a row that I've been here."

"Really?" Jada gave him a surprised look. "So you must like it then."

"Yeah. The paper said they have new membership classes coming up soon." Pete lifted the newspaper slightly and rummaged through the pages. "I might sign up."

Just then, Jada saw Tonya exit the bathroom. Jada had always been into fashion, but Tonya had her beat. Tonya was dressed in a green tee shirt, with a brown, cropped puff sleeve jacket layered over her shirt. Fitted dark blue jeans covered her long, lean legs. Her brown stiletto healed boots perfectly matched her jacket and handbag. Rows of brown necklaces gave her outfit a high fashion look. Tonya's make-up was flawless and her shoulder-length auburn hair bounced lightly around her face. Her beautiful face and stylish appearance reminded Jada of Janice Prishwalko, a fashion model she'd seen hosting chic.tv.

"Hey, Jada!" Tonya said enthusiastically as she stopped where her brother and friend both stood.

The ladies hugged and Jada complimented her on her outfit.

"Oh, this?" Tonya said with a hint of false humility, which she failed to mask with the confident smile and toss of her head that accompanied her response. "Thanks." She then focused her attention to Pete. "So are you ready?'

"Yeah, I was waiting for you. I could have read that whole newspaper stand as long as you took in the bathroom." Pete gave Tonya a teasing grin.

Tonya rolled her eyes at Pete. "Whatever," she said as she gave him a 'talk to the hand' gesture before turning to Jada. "We're going to The Basil Patch to eat. Do you want to come?"

Jada looked at Tonya, and then at Pete. The offer did sound good. Her family was in North Carolina visiting other relatives. She hadn't planned to cook being that she was the only one around to eat it. She smiled slightly. "Sure."

"Great!" Tonya exclaimed. She then linked her arm through Jada's and began walking toward the front doors with Pete following their lead. Tonya turned around to look at Pete. "I'll ride with, Jada," she said.

The two women sauntered to Jada's car and buckled themselves in. Then Jada began to follow the directions of the parking attendant as she waited to exit the church parking lot.

"Pete was saying he's thinking about signing up for the new membership classes." Jada said. "Were you thinking about it too?"

"I'm still not sure," Tonya replied. "My mother would have a fit if she knew that we've been going to such a diverse church."

"Really?" Jada was surprsied. "Why?"

"If you looked up prejudiced in the dictionary, my mother's picture would be there." Tonya sounded displeased. "To her we're increasing the chances that we'll hook up with someone who's not white."

"What makes her think you'd be interested in somebody who's not white?" Jada asked as she turned her Civic onto the main road.

"Because Pete likes black women." Tonya answered casually. "His senior prom date was black."

Jada looked over at Tonya with wide eyes. "Really?" she smirked.

"Yep. And his last girlfriend too." Tonya continued to blab more details. "He didn't tell my parents about his last girlfriend, because he knows how my mom is. She was so mad about senior prom. She puts all of our important photos in a display case in the family room. So she put my junior and senior prom picture in the case, but she only put Pete's junior prom picture in there, because the girl was white. His senior prom picture is nowhere to be found."

Jada's mind absorbed everything she'd just heard. "I was going to ask you if Pete likes black women, and you just confirmed it."

"Why were you going to ask me that?" Tonya curiously asked.

"Remember the night we all went bowling?" Jada glanced over at Tonya. "It seemed like he and Sasha were flirting with each other."

Tonya shrugged. "If you say so. I wasn't looking at my brother. I was too busy checking out Fernando. He's cute."

Jada raised her eyebrows and looked at Tonya. "It looks like your brother's not the only one with jungle fever."

Tonya broke out into laughter. A laugh erupted from Jada's lips as well.

"That's where you're wrong. Fernando's Dominican, not black," Tonya said in a sing song voice.

"Well he's not white." Jada sung back.

Jada parked her car in the first empty spot she saw. Then she and Tonya met Pete at The Basil Patch entrance. They had just managed to beat the crowd and were able to be seated immediately at a small square table. They looked over their menus while the waitress served them their drinks, salad, and breadsticks. Then Jada proceeded to order the Shrimp Mozzerella, Tonya ordered Cheese Ravioli, and Pete selected Shrimp Primavera.

"It would have been nice to sample some of your food today," Jada said to Pete. "Tonya says you're quite the cook."

"I'm all right," Pete replied with a grin. "I'd be happy to whip something up one of these days so you can judge for yourself."

Jada smirked. "I'll hold you to that."

She noticed that Pete was still smiling at her, and she wasn't sure why. As she looked at him, she realized that he somewhat resembled the pop singer, Nick Lachey. Only Pete was a little taller and had reddish brown hair. It was the copper hair, and the dimples that gave him his own unique look.

"So are you coming to the bowling alley again this Thursday?" Pete finally asked.

Suddenly, Mike's image flashed before Jada's eyes. Shaking herself back to reality, she let out a deep breath, wondering if she should tell them what had happened between her and Mike.

The waitress returning with their food delayed Jada's response to the question. When their plates were in place, the waitress left the table.

"I'll bless the food," Pete offered.

They bowed their heads as Pete prayed. After saying a collective, "Amen," silence engulfed the table as they began sampling their entrées.

Tonya finished chewing a bit of ravioli and looked at Jada. "Have you been bowling for Mike lately?" she asked rebirthing the subject of the bowling alley.

"No," Jada replied. "I was just going to hang out." Jada began to slowly twist strands of angel hair pasta around her fork. "Did you know that Mike and I went out a few times?" she asked without looking up from her plate.

Tonya was the first to respond. "Really? I didn't know that."

When Jada finally looked up, Tonya was busy cutting her food, and Pete had placed his fork down, and was looking at her intently.

"We would eat together before going to the bowling alley." Jada picked up her glass and took a few sips of her water.

"Do you like him?" Tonya's voice was laced with curiosity.

"I did," Jada replied sadly.

"What do you mean did?" Tonya put her fork down and stared at her.

Jada hesitated as she thought about how to put her feelings into words. "I did until I found out that he has a son, and he wasn't planning on telling me about him."

Tonya's mouth was now hanging open. "How did you find out about his son?"

Jada took a few more sips of her water. "I kept seeing this picture of a woman and little boy every time he would take out his wallet to pay for dinner. Finally, I asked him who it was and that's how I found out. If I hadn't seen the picture who knows when he would have told me."

Tonya shook her head. "That's messed up."

Jada's eyes grew wide. "That's not the worst of it. On Friday when we went out to eat, he was really supposed to be with his son. When he does go visit his son, he stays with the mother."

Pete dropped his napkin on the table and folded his strong arms across his chest. "I knew he was hiding something. He's always on his cell telling somebody he'll see them tomorrow."

"Right!" Jada exclaimed realizing that she was now smiling at Pete.

They all started laughing. Jada was glad that she could laugh at the whole situation. She wasn't laughing at Mike, because she knew that it must be hard for him being a young single father, but how silly of him to think he could keep such serious attachments a secret.

Calming down, Jada said, "I was angry with him. Now I just hope that he figures out what he wants before trying to get involved with anyone else." She shook her head. "He's a nice guy carrying some serious baggage."

Silence returned as they worked to finish their food. Everyone's spirits were good including Jada's. Talking about her ended relationship with Mike had been therapeutic for her. She now felt release.

"Speaking of baggage," Pete said picking up where the conversation left off, "I've been wanting to take a trip back out to San Francisco for April vacation. I know Tonya hasn't been. How about you, Jada?"

"No, I haven't either," Jada looked at Pete wondering why he was asking.

"If you both want to go out there for spring vacation, I'll show you around," he offered. His eyes had an eager look of anticipation.

"That would be so much fun!" Tonya exclaimed.

Jada thought about how nice it would be to get away for a while. "Yeah. We should go."

A broad grin appeared on Pete's face. "I'll ask Gene if he wants to go too, and then we can start planning.

"Okay," Jada smiled feeling uplifted even more.

Pete was glad to see Jada finally smiling. His mind was occupied with thoughts of her as he attempted to finish the food on his plate. Although Pete felt sad for Jada because she'd been let down by Mike, part of him was glad that she wouldn't be preoccupied by Mike anymore. Pete's thoughts were suddenly interrupted by the sound of Tonya's voice.

"Do you think we should stay out there for the whole week?" Tonya looked at Pete and waited for a response.

He shook his head. "Four or five days would probably be good."

Pete knew that going back to California could end up reminding him of his ex-girlfriend, Stephanie. Ever since things ended with her, he'd sort of forgotten how to have fun. However, when Gene invited him and Tonya to go bowling with them a month ago, that all began to change. Joining the bowling league had allowed Pete to get some fun back into his life. He enjoyed hanging out at the bowling alley on Thursdays, and he had especially liked seeing Jada there. Maybe this trip would finally give him the chance to get to know Jada a little better.

CHAPTER 8

Spring Break

JADA, TONYA, AND NICOLE STOOD OUTSIDE the San Francisco airport, waiting for Pete and Gene to pull up with the car rental. Jada was so glad to be on vacation! The past four weeks had been very hectic for her. She had been working on student files for academic testing, and running the third grade tutoring group before school. She also had substitute bowled every Thursday for Mike because he'd been busy coaching high school basketball tournaments. Jada was mentally drained, and now she was going to have the chance to recuperate.

At seven o'clock that morning, they had all met at Tonya's apartment and car pooled to John F. Kennedy Airport. They arrived at the airport at 8:30 a.m. and by 10:30 a.m. their plane was taking off. The flight had been five hours long, so they had all slept most of the way. Now Jada felt rested and ready to go.

A brown metallic Envoy pulled up to the curb in front of them. Pete and Gene stepped out. With cars still pulling up around them, and people hustling up and down the sidewalk Pete and Gene began loading the suitcases into the back of the SUV.

Jada, along with Nicole and Tonya, climbed into the backseat and waited for the guys to finish loading their luggage. Jada looked at the clock. It was 12:45 p.m. Pacific Time. That meant it was 3:45 p.m. back home. Sunday service was long since over. Jada was glad that according to California time, they still had the whole afternoon ahead of them.

Pete and Gene climbed into the front seat, and buckled in.

"What time's check-in?" Nicole took out her sunglasses and secured them to her face.

"One o' clock," Pete replied as he slowly pulled the car away from the curb.

"We're right on time," Jada's voice was filled with enthusiasm. "Did you plan that, Pete?"

"Yep," Pete looked at Jada through the rearview mirror. "I'm trying to make the most of every moment out here. I'm not trying to waste any time." Excitement rang in Pete's voice. "I want all of you to remember this trip!"

Gene smiled from the passenger side of the vehicle, "I hear that. Out of the four years that I've been teaching, this is the first time I've ever gone away for April vacation."

"I'm so glad you guys invited me to come." Nicole leaned her head back against the head rest. "I could really use this break after training all those new associates at my store."

"So what are we going to do first?" Tonya curiously asked.

Everyone looked at Pete anxiously anticipating his response.

"After everyone gets settled, I thought we could head down to the beach."

A chorus of "okays" filled the vehicle as it coasted down the freeway. A breeze flooded through the lowered windows, and rays of sunshine reflected on the glass. A popular radio station was playing music on the car stereo. As Pete drove, everyone enthusiastically stared out of the windows, taking in the Californian landscape. Three songs later, they were exiting the freeway and approaching an oceanfront inn.

Pete parked the car in the parking garage, and began unloading the luggage with the help of Gene. Then everyone grabbed their suitcases and headed inside.

After a smooth check-in, Jada, Nicole, and Tonya, entered their room located across from Pete and Gene's. The ladies set their bags down and quickly dispersed in different directions. Jada went straight to the window. Nicole went to check out the bathroom. Tonya flopped backwards onto a bed.

"This view is incredible," Jada said as she looked down at the rolling Pacific Ocean, cliffs, and trees.

"The bathroom's clean," Nicole commented, walking over to where Jada stood.

"And the bed's comfortable," Tonya said through a stretch and a yawn.

"We'd better get our bathing suits on," said Nicole. "Pete told us to be ready by two thirty."

They each took a turn entering the bathroom to freshen up, and exiting in their swimwear. Nicole wore a black and white polk-a-dotted tankini top with a black solid bottom. Tonya changed into a peach, yellow, and white plaid tankini top, with a peach skirt bottom. Jada wore a keyholed style tankini top with a curved stripe pattern of red, pink, black, and white. She wore a solid black bottom with ties on the sides.

"Do you think we should bring some cover-up clothes?" Nicole asked.

"Yeah, maybe we should," replied Tonya. "I remember Pete saying the weather can be funny around here."

The ladies stuffed jeans and jackets into their tote bags, grabbed their towels, and left the room.

"It's too cold to be in that water," Nicole said, watching Tonya, Pete and Gene take a swim.

San Francisco had a strong ocean breeze making it still chilly this time of year. Even though the sun was glistening on the water, and the sand was warm, the air was windy and cool. Nicole and Jada were in their bathing suits, lying on their towels. They watched their three friends disappear into the water, and then pop back up to breath.

The wind whipped through Jada's ears as she propped herself up on her elbows to take in the ocean view. "What is Gene doing in the water trying to act like he isn't cold?" she said. "Forget trying to look cute. I'm about to put my jeans and jacket on."

Jada reached into her clear designer tote bag to retrieve her cropped denim jacket.

"That bag is cute. Where'd you get it?" Nicole asked.

"From the tent sale in Norwalk," Jada replied now stepping into her dark blue jeans.

"When was it?"

"They have it every year right after Thanksgiving. The bags can be up to sixty percent off. That's the only way I was getting this bag, because I was not trying to pay full price for some plastic."

Nicole laughed. "I hear you. Well, next time you go, let me know."

As Jada was sitting down, Tonya and Pete strolled up to their towels with Gene shivering behind them.

"I'm going to the beach café to get some snacks," said Pete. "Any requests?"

"What do they have?" asked Nicole.

"Sandwiches, muffins, coffee, tea, hot chocolate," Pete paused. "If you like sweet drinks, they have hot caramel cider."

"Oooh, I'll take that," Nicole said.

"Same here," added Tonya.

"I'll take a hot chocolate, man," Gene said, still shivering.

"I'll just come with you," said Jada. "I need a walk to get myself warm."

As Jada stood up with her tote bag, Pete pulled his red T-shirt over his head and secured his black backpack to his back.

"We'll be back," he said.

Jada and Pete began walking side by side down the beach strip. The sun was still bright, and the wind continued to whip around them. Jada looked over at Pete's shirt. The wind was so strong that his shirt was puffed up with air. She was glad she had tied her hair up into a ponytail on her head. She took out her sunglasses and secured them to her face.

"You were smart to bring some sunglasses," Pete looked at her through squinted eyes. "There's not exactly any shade around here."

"I know," Jada replied through a slight smile.

"I remember when I used to go to the beach as a kid. My mom would be like, 'Come here and let me put your sunblock on!'" Pete said raising his voice up an octave. Jada laughed and looked over at him. "She would put mad sunblock on me. She'd put it on all thick. I'd be walking around the beach all shiny, looking like I just went swimming in some Vaseline."

Jada continued to laugh as she lifted her hand to pull some flyaway bangs away from her face. "I can't say that I had that problem," she said. "I didn't even know what sunblock was when I was a kid."

"Really?" Pete said inquisitively. "Besides having to walk around with a pound of sunblock on, I used to love for summer vacation to come. We would take trips to Misquamicut, Rhode Island and hang out at the beach."

Jada looked over at Pete. "I've never been to Misquamicut."

"It's nice." A nostalgic look came over Pete's face. "They had mini-golf, and rides too. We had mad fun. I loved summer because of those trips. Then when we'd come back, it was time for us to go back to school shopping, and I would be all excited."

"Did you like school?" Jada asked curiously.

"Yeah." Pete replied. "I was like a math wiz in elementary school." Pete rubbed his hands together. "We would do these timed fact tests, and I was always the first one done. I didn't brag about it or anything, but kids would still be hatin' on me."

"How'd you know they were hatin' on you?"

"'Cause they'd suck their teeth and just stare at me when the test was over. I don't know. Math just always came easy for me I guess. That's probably why I love teaching it now." Pete looked at Jada and smiled. "But enough about me. How about you? Did you like school when you were a kid?"

Jada paused for a moment. Thoughts of smirks, rude comments, and teasing faces began to flow through her head. Then she also remembered her kind teachers and honor roll report cards. Finally she said, "School, yes. The kids in the school, not so much." Jada began to look off into the ocean as past memories now flooded her thoughts.

"Why?" Pete asked with curiosity in his voice. "What happened?"

"I was the different one in my class. I was the only black girl in my elementary school classes, and they all made sure I knew it too. I had puffy hair back then that my mom would put in ponytails, and the little girls always gave me ill looks everyday. Eventually, my mother started straightening my hair with hair grease and a hot comb, but the looks didn't change." Jada paused. Though her eyes were still focused on the ocean, she could feel Pete's eyes on her.

"Did the kids do anything else?" he asked with sympathy in his voice.

"Well, once we got to middle school, some of the girls were a lot nicer, but the boys…" Her voice trailed off. She had a faraway look in her eye.

"What about them?" Pete prodded anxiously.

"One time in middle school we were running laps around the field," Jada began to look down at her feet as they made tracks in the sand. "So I'm running with a friend. Then I felt something hard hit my back, and I saw a rock hit the ground."

"What?" Pete's voice was full of shock. "A rock?"

"Yep. I looked around and saw a bunch of the boys laughing behind me," Jada continued. "I didn't see who threw it, but I believe it was one of them." Jada hadn't planned on going into that much detail, but something about Pete's presence was so comfortable. She could tell he was listening intently to her every word. "I think they were aiming for my butt."

"For real?" Pete's tone was low. He sounded as if he were in utter disbelief.

"Yeah, because they would always say things like, 'what's going on with your butt, Jada? Is it swollen or something? If I poke it will it pop?'"

Pete let out a long, low whistle. "No they didn't," he said.

"I remember times when I would be talking to a boy about something, and they would interrupt me and say, 'Why's your hair so greasy? Go wash your hair.' Then a bunch of them would bust out laughing." Jada now wanted to end the conversation of her negative past. Uncomfortable memories currently clouded her mind. For the moment, she was finding it hard to focus on anything else. "How much farther to the café?" she asked attempting to change the subject.

"We should be there in a minute or two," Pete replied.

Jada watched a group of white teenaged boys pass them with their surfboards. She found herself remembering her eighth grade end of the year trip. "This reminds me of the class trip to Cape Cod we took at the end of eighth grade," she said.

Pete looked over at Jada. "Did you have fun?"

Jada shrugged. "It was okay."

"Did any of those boys harass you while you were there?" Pete sounded somewhat worried.

"A little," Jada watched a few surfers as they rode the rolling waves.

"What did they do?" The worry in his voice increased.

Jada sighed. "I remember I wanted to go in the water, but I had just gotten my hair done. I didn't want it to get wet. Freshly done black hair and water don't mix, so I pulled it up into a high ponytail."

Pete glanced at Jada. "Like you have it now?"

Jada felt the top of her head where her blown-out straight hair cascaded out of a neat ponytail. "Yeah. It was high like this so it wouldn't get wet," she explained. "I was just in the water talking to my friend, Felicia, when all of a sudden, I was yanked underneath the water. I couldn't see who did it, because they came from underwater. The water in Cape Cod was not exactly clear. But when I finally popped up, a bunch of the boys off to the side were laughing, as usual."

Pete looked at Jada with wide eyes. "That's pretty messed up. Is that why you don't get in the water now?"

Jada chuckled, suddenly amused at Pete's assumption. "No. First, I can't swim. Second, it's way too cold to get in this water."

"Wait, you can't swim, and they pulled you under like that?" Pete shook his head vigorously, apparently not amused. "That makes it even worse, Jada. A wave could have pulled you in deeper. Did you tell anyone?"

Jada's face became serious again. "No. I was Little Miss Independent back then. I didn't want any help trying to solve my problems. I don't know what was so ugly about me that they had to do those things to me," She looked off into the distance where the water met the horizon.

"I think you're beautiful, Jada."

She looked over at Pete. Beneath her shades, her eyes met his light brown eyes that now looked at her from his tanned ivory face. Suddenly, she couldn't believe she had just shared all of those memories with a white man. As she talked to him, she had forgotten that he was white. He had listened understandingly and not defensively. The concern he had shown made it easy for Jada to open up to him. She felt like she had known him for a long time. Jada looked at Pete surprised by the comment he'd just made.

Pete smiled calmly, "Black women work hard, have great skin, and beautiful figures. I've always been attracted to black women."

Pete saw a glimpse of a grin appear on Jada's face. He couldn't help but wonder if she was amused by what he'd just said. Still, the stories that Jada had just shared with him made him feel that deep inside, she had a chip on her shoulder that wasn't going to be easily brushed off. At times when she had been talking, he'd detected bitterness in her voice.

"Not all white guys are like those jerks you went to school with, Jada," he said.

"I know," Jada looked down at her feet.

Somehow Pete wasn't convinced. "Let's cross here. The café's coming up on the other side."

Pete crossed the street with Jada and approached the busy café. A few people were seated at the outdoor tables eating, drinking, or reading newspapers and books. Pete opened the door, and waited for Jada to pass through.

"It smells good in here," Jada said.

"Let's check out the menu." Pete maneuvered around customers and tables to give them a clear view.

He ordered two hot chocolates and three hot caramel ciders. Then he selected a few cookies. As Pete's order was being prepared, Jada chose a few maple bars she thought Nicole and Tonya might also want to try. Pete watched Jada begin to place a ten-dollar bill on the counter next to his order.

"I got it," he said, smiling at Jada. He handed two bills to the clerk and waited for his change. He couldn't help but be amused by the surprised look Jada now wore on her face. He saw her open mouth slowly form into a smile.

"Thanks," she said as she put her money away and put the maple bars into her bag.

Pete put the cookies in his backpack, and picked up the carrying tray full of drinks. They left the café with their snacks and began the walk back to their friends.

"I'm really enjoying getting to know you, Jada." Pete said as they crossed the street toward the beach. "What was high school like for you?"

Jada looked at him with a creased brow. "What do you want to know?"

Pete thought for a moment. "I played football in the fall and baseball in the spring. How about you?"

"Track," Jada smirked. "It sounds like you were a jock."

Pete laughed. "Guilty as charged. I loved hanging out with my football buddies. Those were some good days."

"What do you remember most about them," Jada asked curiously.

A mischievous look came over Pete's face. "I'm going to be honest with you. A lot of my football buddies were black. I spent a lot of time hanging out at their houses. One of them had an older sister that I had a major crush on." He chuckled and paused. "I was the victim of a lot of jokes, because of how nervous I would get around her."

Jada grinned and looked at Pete, "I wish I could've seen that." She raised her eyebrows. "You don't seem like the nervous type."

Pete smiled. "Well back then I was." His smile widened as he looked at Jada. "What do you remember most about your track days?"

Pete attentively watched Jada as she shared happier memories of being a star on the high school track team. He walked and listened closely as she chatted about her track and field events. He was somewhat disappointed when they made it back to their towels, bringing their conversation to an end.

"Where have you two been?" Nicole asked, quickly sitting up.

"Sorry. We walked slow," Pete replied as he began passing out the beverages.

"My hot chocolate's probably iced chocolate by now," Gene said from his seated shivering position on his towel. Gene immediately took a sip after Pete handed him his drink. "It's straight," he said.

"This is good," Nicole said after taking a sip of her hot caramel cider.

Pete and Jada took the cookies and maple bars out of their bags for everyone to try. They sat on the beach and ate their snacks, watching the activity around them. Dedicated surfers battled waves, locals from the neighborhood walked dogs, and couples walked together along the shore.

Pete was still thinking about the conversation he'd had with Jada. He knew he'd never been like the white boys she described. Growing up, he had always been cool with black, white and Hispanic kids. He and Tonya had listened to all kinds of music like pop, hip-hop, and R&B. In high school, they even watched the music videos on BET.

Pete had always found the brown skin, and curvy figures of black women attractive. During his high school senior year, he'd had a crush on his lab partner, Monica. She was the smart, beautiful, African American girl he took to his senior prom. Going to the prom with Monica had given Pete the courage to pursue black women.

Jada seemed like the type of woman he'd be interested in, but Pete decided he should probably forget about pursuing her. After hearing Jada talk about her past, he figured that she'd never consider going out with him.

"Let's take some pictures," Tonya said, breaking the silence.

Pete looked at his watch and saw that it was 4:30 p.m.. "Okay. Then we can head back to the hotel and clean up before we go out to eat."

Pete smiled as he took pictures of the ladies posing in their swimsuits with the ocean behind them. Then Tonya took pictures of Pete and Gene standing in the water with their muscles flexed. Jada and Nicole could be seen laughing at the guy's supermodel attempts, and the guys couldn't help but laugh at themselves. Their laughter continued even as they all packed up and headed back to the hotel.

The bang on the door startled Pete from his thoughts. He didn't know how long he had been in the bathroom, but he assumed Gene was trying to tell him it had been too long.

"Hurry up in there, man," Gene yelled through the bathroom door.

Pete quickly rubbed his deodorant under his arms and secured the towel around his waist. Cool air hit him as he opened the bathroom door.

"It's about time," Gene said "What were you doing in there?" He gave Pete a peculiar look.

Pete shrugged. "I guess I zoned out for a minute." The truth was he had just spent a good five minutes simply standing at the sink thinking about Jada. She had looked so cute that afternoon. The way her hair was pulled up, with the wind blowing strands of hair down onto her neck. Yet, she didn't even seem to know how attractive she really was.

As Gene went into the bathroom, Pete began to lay out the clothes he planned to wear for dinner. He put on some loose fitting blue jeans, and a slick, gold, crewneck short sleeve shirt. He took out his bottle of Curve Soul, his favorite fragrance, and sprayed two squirts on his neck. Then he sat down at the circular table by the window. He leaned back in the chair and began absentmindedly drumming his fingers on the table as he stared at the TV. Images of Jada continued to try to occupy his mind. He found her easy to talk to, and he had enjoyed some of the laughs they had shared.

Though Jada seemed like his type, he was pretty sure she did not feel the same way about him. He began to wonder why he was still thinking about her. He was here to relax, not to get hooked up. He needed to focus on showing them around and that's it.

Gene exited the bathroom just as Pete was ending his silent pep talk to himself.

As much as Pete tried not to, he had to bring Jada up. "I was talking to Jada this afternoon, and she's really been through a lot."

Gene began to rummage through his suitcase. "What do you mean?"

"She said some of the white kids used to harass her when she was in elementary and middle school." Pete's tone was sympathetic.

Gene gave Pete a surprised look. "She told you about that?"

Pete nodded. "She still seemed a little upset about it."

"She doesn't usually talk about that." Gene's eyes widened. "No offense man, but I'm really surprised she told you!" He smirked a little.

Pete laughed. "I was just as surprised as you." He paused thoughtfully. "Do you think she'd ever consider going out with a white guy?"

Gene shook his head. "I don't think so."

As Gene finished dressing, Pete flipped through the channels while waiting to take everyone to their first restaurant of the trip. Just as Gene sat down, there was a knock on the door.

"I'll get it," Pete said. He walked over to the door. As he opened it, his jaw dropped. He knew Tonya was standing in front of him, but it was the image next to Tonya that had him speechless. He was aware that the image was Jada, but he had never seen her look so good. Her shiny black hair came down over her shoulders, and the gold shirt she wore was hugging her shapely figure. He must have looked her up and down, because he saw gold sandals that laced around her ankles. "Wow!" he finally said. "I almost didn't recognize all of you."

"Whatever, Pete" said Tonya.

"So you're all ready?" Pete asked.

"No. We're standing here, because we want a tour of your room," Tonya said sarcastically. "Heck, yeah we're ready," she added with a smile.

"Well, all right," Gene said, coming up behind Pete. "Let's go."

After loading into the Envoy, Pete drove over to the Cliff House, overlooking Ocean Beach. Of the two restaurants located in the Cliff House, they chose the Bistro. They were seated at a window table with a direct ocean view.

Once they'd read their menus, the waitress came and took their orders of Grilled Salmon, Sauteed Prawns Scampi, Ceasar Salad with Shrimp, "Fish and Chips", and Roasted Chicken Breast. Tonya took a few table pictures while they all waited for their food. After, she handed the camera to Pete so that she could get in some of the shots.

With the photos complete, Pete gave the camera back to Tonya and returned to his seat across from Jada. He was having a hard time keeping his eyes off of her. Thankfully the waitress returned with their orders. Gene volunteered to bless the food, and they all dug in.

Gene took a sip of his beverage and looked at Pete, "Do you miss living out here?"

Pete shook his head. "After my ex-girlfriend broke up with me, there wasn't anything here for me anymore." Pete saw sympathetic looks engross the faces of everyone around the table. "It took me a while, but I'm over it now."

Tonya looked up from her plate. "All three of the boyfriends I've ever had have broken up with me. They all said that I rushed them into a relationship." She rolled her eyes. "I know it just means that they were afraid to commit."

Gene smirked mischievously. "I have to agree with you on that one. I've used that line a few times myself." His mischievous grin began to fade. "I think I'm ready to put those days behind me now."

Pete looked across the table at Gene and Jada. "Were you two close growing up?"

Jada looked at Gene and smiled. "Yeah. We would go over each other's houses a lot when we were kids. I was a bit of a tomboy back then."

Gene nodded. "She'd always play football with my brothers and me," he said with a smile. "But we didn't grow up in the boonies like Jada did. My younger brothers and I came from a more simple background. My dad's a police officer and my mom's a teacher."

Jada glanced up from her food to look at Pete. "His mother is the one who inspired me to become a teacher."

Gene continued where he left off. "When we were kids I used to wish my house was as big as Jada's. He smirked. "That's why we always have family dinners at her parents' house. It's the only place we can all fit!"

A chorus of laughter erupted around the table. Napkins went up to cover mouths full of food.

As her laughter faded, Jada placed her napkin down and looked out at the ocean. "One thing I'll definitely remember about this trip is how cold it was on that beach!"

Pete laughed. "I told you the weather could be funny around here."

Nicole held her hands in front of her as if holding a platter. "Funny. Cold. Doesn't exactly sound the same to me!" She gave Pete a playful glare.

Pete just maintained his dimpled grin. "Just make sure you bring a jacket for the rest of the trip."

As Pete took a bite of his Grilled Salmon, he watched Jada carefully twist strands of pasta around her fork before bringing the food to her mouth. Then she chewed slowly as she looked at the view. Even after she had finished chewing, she continued to watch the waves ripple over the large ocean rocks. He saw a slight smile appear on her face as she returned to eating her food. Seeing that Jada was enjoying herself was making Pete feel good inside.

CHAPTER 9

Let The Tours Begin

PETE AWOKE TO THE SOUND OF his growling stomach. He couldn't believe he was hungry after all he'd eaten last night. But then he remembered that seafood usually went right through him.

As he opened his eyes, he could see that it was still early by the scarce light in the room. The only sounds he could hear besides his stomach were the low voices from the TV and Gene's snoring.

He reached over to the nightstand and lifted his watch. It was 6:30 a.m.. He had told the ladies to be ready by 7:30 so they could go down for breakfast. He looked across the room at Gene who was still sleeping, and decided to get a head start in the bathroom.

Pete quickly brushed his teeth, washed up, and shaved his face. When he opened the bathroom door, Gene hadn't even flinched.

"Gene! Let's go, man," Pete said. "We got things to do."

Gene sat up scratching his head. "What are we doing today again?" he asked.

"The Alcatraz and Angel Island Tour. But first we've got to get down to breakfast."

"You don't have to tell me twice," Gene said jumping out of bed. "They're both number one on my list," he continued as he disappeared into the bathroom.

Pete chuckled. He knew that would be all it took to get Gene amped up. First of all, he'd learned that Gene loved to eat, though one would never know by looking at his athletic build. Second, being the history teacher that Gene was, he'd been extra excited when Pete told him about the tour.

Pete put on a pair of blue jeans, a brown T-shirt, and matching Nike's. After a few squirts of cologne, he and Gene were ready to go.

"That omelet was off the chain!" Nicole said as she savored the last bite of her Hawaiian omelet.

Pete looked around at the empty plates. He and Gene had been done with their Mexican omelets ten minutes ago, and Tonya only had a couple bites left of her French toast. But when he looked at Jada's plate, she looked like she had just started.

"You're a slow eater, aren't you, Jada?" Pete asked, looking at her.

Jada nodded her head while chewing on a bite of cheesy egg, ham, and pineapple. "Yep," she finally replied with a smile.

Pete smiled and shook his head. He thought it was cute the way Jada took her time to eat. It was like she would take perfect little bites every time she ate. "I hate to rush you, Jada. But if we're going to get to the tour on time, you're going to have to finish that in five minutes or less."

After watching Jada unsuccessfully attempt to finish her omelet, they all climbed into the Envoy and drove to San Francisco's Pier 33. The wind whipped around them as they stood on the pier waiting for the tour to begin.

At about 9:30 a.m., Pete, Gene, and the ladies joined flocks of other tourists on a ferry ride across the San Francisco bay to Alcatraz Island. Pete enjoyed watching the peaceful look Jada wore on her face as the tour boat rode across the bay.

Once on Alcatraz, there was a 45 minute audio tour of the areas historically used as a civil war fort, military prison, and federal penitentiary. Pete watched Gene become completely absorbed into the moment. They were then shown a video presentation before viewing some of the island's historic gardens and wildlife.

At about 12:15 p.m., they left Alcatraz and arrived at Angel Island State Park. They took a tour of the island, viewing the spot where thousands of Chinese immigrants passed through. They were also informed of the Japanese and German Prisoners of War that were historically held on the island and shown the former location of the Nike missile base that occupied Angel Island in the 1950's and 1960's. Pete suggested that they stop at the island's Cove Café. They ate sandwiches for lunch. By the time they made it back to Pier 33, it was three o'clock.

"That was fun," Gene announced smiling.

There wasn't much of a response from the others, so Pete got the feeling they weren't as impressed. "I'm glad you liked it, Gene."

"It was interesting," Jada added casually.

Pete smiled at Jada. "I thought you'd like it."

Pete then led Gene and the ladies on a walk down Fisherman's Wharf. They stopped to walk on some of the tall ships on Hyde Street Pier, and then they walked over to Pier 39. Tonya, the animal lover of the group, took pictures of a few sea lions dancing around in the bay.

After stopping in a few shops to buy souvenirs, it was five o'clock. Pete walked the group to The Franciscan for dinner. They each enjoyed a plate full of shrimp. From their table they were able to look out at Alcatraz, and the Golden Gate Bridge.

Pete saw Jada look out at the bridge multiple times during their meal. He knew she would enjoy it even more, if she had a closer view.

"We'll probably check out the Golden Gate Bridge tomorrow," he said, smiling at Jada.

"I can't wait," Jada said, looking at him with a sparkle in her eye.

CHAPTER 10

Forty-niners

JADA PUT HER SUNGLASSES ON AND leaned her head against the backseat of the Envoy. She was truly enjoying this vacation. She had no idea that San Francisco was such a unique city, and she was looking forward to seeing what today had in store.

"So does everybody have everything? Anybody need to go back up to use the bathroom?" Pete asked, looking through the rear view mirror.

"Pete," Tonya's voice was steady and calm "we're not your students, and you're not the bus driver. Just start the car!" she suddenly exclaimed.

"Okay," Pete slowly replied. "But the forty-nine mile drive is not short." He smirked. "If you thought yesterday's tour was long, you ain't seen nothin'."

With the ladies relaxing in the backseat, and Gene operating as co-navigator, Pete drove down Point Lobos Avenue toward the Downtown area. He managed to find parking near the Civic Center. They exited the vehicle to take a walking tour of Japantown.

They walked past Japanese restaurants, sushi bars, and karaoke lounges. Eventually they reached an area full of Japanese shops. As they prepared to enter one of the shops, Jada decided to purchase a few items to share with her first grade class. She knew they would be excited to see items from the Japanese culture.

Inside the shop, everyone browsed around by themselves for a while. Jada ended up buying a painting, a colorful kimono, a necklace, and a variety of Japanese children's books. She also bought a Japanese toy, a CD of instrumental Japanese music, and an educational Japanese DVD.

After completing their shopping, they stopped to watch dancers perform to traditional Japanese music and a martial arts presentation. Jada took pictures of the dancers and the martial arts performers. Then they followed Pete's lead as they began to walk toward Union Square.

"So how'd you like Japantown?" Pete asked, looking directly back at Jada.

"It was great," Jada replied as she inched up to walk next to him.

"Did you buy anything?" Pete continued.

"The question is, what didn't I buy?" Jada held out her heavy tote bag full of purchases. "I plan on showing a lot of these things to my students when we get back to Connecticut."

Pete smiled at her, but did not respond with words. Something about his smile caused Jada to quickly look away to escape the awkwardness she suddenly felt. She continued to walk next to Pete, but only stores and strangers now occupied her view.

"This is Union Square," Pete said as he turned around to look at the group.

As Pete led them toward Crocker Galleria, the spectacular glass pavilion of shops, they approached three men who looked of Asian decent, seated along the sidewalk. They each had easels and caricature drawings on display.

"Excuse me," one said. "May I draw picture?" He looked directly at Jada with a smile and a pleading look in his eye.

Pete saw Jada look at the drawings and then up at him. He smiled and shrugged.

"Okay, I guess," Jada replied.

The man motioned to the high stool next to his easel. "Have a seat," he said.

Jada sat on the stool and smiled at Nicole and Tonya who then walked to the other side of the easel to see the work in progress. They watched the cartoon image of Jada begin to appear on the page.

"Ooh, that's coming out good!" said Nicole. She looked over at one of the other artists. He was finishing with his customer. He motioned to his stool, and Nicole sat down to get her own drawing done.

Tonya also replaced the stool of the third artist who had just finished with his last customer as well.

Pete and Gene began to cross the sidewalk so they could wait against the building and be out of the way. As they crossed the pavement, a stiff man painted in silver turned his head and blinked at them.

"What was that?" asked Gene. He sounded surprised.

"A mime," replied Pete with a smile. "He'll probably try to entertain you for a few minutes, and then he's going to want some money in his cup."

"That mess was freaky," said Gene.

Pete no longer found mimes entertaining, as he had walked by them for five straight years when he lived in the city. While Gene was busy watching the mime perform his silent comedy, Pete glanced over at the chair where Jada was seasted. She sat motionless, allowing the artist to complete his cartoon interpretation of her. She looked beautiful as usual. Thick, dark lashes surrounded her bright eyes, and her shiny black hair rested on her shoulders. He didn't know how she was able to hold such a perfect smile for so long, but he was enjoying looking at her perfectly straight, white teeth.

Suddenly she handed the artist a bill, took her drawing, and began walking toward them. She stopped in front of him and held up the drawing.

Pete immediately felt himself smile. The artist had succeeded in making her look like a cartoon version of a Barbie doll.

"Are you laughing at my picture?" Jada asked smiling.

"No!" Pete said, suddenly worried that he may have offended her. "It looks really good."

"Oh. Okay," Jada replied. She gave one last look at the drawing of her head and shoulders complete with a small sketch of the Golden Gate Bridge in the background, before rolling it up, and placing in her bag.

"Why don't we play this while we wait?" Pete took out his cell phone.

"Play what?" Gene asked with a furrowed brow.

Pete held up his cell phone screen. "Who Wants To Be A Millionaire?"

The three worked together to answer the game's questions until Nicole and Tonya's drawings were done. They all proceeded to browse Crocker Galleria, before stopping at Pizzelle for some lunch.

After they had finished their pizza and pasta, Pete led them back to the car so they could hit their next destination on the forty-nine mile tour. Pete drove them through Chinatown, Jackson Square, and North Beach. They drove past Fisherman's Wharf and Fort Mason to Marina Boulevard where they took pictures in front of the Palace of Fine Arts Theater. Then they stopped at the Letterman Digital Arts Center where they toured the gallery of props and costumes from the Star Wars film series.

Finally they reached the destination that Pete knew Jada had been waiting for. He parked in the visitor parking of the Golden Gate Bridge.

"You guys up for an adventure?" Pete asked, turning around in his seat. Blank stares were all that could be seen throughout the vehicle. "We're going to walk across the bridge," Pete continued. He saw Jada's eyes light up.

"Is that safe?" asked Tonya.

"Very," Pete said reassuringly. "I wouldn't take you if it wasn't. "If any of you are afraid of heights, you can stay in the car."

"I don't even do roller coasters, Pete, and you expect me to walk across a bridge?" Tonya asked with concern in her voice and eyes.

"If I can do it, you can do it," Nicole cheered.

With their arms linked through Tonya's, Nicole and Jada followed Pete and Gene to the pedestrian entrance of the bridge. They followed other adventurous tourists as they walked the tall sturdy structure, which brought them out over the San Francisco bay.

Pete snapped a photo of the girls holding onto Tonya. His sister had always been less adventurous than him. He found it amusing those things still hadn't changed. Jada volunteered to take a picture of him and Gene standing on the bridge with the water and boats that looked as small as toys in the background. She then took a picture of Pete, Gene, Nicole, and nervous Tonya against the San Francisco skyline. Pete could tell by the look on Jada's face that this would be an experience she'd never forget.

By the time they made it back to the car, it was almost four o' clock. They were only halfway through the tour. At least they had completed the most time consuming and memorable events, Pete reasoned.

Pete drove past Sea Cliff, where their hotel and The Cliff House restaurants were located, and onto Great Highway. There they rode along the Pacific Ocean past Ocean Beach. They proceeded onto Sunset Boulevard and stopped at Golden Gate Park. Pete took the group through the Japanese Tea Garden for great photos, tea, and cookies.

Pete then drove them to Twin Peaks' 910-foot summit where they stopped for a three hundred sixty degree panoramic view of the city. He watched Jada and Tonya explode through picture after picture of the view. Afterward they drove past Mission Delores and AT&T Park, home of the San Francisco Giants. Then they drove across the Oakland Bay Bridge and past the Ferry Building and Embarcadero Center, both popular San Francisco landmarks for shopping and dining. Finally they passed the Moscone Center, San Francisco's largest convention and exhibition complex, and the San Francisco Museum of Modern Art. With that, their forty-nine mile tour was complete.

It was almost eight o'clock, so Pete decided to officially end their tour by driving to Ghirardelli Square for dinner. He took the group to Lori's Diner, the San Francisco spot designed to pay homage to the 1950s, for burgers and fries.

After dinner they walked over to the Ghirardelli Ice Cream and Chocolate Shop where they viewed the original chocolate manufacturing equipment, and sampled chocolate squares. They each devoured hot fudge sundaes before heading back to the hotel for some much needed rest.

Jada, Nicole and Tonya each lay stretched out on the comfortable hotel beds. While resting their tired limbs, they had been watching the movie, Hitch. Hysterical laughter currently rang throughout the room as they watched the movie's concluding soul train line.

When her laughter subsided, Nicole sat up and leaned her back against the headboard. "That was so beautiful. Why can't I find a man who's going to respect me and treat me right?"

Jada quickly sat up and looked at Nicole. "You and Gene should go out sometime. I think you two would hit it off."

"Me and Gene?" Nicole sounded surprised. "He's cute, but he's always been like a little brother to me."

Jada rolled her eyes. "Come on, Nicole. He's only two years younger than you." She smiled. "And you're both virgins."

Tonya's eyes nearly popped out of her head. "Gene's a virgin? Your cousin looks really good, Jada. I never would have thought that he's a virgin."

Jada laughed. "Looks can be deceiving."

Nicole shrugged. "Gene's never showed any signs that he's interested in me." She looked at Tonya and eyeballed her. "Are you interested in him?"

Tonya shook her head vigorously. "No. I've had my eye on someone else recently." She paused and looked at Nicole. "Why didn't Fernando come?"

"He couldn't get the time off." A look of pride came into Nicole's eyes. "The restaurant where he works just promoted him to head chef. He's been so busy working that he barely has time for anything." Her tone became exasperated. "He doesn't go out much. He doesn't have a girlfriend. All he does is work."

"Oh." Tonya said thoughtfully. She appeared to be taking in all the information she'd just heard. "We should probably go to bed," she said through a yawn. "You know how Pete like's to plan everything early."

"Pete's been a great tour guide." Jada propped herself up on one elbow and looked over at Tonya.

Nicole began weaving her hair into a long, thick single braid. "I agree. This has been one of my favorite trips so far." She smiled and looked at Tonya. "Your brother's cool people."

Jada squinted thoughtfully. "He seems like a really nice guy. I wonder why his last girlfriend broke up with him."

A mischievous grin appeared on Tonya's face. "He's always been into black women, Jada. Maybe you're next."

CHAPTER 11

Shop 'Til You Drop

PETE PUT HIS CHANGE IN HIS wallet and stood up to leave the hotel restaurant.

"I can't believe this is the last day of our trip," said Tonya.

"Yeah, and Jada still hasn't finished any of her food," Gene said as they walked away from a table of empty breakfast plates, excluding Jada's.

Pete couldn't believe it was the fourth and final day either. It had been a great trip so far. He didn't remember having that much fun even when he lived out there.

"Last day," Pete said as they climbed into the Envoy. "Let's make it count. How about we check out the places we didn't make it to yesterday?"

"Can we finish shopping first?" asked Nicole.

"You got it," Pete replied as he started the car and pulled out onto the main road.

As Pete stopped at a traffic light on Geary Boulevard, he stole a look at Jada through the rear view mirror. She was moving strands of hair that had blown across her face as she looked out the window. She is gorgeous, he thought to himself. Sweet, smart, and gorgeous. Beauty and brains...

"The light's green, man," Gene announced, interrupting Pete's thoughts.

Hoping Gene hadn't noticed him daydreaming about his cousin, Pete continued to drive toward downtown. He took the group to the Embarcadero Center, since they had only driven by it yesterday. After parking the car, they headed to the first shopping level.

"Go ahead. Shop 'til you drop," said Pete, looking at the ladies.

"Man, why'd you say that?" Gene said, giving Pete a playful shove in the back.

"I don't know!" Pete replied, playfully shoving him back.

"Now we're gonna be here all day," Gene complained.

"Not unless they want to walk back to the hotel," Pete said dangling his keys.

Gene smiled and smacked hands with Pete. But the truth was, as much as Pete liked making his shopping quick, today he really could care less how long the ladies took. Pete knew this would be the last day he'd get to spend this much time around Jada. He had to admit it to himself; he was falling for her.

Jada savored the taste of the most unique shrimp pasta dish she had ever eaten. Pete had brought them to McCormick and Kuleto's for their last dinner out in San Francisco. As the flavor of juicy shrimp, tender linguine, and fresh basil filled her mouth, she took in the incredible view of the San Francisco bay. Between the food, tours, shopping, and great company, Jada new this had to be the best vacation she'd ever had.

"You guys need to be banned from any more stores," Gene said after taking a long drink of his soda.

"Well you guys need to be banned from movie theaters," Tonya replied as a comeback. "Here we don't know anything about this city, and I get a text message saying that you guys were watching a movie while we shop. Our tour guide ditched us! How messed up is that?"

"It was Gene's idea," Pete said, looking down sheepishly. "But, we were still in the same building," he continued, trying to justify himself.

"But we didn't know where you guys were," added Tonya.

"Look," began Gene. "You all spent forty-five minutes in one store. What did you expect us to do? We're men. We don't take five hours to shop."

"Was it really five hours?" asked Jada.

"Three in the Embarcadero Center, and two in Ghirardelli Square," Pete said with a grin.

Jada smiled and looked at Tonya and Nicole. "Maybe we did get carried away," she relented.

Everyone laughed and went back to eating. For the first time since they'd arrived in San Francisco, Jada actually finished all of her food.

CHAPTER 12

Sea of Bitterness

JADA PUT HER SUITCASES DOWN IN front of the sunlit window, and collapsed onto her bed. Her bed. Boy, did it feel good. She had just been on the most exciting trip of her twenty-seven years, but it sure did feel good to be home. Whether it was jet lag she was feeling, or fatigue from the long action packed days of their trip, Jada could think of nothing she'd rather do right now than sleep.

As she stretched her tired limbs and turned on the TV, her cell phone began to ring. She grabbed it from her nightstand and looked at the screen.

"Hey, Tonya," she answered through the receiver.

"Hey. Did you notice that you don't have your cell phone charger?"

"No," Jada answered slowly.

"You haven't started unpacking yet, huh?"

"Nope. I'm lying down." Jada said wearily. Tonya seemed to have just a little bit too much energy for her right now. All she wanted to do was rest.

"I accidentally put both of our chargers in my suitcase," Tonya explained. "Pete said he'll bring it to you on his way to bowling in a couple of hours if you're going to be around."

"Yeah, I'll be here." Jada hung up the phone.

She continued to lay there. She was glad they had decided to come back on a Thursday. That way she could go back to school on Monday feeling refreshed. Within moments, she drifted off to sleep.

Sunlight no longer streamed through her room when Jada opened her eyes. Afternoon had crept into evening. She looked at the clock and saw that it was after seven. Feeling more rested, but now hungry, Jada made her way into the kitchen to see what there was to eat.

Her dad was in the kitchen washing dishes, and there was a covered plate of chicken and mashed potatoes at the table where she normally sat.

"Hey, Dad," she said as she stopped by the kitchen table. "Is this for me?"

"Hey!" Charles replied enthusiastically. "We didn't think we were going to see you until morning." A teasing grin appeared on his face as he walked over to the plate and picked it up. "So we didn't leave you any food. This plate's for me."

"Oh," Jada replied, slightly disappointed.

"I'm only playing with you," Charles replied, setting the plate back on the table.

Jada smiled and sat down. "All right. Your turn is coming," she said with a similar teasing grin she most likely inherited from her father. She began putting a fork of potatoes into her mouth. "Where's Mom?"

"She went for her evening walk." Charles sat himself down across from Jada. "How was your trip?"

"Great! I never knew San Francisco could be so exciting. I think Pete showed us everything there is to know about that city."

"I almost forgot; Pete dropped your cell phone charger off about an hour ago."

"Okay," Jada replied continuing to alternate between bites of chicken and potatoes.

"Is something going on between you two?" Charles curiously asked.

Jada immediately looked up from her food. "What? No! He's just a friend, Dad."

"If I didn't know any better, I'd say he likes you," Charles looked into his daughter's eyes. "The disappointed look on his face when I told him you were asleep said it all. I felt so bad for him I offered to go wake you up, but he said no."

Jada went back to eating her food. "Dad, please. I'm not interested in dating a white guy. And I highly doubt that he likes me like that."

"What makes you so sure?"

"You know white people think they're better than us," Jada explained.

Charles' eyes immediately widened. "What's going on with you, Jada? Where is this coming from?"

"Come on, Dad. You told me yourself you were called a Nigger when you were growing up. You were laughed at, because you had to walk miles to school while all the little white kids rode by on the bus laughing out the window. And I dealt with their taunting me and physically bullying me all of elementary and middle school. White people think we're less than them, and I don't want to have anything to do with that."

"What about Tonya?" Charles asked, appearing concerned by the harshness he heard in his daughter's voice.

Jada took a deep breath. "She's different. We teach in an urban school district, so she's used to being around diverse people."

"What about your white students?" Charles prodded.

"They're different too." Jada smiled slightly. "I'm able to teach them about seeing everyone as special and liking each other just the way they are."

"Jada," Charles' tone was compassionate. "Those things I told you happened years ago. I've learned to forgive and forget the past. Most white people that I've come across since I've been an adult are nothing like the kids and their parents I dealt with growing up. I had to learn to give each person a fair chance. I'd be just as ignorant if I judged every white person by thinking they're prejudiced without getting to know them. Once I stopped judging them, I began to have nothing but good friendships come out of it."

Jada sighed deeply. "I've done that, Dad. I got to know Tonya, and she's not prejudiced. But she told me that her mother is. Time may only tell before Pete's true colors may come out."

"You've got to give people a chance, Jada. And even if you do come across someone with a prejudiced attitude, no matter what their race may be, you can't go around being hateful and judging every other person from that race. That makes you just as prejudiced as anyone else."

Jada continued to eat in silence. She could feel her dad's eyes still on her. She knew he wasn't done. She looked up when she saw him leave the kitchen. Charles returned to the table with an open Bible in his hand. "*Do not judge, and you will not be judged. Do not condemn and you will not be condemned. Forgive and you will be forgiven.* Luke 6:37." He looked up at Jada before flipping over to a new passage. *Get rid of all bitterness, rage and anger, brawling and slander, along with every form of malice. Be kind and compassionate to one another forgiving each other, just as in Christ God forgave you. Be imitators of God, therefore, as dearly loved children and live a life of love, just as Christ loved us and gave himself up for us as a fragrant offering and sacrifice to God.* Ephesians 4:31-5:2." Charles closed his Bible and watched Jada slowly attempt to finish her food. "Those are two things I always try to remember. If someone does you wrong, no matter how hard it may be, you've got to forgive them, and love them anyway."

Jada put her fork down on her plate and looked at her dad. She saw tenderness in his eyes.

"Are you going to stop hating and judging and do more loving?" Charles asked with a gentle smile.

Jada sighed. "I'll try."

"Your test may come sooner than you think," Charles said with a wink.

CHAPTER 13

A Meeting of Strangers

MIKE HAD BEEN BORED FOR MOST of his April vacation. Bowling was the only fun thing he had done all week. Now that basketball tournaments were over, he had been able to go bowling yesterday. There he'd found out that Gene and Pete had just gotten back from San Francisco. He had also been informed by them that Jada had gone as well. It had now been five weeks since the night Jada had said that she didn't want to keep seeing him. A few times Mike had thought about calling her to see if they could start over. However he had never been able to bring himself to actually call. He decided to face the fact that he had been rejected.

Lately, Jada wasn't the only one who was rejecting Mike. Last week, Brenda had told him that he couldn't stay at her house that weekend, because she had plans. So he had picked Mike Jr. up and brought him to Connecticut for the weekend. This weekend, Brenda said that she had plans again, so Mike couldn't stay at her house. He was beginning to wonder what was going on.

Mike saw that it was almost five o'clock as he exited I-95 in Mount Vernon, New York. He had agreed to arrive at Brenda's house by four o' clock to pick up Mike Jr., but he had left work later than he was supposed to. Brenda had been calling his cell phone every ten minutes for the past hour asking him where he was.

Mike turned onto the street where Brenda and Mike Jr. lived in a two family house. Brenda's landlord lived on the second floor, and she rented the bottom level. Mike was used to the street being crowded with parked cars, but he wasn't used to seeing a car parked in the space directly in front of Brenda's house. He usually parked there, however today he ended up having to park way down the street.

Mike locked his car, and began to walk up the street toward Brenda's house. He walked up the steps and rang the doorbell. The door opened, and Brenda stood glaring at him. Her short hair looked freshly done, and she wore a patterned casual dress with matching earrings.

"Hi," Mike said casually. "Sorry I'm late."

Brenda shook her head. "I was supposed to go to a Broadway show tonight. Now we might be late."

Mike's brows raised at the 'we' that he had just heard. "I'm sorry. I got caught up at work."

Brenda sighed in frustration. "I'll go get Junior." She opened the door wider to let Mike in.

Mike stepped inside and his eyes immediately widened. Off to the left in the living room, he could see a man sitting on the couch. He closed the front door, and followed Brenda into the neatly decorated living room.

Brenda stopped next to the couch. "Shawn, this is Mike, my son's father." She announced. "Mike, this is my friend, Shawn." Brenda gave them both a quick nervous grin.

Shawn stood up and extended his hand to Mike. "Nice to meet you."

Mike took Shawn's extended hand and forced politeness into his voice. "You too."

After the two shook hands, Brenda quickly left the room. Mike stood there, not knowing what to say or do next. Shawn sat back down on the couch, and Mike walked over to a chair in the corner and sat down. The local news was playing on TV. Mike immediately looked at the news anchorman to avoid making eye contact with this stranger he had just met. Silent tension began to build in the room as they both sat quietly staring at the screen.

Just then, Brenda reemerged with a suitcase and Mike Jr. beside her. Mike Jr.'s face lit up and he ran to his dad.

"Daddy!" he yelled.

Mike scooped up his son and gave him a big hug. "Hey, sport!" He placed Mike Jr. back on the ground and gave his head a quick rub. "You ready to go?"

Mike Jr. nodded. "Can we have pizza again tonight?" He looked up at his dad excitedly.

"We sure can." Mike grinned at the sight of his son's widening smile. "Go say goodbye to your mom."

Mike Jr. walked back over to Brenda. She kneeled down and wrapped her arms around her son. "Bye, sweetie. I love you."

"Love you too, Mom." He wrapped his small arms around his mom's neck.

Brenda stood up and looked at her son. "Say goodbye to Mr. Shawn."

Mike Jr. turned around and looked at the couch. "Bye, Mr. Shawn," he said in a timid voice.

Shawn smiled. "Bye, kiddo."

Mike held back a frown. He didn't like the idea of this stranger calling his son kiddo. He walked over to Brenda and took Mike Jr.'s suitcase. Then he turned and looked at Shawn. "Take care," he said flatly.

"All right." Shawn grinned. "You too."

Mike turned back to Brenda. "I'll see you on Sunday."

Brenda followed Mike and her son to the front door. She watched them walk outside and closed the door behind them.

Mike quietly walked his son down the street toward his car. Now Mike knew what was going on with Brenda. She was dating this guy, Shawn. Mike was disturbed by what he had just seen. He wasn't sure he liked seeing a man in Brenda's house. He definitely didn't like the idea of another man being around his son.

CHAPTER 14

New Beginnings

JADA STOOD IN CHURCH AND FOUND her mind drifting to the conversation she'd had with her dad a few days ago. Here people of many races surrounded her. Yet none of them probably had any idea of what she had been struggling with in her heart. For the past three days, Jada had prayed and asked God to forgive her for having bitterness in her heart. Previously, every time she looked at a white face she had to battle feelings of disgust. Today, she felt as if she'd finally won her battle of resentment. During her prayer time, God had reminded her of his scripture that says, *"For you created my inmost being; you knit me together in my mother's womb. I praise you because I am fearfully and wonderfully made."* Psalm 139:13-14. God had also reminded Jada of the scriptures her dad had shared with her. Jada realized that she couldn't spend the rest of her life resenting white people because of the way she had been treated in her past. She knew she couldn't argue with God's Word, so she decided to forgive those who had tried to tear her down. As she looked around the congregation, she knew that something inside of her had been released.

Jada closed her eyes and lifted her hands as the worship team led the congregation in singing Because of Who You Are. The pastor taught on the source of your strength. He had said that God doesn't expect us to meet his expectations on our own, but God will give us the strength to meet his expectations. By the end of the service, Jada felt confident that God would give her the strength to fight the temptation to be bitter.

As the pastor dismissed the congregation, Jada began to walk out of the sanctuary feeling better than ever. She knew she looked good this morning due to the new dress she had on. But right now, she felt beautiful on the inside, too.

"Jada?" A familiar male voice called from behind.

Jada turned around and saw Pete approaching her. "Hi, Pete," she replied. She moved to the side of the lobby to let other church members precede toward the exit doors. "Where's Tonya?" she asked.

"She's up visiting our parents," Pete answered through a slight smile. His eyes searched Jada's face. "You're smiling awfully hard, Jada. What's up?"

Unaware of how big her smile was, Jada responded by saying, "I just feel really good today. This service really blessed my spirit."

"Well you look good too," Pete added.

"Thank you," Jada replied, slightly embarrassed, but still wearing a smile.

"Would you like to go somewhere to get something to eat?" Pete asked, trying to appear confident through a shy grin.

Jada felt her smile weaken slightly as a small ripple went through her stomach. The words of her father replayed in her mind. 'If I didn't know any better, I'd say he likes you.' Then Tonya's words quickly jogged into her memory, 'Pete likes black women.' Jada didn't know what to say. She stood there speechless.

"That is if you're not having dinner with your family today," Pete nervously added.

What a coincidence that she was invited out to eat when her family wasn't around again. Her parents had left on Saturday to visit her father's family in South Carolina. Uncle Jack and Aunt Tina were celebrating their tenth wedding anniversary in Cape May, New Jersey. Grandma and Aunt Ira were at a women's luncheon at their church. Gene, Joe, and Tyrese had gotten tickets to a Celtics game in Boston. It seemed Jada had no excuse.

"Sure," Jada finally replied.

With a more confident smile, Pete escorted Jada out of the church lobby and walked her to her car. They agreed to drive their own vehicles and meet at The Basil Patch.

A touch of déjà vu hit Jada as she made the drive. Same route, same restaurant, only this time, Tonya wasn't there. She parked her car in the parking lot and walked up to the restaurant entrance where Pete was there waiting. For some reason, *GQ* magazine flashed into her mind. She hadn't paid attention to his appearance earlier, but right now Pete stood out. He was standing with his hands in the pockets of his black dress slacks, and a slick brown crew neck T-shirt displayed his strong arms. A smile appeared on his face as Jada approached him.

"Feels like we were just here," Pete said as he held the door open for Jada.

"I was just thinking the same thing," admitted Jada.

After being seated at a table by the window, a waitress arrived to take their orders. The moment became even more familiar when Jada once again ordered the shrimp mozzerella, and Pete ordered shrimp primavera.

As they waited for their orders to come, Jada found herself looking out the window at the comings and goings of the restaurant diners. Then she found herself admiring the trees that were now budding with clusters of pink and white flowers to display the full arrival of spring. Jada suddenly noticed that while she gazed out the window, Pete was busy gazing at her.

"Thanks for coming to eat with me," Pete said through a smile. "I would have been bored today at home all by myself."

Jada grinned slightly. "Yeah, me too. All of my family had plans today except me."

The waitress returned with their orders, and they each silently blessed their food. Then Jada felt herself wanting to know more about Pete.

"So why'd you move to California and then back to Connecticut?" she asked.

"That's a long story, Jada," Pete looked at her with a grin.

Jada dipped her fork into her pasta and glanced back up at Pete. "I have time."

"Well, I was dating this girl in college," Pete appeared to be thinking about his words.

"What was her name?" Jada inquired.

"Stephanie," Pete replied calmly.

Jada nodded as she chewed her food. She waited eagerly for Pete to continue.

"I met her in one of my engineering classes. I was an electrical engineer major, and she was a civil engineer major. So when it was getting time for us to graduate, I asked her what her plans were. She said she really wanted to live out west, so she started applying for jobs in California. I was really into her, so I applied out there too."

Jada placed her fork down and looked directly at Pete. She was becoming completely intrigued by this story.

"So we both ended up getting jobs in San Francisco," continued Pete. "We decide to get an apartment together, and everything was cool. Then she meets this new friend at work. She would say that this girl was so nice. Stephanie started hanging out with her and found out that the girl was a Christian. So the girl invited Stephanie to a concert at her church one night. After that, Stephanie started wanting to go to church and stuff."

Jada watched Pete pause to take a few quick bites of his food. She was fully engrossed in the story and didn't want him to stop.

Pete cleared his throat, preparing to continue. "So I went with Stephanie to church trying to be the supportive boyfriend. I was like, 'I grew up Catholic. I'm used to church.' But this church was different. They kept talking about having a personal relationship with Jesus Christ, and I was like, 'What's that? How can you have a relationship with someone you can't see?' So they started preaching on repentance. They said the first step is to be sorry for your sins and ask Jesus to forgive you and come into your life as your personal savior. I was like, 'Well I've been to confession'. But the personal savior for your sins part had me stumped."

Jada watched Pete take a long drink of soda, set his glass down, and look her deep in the eyes.

"Do you want me to keep going?" he asked. "You haven't really touched your food."

Jada looked down at her plate. He was right. She had been so into his story that she had forgotten to keep eating. "Go ahead," she said, putting a forkful of food into her mouth.

Pete took another quick drink and picked up where he left off. "So I was stumped, but Stephanie was getting it. She kept coming at me like,

'We're living in sin.' I refused to listen to her because I believed it was okay to test things out before getting married. I wanted to keep shacking up for a while. I figured it wouldn't matter as long as we confessed it eventually. Then one day, she told me she had accepted a job back home in New Jersey, and she left."

Jada's eyes widened as she stared at Pete.

Pete leaned in a little closer to Jada. "One thing she told me before she left stuck with me. She said, 'You need to know God for yourself. You need a relationship with God, not me.' But again I was like, 'How can I have a relationship with somebody I can't see?' So I really needed to understand this. I was like, 'This girl left me for another man.' I needed to know this man. So I kept going to that church, and then one Sunday the pastor taught on sins of the flesh."

"I was just reading about that last week," said Jada. "Those are sexual immorality, lust, greed, right?"

"Yeah, and others I'd have to look up," replied Pete. "Usually if I Google it on the computer it shows the scriptures."

"I do that too!" Jada uttered excitedly.

Pete smiled. "So the pastor was like, 'You can get rid of your old self and receive salvation and eternal life right where you're standing.' I prayed with the congregation that Jesus would come into my heart and forgive me of my sins."

Jada smiled, happy to hear that Pete's move to California had resulted in him giving his life to Christ. "So you've covered why you moved to California, but you still haven't said why you moved back."

"I'm getting there," Pete said in his higher octave voice.

Jada laughed, and Pete winked at her. She suddenly remembered the last time she'd heard him use that silly voice. Her mind retreated to their walk on the beach when he told her about his mother's obsession with sunscreen. Jada was really beginning to enjoy Pete's sense of humor.

Turning serious again, Pete began to share his motives for moving back. "Before Stephanie left, we were about to make an offer for a condo," he said. "So I was like, 'I can't get it now. Not on my own income.' So a few

Sundays later the pastor was preaching on obedience, He read the scripture *Bring the whole tithe into the storehouse, that there may be food in my house. Test me in this,"* says the Lord Almighty *"and see if I will not throw open the floodgates of Heaven and pour out so much blessing that you will not have room enough for it.* I know that's somewhere in Malachi."

Pete paused and looked away, appearing to be in deep thought. Then his eyes met Jada's again. "The pastor said if you don't trust and obey God with your finances, how are you going to trust and obey him in anything else. So I saw the *test me in this*, and I said 'Okay.' I gave my ten percent tithe and a ten percent offering every week, and do you know two weeks later they dropped the price of the condo by twenty percent?"

"What?" Jada said in her sing song voice.

"So I bought the condo and I kept tithing. Then a month later I got a ten percent raise. I was able to double some of my mortgage payments.

"That's deep."

"Yeah. So now I'm like, 'I get this relationship thing. God wants to bless us, all we have to do is obey him.'"

Jada smiled. She could see and hear Pete's passion as he spoke. She absentmindedly poked her fork through her pasta while Pete took another long drink of soda.

He then returned his eyes to Jada's as he spoke. "So after that I was talking to God everyday. Thanking him and stuff. So I was like, 'God, I have a relationship with you now. I want to obey you now. I can find Stephanie and tell her I get it now. Maybe we can work things out.' I tried to find her, but all her old numbers were changed, her e-mail, everything. So I was asking God, 'Why?'"

Pete paused to finish up his last bit of food and Jada realized she should probably try to eat her food too, which was now cold from the time she had spent listening instead of eating. She didn't care, though. To her, Pete's story was better than the food right now.

"I was reading 2 Corinthians 5:17," Pete said pausing as if to gather his thoughts. "*If anyone be in Christ he is a new creation. The old has gone, the new has come!* I read it, and I was like, 'Yeah, Lord, I can be my new self with Stephanie. We can start over and have a new relationship doing it right this time. Separate places and everything.'"

"Wow!" exclaimed Jada. "You were sprung!"

Pete raised his eyebrows. "I was," he admitted. "But then the pastor taught on Jeremiah." Pete squinted his eyes. "I think it's Jeremiah 29:11-13, *For I know the plans I have for you," declares the Lord, "plans to prosper you and not to harm you, plans to give you hope and a future. Then you will call upon me and come and pray to me, and I will listen to you. You will seek me and find me when you seek me with all your heart.* I don't have as many scriptures memorized as I probably should, but those that I quoted for you are my favorite scriptures because they've changed my life. I know them from beginning to end._

Jada smiled and reached for her soda.

"Now I'll answer your question," said Pete. "The pastor was like, 'That same scripture applies today.' So I said, 'Maybe the Lord wants me to have a completely new start.' I stopped trying to contact Stephanie. I went back to Connecticut for Christmas and stayed for two weeks. I started thinking it would be good to move back to Connecticut to start brand new. That's when I got hired for the permanent substitute position and gave my job two weeks notice. When the school hired me for a permanent position, I sold my condo and here I am."

"Wow," Jada said with wide eyes.

"To sum it all up, I think God wanted me to follow him instead of a woman."

Jada smiled. "I know exactly what you mean," she sighed. "One day I'll tell you my story."

Pete grinned and finished the last of his soda. "All right," he said through smiling eyes.

Jada drove home thinking about how sincere Pete was. He was so open and honest about all he had been through in his past. She really admired that about him. After walking her to her car, Pete had asked Jada if he could call her sometime. Jada had slowly agreed, but now she was having regrets. Although she enjoyed Pete's company, dating a white guy had never been part of her plan.

Pete dropped his keys on the coffee table and sat down on the couch. He couldn't get the funny look Jada had given him out of his head. After he'd asked her if he could call her sometime, Jada's eyebrows had gone halfway up her head before she finally agreed. The look on her face had made him completely forget to ask for her number. Maybe he could get it from Tonya. He had gotten to know a great woman, and he didn't want this one to get away.

CHAPTER 15

Just Friends

JADA CAPPED HER PEN, AND TUCKED the newspaper's real estate section into the back of her spiral notebook. She had successfully listed three properties she planned to e-mail to her realtor. She really was getting tired of not having a place of her own. Jada looked around her neat bedroom. She had managed to fit a queen-sized bed, mini-entertainment center, large desk, and office chair into the spacious room. Her room was in a house large enough where she often felt as if she were the only one there. She had a great relationship with her parents, but Jada was feeling ready for a change. She now had enough money in her savings, so finances were no longer an issue. Her parents hadn't been charging her much rent, so she had been able to save large chunks of each paycheck. All she had to do was find a place and make the move.

Jada leaned back and began to absentmindedly rock in her office style desk chair. She was beginning to notice the anxious feeling she had been dealing with all week. Pete had called her on Monday to tell her what a nice time he'd had with her after church on Sunday. Then he'd suggested they get together again to do something fun. He'd suggested mini golf if it was nice on Saturday. Jada had accepted his invitation. Now it was a bright, sunny, Saturday afternoon, and Jada wondered if she knew what she was getting herself into.

Like a breath of fresh air, the scripture Jada had read in her personal devotion that morning flooded into her spirit. Jada reached for her Bible and decided to read it again. *Do not be anxious about anything, but in everything, by prayer and petition, with thanksgiving, present your requests to God.* Philippians 4:6. Jada closed her Bible.

Just go to relax and have a good time, she thought. She silently thanked the Lord for blessing her with a new friend. She prayed that her eyes would be open to see God's plan for her.

Then Jada heard a voice in her spirit say, "What do you want?"

Without knowing exactly why, Jada opened her notebook and began to make a list. She wrote the words love, laughter, kindness, devoted to God, husband, family.

Just as she'd finished writing, the doorbell rang. Jada quickly stood up and rushed over to her full-length mirror. Not a wrinkle could be found in her jeans. She pulled her cropped jean jacket over her yellow shirt and slipped her French manicured toes into her studded thonged sandals. Then she scampered down the hall and hurried down the stairs, slowing when she had almost reached the living room. She walked into the room to find Pete sitting on the loveseat, chatting with her mom and dad. She cleared her throat.

Pete looked over at Jada. "Looks like you're ready," he said through a smile. He stood up and walked over to shake Charles and Dana's hands. "I'll take good care of your daughter," he assured them.

Charles patted Pete on the back. "That's what I like to here." He gave Pete a firm handshake.

Feeling somewhat like a teenager going on a first date, Jada walked with Pete to his car. She had never paid attention to his car before, but it was nice. He was driving a newer cranberry colored Nissan Maxima with gray interior. He must've had a new car scent air freshener somewhere in the vehicle, because the car smelled brand new. It was also extremely clean. That's a plus, Jada thought. She didn't want no Messy Marvin. Suddenly Jada was aware that she had just made a reference to wanting Pete. Well where did that come from? A pondering look came over her face.

"You're awfully quiet," Pete said cutting through the silence.

"I was just thinking about how much I like your car."

Pete smiled and looked over at her. "Is that all you like?"

Jada glanced in Pete's direction, noticing the dimple that now rested in his cheek. "You're okay, too, I guess," she said, returning her eyes to the window.

"I'll settle for that. For now," Pete said as he pulled the car into the sports complex and quickly found a park.

Jada was prepared to pay for her game of mini-golf. She didn't want to consider this a date, because Pete wasn't the type of guy she planned to be in a relationship with. However, she had to admit that she enjoyed being around him. As she looked down to pull her wallet out of her purse, she saw Pete's hand rest on hers. Her hand froze as she looked up at him.

"Everything's my treat today," he said. Then he paid the clerk, and asked for a red ball.

Jada took a green ball, and went with Pete to choose a golf club. "Do you play mini-golf a lot?" she asked.

"Not really. I'm into real golf mostly. That's what I usually do on Saturdays. I play with one of the other math teachers." Pete paused as Jada looked up at him and nodded. "But I'd much rather be playing mini golf with someone as gorgeous as you," he crooned.

Jada didn't know what to say. She gave Pete a faint smile and said, "That's sweet."

Jada watched Pete effortlessly put the ball within centimeters of the first hole. He managed to give his ball just enough power to make it up the hill, but not too much power that it would roll back down. Then Jada made her attempt. Her ball rolled up the hill, hit the back barrier, and began to roll backwards until the ball landed back where it started. She looked over at Pete who was standing off to the side.

Both hands rested on Pete's golf club as he smiled at her silently. "Just try not to hit it as hard this time," he patiently said.

Jada repositioned herself and took her best golfer's stance. With a lighter, firm tap, her ball went up the hill, and hit Pete's ball sending his ball against the barrier and back down the hill, while hers stopped within inches from the hole.

"What!" Pete shouted in his now all too familiar high octave voice. "Oh, it's on now, Jada," he said with a grin.

Jada found herself laughing almost uncontrollably at the irony of how her ball was now closer to the hole than Pete's. Calming down, she watched a determined look appear on Pete's face. The muscles in his arms flexed as he prepared to bring his club in contact with the ball. As Jada watched him, she realized that Pete's car wasn't the only thing she liked. He was looking really good today.

Pete managed to make a comeback by hitting his ball directly into the hole, and Jada tapped hers in as well. They continued to navigate the course full of sand traps, hidden rivers, and miniature buildings. For the most part, Pete stood off to the side watching Jada as she took her strokes, giving her advice now and then. Once or twice, he stood behind her, placed his hands on hers, and assisted her in hitting the ball.

Jada watched Pete make four hole in ones. Whenever he felt he had made a bad shot, she would chuckle, and he would playfully eyeball her. She found herself laughing at the various facial expressions he would make.

Finally, Jada made her first hole in one at the last hole.

"Good job," Pete said putting his arm around Jada.

"Thanks, but you still beat the mess out of me" They returned their clubs and began walking to the car.

"You'll do better next time," Pete gave Jada's shoulder a squeeze.

After Pete unlocked and opened her door, Jada sat on the passenger side and waited for him to get in.

Pete sat down on the driver's side, and started the car. "Did you have fun?" Pete asked looking at her with his light brown eyes.

"Definitely." Jada smiled. "We should do this again."

Pete nodded and grinned. "How about we go get something to eat at Mama's Place?"

Sure," Jada exclaimed with much more excitement than she had intended.

***

Jada watched Pete get out of the car and walk over towards her as she stood in the driveway holding her leftover sweet potato pie. Then they walked across the driveway and up the steps to Jada's front door.

"Thank you for spending the day with me, Jada,." Pete said. " I had a really nice time."

Jada smiled and looked up at him. "Me too."

The setting sun added a glow to Pete's slightly tanned face as he leaned in and kissed Jada on the cheek. "I'll call you tomorrow."

"Okay," Jada almost whispered. She turned her key, and entered the front door. She quickly pulled the curtain away from the side window to watch Pete walk back to his car. When he had driven away, Jada sighed happily and walked up to her room.

She turned on her light, and walked over to her desk to check for messages. As she sat down, the list she had made before she'd left caught her eye. She saw the words kindness and laughter. She thought about how kind Pete was and how much he had made her laugh today. He has such a great sense of humor, she thought. Then Jada saw the words devoted to God. She believed that Pete had his devotion to God under control. His church attendance seemed regular, and he had talked bout obeying and following God so passionately when they had gone out to eat last Sunday. Jada's mind and heart were now racing. Could she and Pete really become more than just friends?

CHAPTER 16

Family Sunday

AFTER SPENDING THE DAY TOGETHER LAST Saturday, Pete had done just as he'd said he would. He had called Jada the next day, and told her how much he enjoyed spending time with her. He had also called her on Monday to see how her day had been. Jada found it so easy to talk to him, and Pete would just patiently listen.

On Tuesday, they'd had a more intimate phone conversation. Just as Pete had opened up about his past relationship, Jada decided to finally open up about hers.

"Remember how you said that your break-up with Stephanie brought you closer to God?" Jada had asked.

"Yeah," Pete had replied.

"When I broke up with my high school sweet heart, it brought me closer to God too," Jada had explained. "I had grown up being taught that I should wait until marriage to have sex. I had planned to do that, until I met Tony. He was one of the stars on the basketball team, and we started dating in my junior year of high school. We went to both proms together, and ended up going to the same college. By then, I was convinced that we were meant to be together, and he would hint at it too. He would say that he wanted to marry me when we were done with college, so it wouldn't matter if we went ahead and started having sex."

Jada had paused at this point. She had been a little nervous about continuing. She had never told any other man this much detailed information about her relationship with Tony.

"Are you still there?" Pete had asked.

"Yeah." Jada had sighed before continuing. "So I gave my virginity to him in our freshman year of college. Then a year later, I started hearing from a friend that he was messing around with another girl. I didn't believe it at first. When we started spending less time together, I started getting suspicious. Two more friends of mine then told me of a girl they each knew that he was messing around with. That was enough for me to believe that it was true. He never admitted to it, but I left him alone anyway. I didn't need the drama."

"Too many women accept that kind of drama," Pete had reasoned.

"I know," Jada had agreed. "I realized that I had neglected my relationship with God when I got in a relationship with Tony. After I ended things with him, I decided that I wouldn't let another man come between my relationship with God." Jada was glad that she had decided to tell Pete more about herself. She felt comfortable with him, and they were becoming close friends. Pete had continued to faithfully call Jada every other day that week.

Now it was the first Sunday of May and as Jada entered the sanctuary for praise and worship, she was hoping she would see Pete today in church.

Jada lifted her voice as the praise and worship team sang All Praise and Honor by Paul Baloche.

As Jada rocked to the music and prepared to sing the verse, she suddenly noticed the male voice that joined in beside her.

Jada looked over and saw Pete standing next to her. How'd he know where she was sitting? She wondered. Then she remembered that in one of their phone conversations he'd asked her where she usually sat on Sundays. Jada quickly recovered from the initial shock and began to lift her voice again in worship. She imagined that it was just her singing praises to God.

When the song was completed, the pastor asked them to turn and greet someone near them. Jada turned to Pete as they each extended their arms to give a nice brother-and-sister-in-Christ hug. They also turned to greet other worshipers in the congregation.

Although Pete looked very good to Jada dressed in khaki pants, and a ribbed white crew neck shirt, she was able to keep her composure and focus on the sermon. Pastor John extended on the resurrection sermon by preaching on the power of God. His message was, If God had the power to perform the miracle of raising Jesus from the dead, then surely he has the power to work things out according to his will. Jada allowed the message to sink into her heart. Soon, Pastor John was closing in prayer and the congregation was dismissed.

Jada looked up at Pete. "Are you following me?" she asked with her teasing grin.

"Something like that," Pete playfully responded.

"Is Tonya at your parents' house again?" asked Jada.

"Yeah. She said an old high school friend just moved back into that area, and they were going to hang out this weekend." Pete smiled. "Sometimes I think she's been going up there to get away from me."

"Now what would make you think that?" Jada asked sarcastically. Pete had already told her that he was aware of Tonya's disappointment when he had finally moved into her apartment. Without waiting for him to respond, Jada continued. "I'm scheduled to look at some condos this week with my realtor. I can give you her name and number, if you want."

Pete thoughtfully nodded. "So, can I interest you in going to eat with me again?"

"Well, my family is supposed to be getting together for dinner again today. I'm sure you've noticed how my family loves to eat."

Pete's eyes grew wide. "Oh, I've noticed."

"Do you want to come?" the words seemed to fly out of Jada's mouth. Pete stood there appearing to be somewhat shocked. "I get the feeling my family likes you," Jada explained. "I'm sure they'd be glad to see you."

"Cool," Pete said with a smile.

"There's my little boy!" Grandma exclaimed when she saw Pete walk into the living room with Jada.

Pete scanned the area to see who else the woman could be referring to, but there weren't any other males around. Somewhat surprised by the greeting, Pete smiled and walked over to Jada's grandmother who was sitting in a chair by the window. He bent down to give her a hug. "How are you Ms...?"

"Grandma," she said, looking at him as she held onto his hands. "You call me Grandma."

"All right, Grandma," Pete said with a smile. He began to walk over to the couch where Jada was now seated.

"Am I invisible?" an elderly voice cried out.

Pete quickly looked in the direction of the voice, and saw Jada's great aunt sitting on the loveseat. He quickly looked back at Jada who mouthed, "She's kidding."

Not wanting to take any chances, Pete walked over to the elderly lady and gave her a hug. "Nice to see you Ms...?"

"Aunt Ira," she answered in a sweet voice.

Pete was confused. One minute she sounded like she was going to knock him upside the head with her cane, and the next minute she sounded like a sweet little old lady. Nevertheless, he sat down next to Jada and tried to relax.

Just then Jada turned and looked at him. "I'm going to go see if my mother needs any help with anything," she said.

Pete smiled at her as she left him with the two elderly family matriarchs.

Grandma looked at Pete with a sweet smile. "So you like my granddaughter, don't you?" she asked.

"Yes, ma'am. I do," Pete responded in a genuine voice.

"You seem very respectseful," Grandma said.

"Yes, ma'am. I try to be respectful."

"Don't come 'round here correcting folks now," Aunt Ira chimed in. "We talk how we wants to talk around here. This ain't school."

Pete began to vigorously shake his head, "Oh, no, ma'am. I wasn't trying to correct anyone."

"Well, all right," Aunt Ira replied in her sweet tone.

Pete exhaled deeply. He knew it was going to take some time to get used to the ways of Jada's family, but he was more than willing to put in the effort. He saw a future with Jada, whether she saw it yet or not.

At that moment, Jada reentered the living room. "As soon as the rest of the family gets here we can all go eat," she said returning to her seat next to Pete.

"Ya'll went to church today?" Grandma asked looking at Jada and Pete.

"Yes, we did, Grandma," Jada replied.

Grandma silently nodded as she looked at them and smiled. Then the doorbell rang announcing the arrival of the rest of Jada's family. Gene, Joe, Tyrese, and their parents Uncle Bob and Aunt Linda walked in with Unlce Jack and Aunt Tina following behind. They all made their way into the kitchen where the food was blessed by Jada's dad. Then they all began piling their plates with lasagna, salad, and Italian bread.

The family divided itself among the kitchen and dining room tables. Grandma, Aunt Ira, Dana, Charles, Uncle Bob, and Aunt Linda chatted around the dining room table. Pete and Jada ate in the kitchen with the younger half of the family. Conversation drifted to the highlights of their San Francisco trip. As they all consumed the food, laughter rang through the Calloway home. Pete sat there enjoying every minute of it. He had found a beautiful woman with a great family. What more could he ask for?

CHAPTER 17

New York City

"I'M GLAD WE DECIDED TO COME down here," Jada told Tonya as they stepped off the Metro North train.

Tonya smiled. "We were overdue for another shopping trip. We haven't gone shopping since San Francisco."

"I can't believe that was a month ago already." Jada pulled a pack of gum out of her purse. She placed a stick of gum into her mouth and handed the pack to Tonya.

They exited the crowded terminal and entered Grand Central Station. Activity surrounded them as they navigated through the sea of people toward the 42nd Street exit. From there they planned to walk to Macy's and then H&M. They liked shopping at the Manhattan locations, because the stores were significantly larger and always had a wider selection. The Macy's at 34th and Broadway had ten shopping levels, three of which all sold women's clothing. Jada was excited about shopping on the third and fourth floors for her clothes and shoes. After, she'd check out the main floor for perfume, cosmetics, and accessories.

The sun was shining brightly as the ladies walked onto the busy sidewalk. Crowds of people surrounded them as they headed toward 34th Street.

"San Francisco's a nice city." Jada continued. "Nicole said she liked it too."

"I had fun hanging out with you two. That was actually the first trip that I've gone on where I didn't go drinking or clubbing. " Tonya looked at Jada thoughtfully. "You and Nicole actually live what you believe. I might start going to your church more often. I need some of that to rub off on me."

Jada smiled. "I was never into drinking, but I stopped clubbing in my college days. I don't miss it either."

"Pete's a lot different than he was when he finished college." Tonya seemed to pause and think about her words. "It's like I'm getting to know him all over again. He doesn't go drinking or clubbing anymore, and he actually enjoys going to church. That's a sight to see."

"Is it still annoying living with him?" Jada glanced at Tonya curiously.

Tonya rolled her eyes. "Yes! That's why I'm glad we decided to go shopping today. I can only take but so much of him." Her mouth formed into a pout. "He's invading my space."

Jada laughed. "Well if it makes you feel any better, I gave him the name of my realtor on Sunday."

Tonya's eyes lit up, "Oh, good!"

"I'm supposed to go look at a few condos next weekend actually," added Jada.

Tonya chuckled. "Can you take him with you?" A hint of sarcasm laced her tone.

A thoughtful look came over Jada's face, "Maybe I should. My dad's going to be working and I could use a male opinion."

Having reached 34th and Broadway, Jada and Tonya followed a few other pedestrians into the multi-leveled Macy's store. They walked past a few men and women handing out fragrance cards as they headed for the escalators. Jada accepted a card for a new women's fragrance. She held it to her nose and inhaled softly.

Tonya began to rekindle the conversation. "You and Pete have been spending a lot of time together." She smiled slightly. "What's going on with you two?"

Jada shrugged. "We're just friends."

Tonya raised her eyebrows. "Are you sure that's all you guys are?"

"For now," Jada added casually. She stepped onto the escalator and turned to look at Tonya.

"Come on, Jada. Admit it. You like him, don't you?" Tonya grinned knowingly. "I can tell he likes you. I see it in the way he looks at you."

Jada couldn't hold back the grin that was appearing on her face. "Okay, I'll admit it! I do like him," she relented. "He's nice, he's funny," She smirked slowly, "and he's super fine. I don't care that he's a white guy. Your brother's got it goin' on!"

Tonya laughed as she stepped onto the next escalator. "I'm so happy for you guys."

"You are?" Jada smiled shyly. "I didn't know how you would feel."

"I think you both seem good for each other." Tonya paused and took a deep breath. "But I have to warn you. I don't think my mother's going to agree."

Jada and Tonya stepped off of the escalator onto the abundantly stocked third floor. As they walked the isle toward the casual clothing, Jada realized that the thought of having to meet Pete's parents made her nervous . She remembered Tonya mentioning that their mother didn't approve of interracial dating. If Jada was right about where things were going with her and Pete, she would have to meet his mother eventually. Jada's body tensed with anxiety.

A sympathetic look came over Tonya's face. "My mother might give you a hard time. Just make sure you're ready."

CHAPTER 18

A Night with the McKnights

PETE WAS POSITIVE THAT HE WANTED to move into a more serious relationship with Jada. He was sure he had picked up signals that she felt the same way. Pete had found out that the comedian who visited the church a while ago was going to be back in Connecticut. Jada had agreed to go watch the show with him. Then the hard part came. Since the comedy club was near his parents' house, he'd asked Jada if she wanted to meet them before the show. Though she hesitated, she had agreed. That confirmed for Pete that the feelings he had for her were mutual. Any woman in her right mind would not want to meet a woman with his mother's reputation, unless they wanted the relationship to go further.

Pete was sure Tonya had mentioned a few things to Jada about their mother by now. Tonya had probably told Jada about his mother's prejudiced attitude. Since becoming saved, Pete had prayed for his mother daily that she would no longer be narrow-minded. He hoped that she had changed her ways and become less proud and judgmental about others.

As part of the visit, his mother had offered to cook them dinner before the show. Dressed in dark tan khaki pants, and a brown ribbed crew neck shirt, Pete grabbed his keys, and headed to his car to pick up Jada.

Jada nervously squeezed Pete's hand as she stood next to him on the steps of the McKnight home. He released her hand, put his arm around her and began to gently rub her shoulder.

"Try to relax," he said. "It'll be okay."

Jada wasn't convinced. Suddenly the door opened. Jada immediately noticed the beautiful woman standing in front her. Next to her was a tall, broad white man. Thick auburn hair hung over the woman's shoulders, and she looked at Jada through bright green eyes. Suddenly the pearly white smile she wore began to fade, and her green eyes seemed to darken a bit.

"Mom, Dad, this is Jada. The girl I was telling you about," Pete said cheerfully.

"Yeah, come on in," Mr. McKnight said through a slight smile as he stepped to the side to let Jada and Pete through.

As they walked past Mrs. McKnight, she folded her arms and looked at them with a grimace on her face. Jada immediately knew that this woman was going to be trouble.

"Have a seat. Make yourselves comfortable," Mr. McKnight said, pointing to a long, white couch. He then put his arm around his wife and walked over to a love seat angled to the right of the couch.

They all sat down in an awkward silence. Jada wanted to grab her purse and run straight for the door. She was convinced that her coming there had been a bad idea.

Mrs. McKnight abruptly stood up. "I think we should go ahead and eat," she said, turning to walk toward the kitchen.

Jada was sure Mrs. McKnight wanted her to get out of there just as much as she wanted to leave. She and Pete followed Mr. and Mrs. McKnight into the dining room. Jada seated herself next to Pete at the long dining room table. Mr. McKnight sat at the head. Mrs. McKnight placed a glass pan of chicken parmesan on the table next to a plate of dinner rolls. Then she placed a bowl of pasta and a bowl of salad on either side, and sat across from her husband.

"Would either of you like wine?" Mr. McKnight asked, picking up the bottle of Merlot.

"No, thanks," Jada and Pete answered almost in unison.

Mr. McKnight poured some for himself and passed the bottle to his wife. Pete picked up the glass picture of lemonade and poured some into Jada's glass, and then into his own.

"You can serve yourselves," Mrs. McKnight said.

Jada filled her plate with salad, chicken, pasta, and bread. Then she silently bowed her head to bless her food. When she lifted her head, she saw Mr. McKnight looking at his son bewildered as Pete did the same. Mrs. McKnight was already looking down at her plate and eating.

"So," Mr. McKnight began breaking the silence. "Tell us a little about yourself, Jada. What do you do?"

"I teach first grade," Jada replied.

"Oh. That's nice," encouraged Mr. McKnight. "How many students do you have in your class?"

"Twenty-one," Jada answered, smiling at Mr. McKnight. She was trying her best to sound as pleasant as possible despite how uncomfortable she felt.

"Do you have any children of your own," Mrs. McKnight suddenly interjected. "Because you girls seem to have children so young and then end up being single moms."

Jada's eyes widened as she looked at Mrs. McKnight. "No, I don't have any children," she politely replied.

"Is your mother single?" Mrs. McKnight continued.

"No," answered Jada. "My parents have been happily married for twenty-nine years.

Mrs. McKnight had now put her fork down, and was looking at Jada with her arms folded. "Oh. Well so many of you people come from single moms, who keep having babies, and then you end up the same way."

Jada looked over at Pete's dad. His face was as red as could be, and he was looking at his wife with a scowl. Then Jada looked at Pete who looked more hurt, than angry. He was looking at his mother with a pleading look in his eyes as if he were silently begging her to stop.

"Do you have brothers and sisters?" Mrs. McKnight asked.

Jada let out a breath relieved that Mrs. McKnight had asked a normal question. "No. I'm an only child," she replied.

"That's surprising," Mrs. McKnight snickered. "Because so many of you women have multiple children with more than one baby's dad. That is what you call it now, right?"

No one responded. It seemed to Jada that Mrs. McKnight was trying to find out something about her or her family that would make Jada unqualified for her son in her eyes.

Mrs. McKnight cleared her throat and continued. "Well, Pete went to his senior prom with this black girl named Monica who used to live a couple streets away from here. Her mother was single, and her sister has two children by two different men. The mother and sister still live there, and I see the sister's wild kids playing outside when I drive through the neighborhood." Mrs. McKnight took a long sip of wine and placed her glass down. "I'm so glad Pete didn't take things seriously with that girl."

Pete put his fork down and dropped his napkin onto his plate. "We should get going so we don't miss the show." He looked over at Jada. "Do you need a few more minutes to finish your food?"

Jada knew it was still early. She hadn't even finished half of her food, but she jumped on the opportunity to get as far away from Mrs. McKnight as possible. "No," she said. Looking at Mrs. McKnight, she continued. "Thank you for dinner," Jada forced a smile.

The grimace Mrs. McKnight had worn earlier returned.

"I'm going to use the bathroom, and then we're leaving," said Pete. "Do you need to use the restroom?" Pete asked, looking at Jada.

Jada didn't really need to go, but she didn't want to be left alone with Pete's parents, so she nodded yes. She then followed Pete into the kitchen where he pointed to a hall off to the right.

"It's down that hall," he instructed.

"You can go first," Jada offered.

While Pete went to the bathroom, Jada gazed around the McKnight home. Because of the open floor plan, she could see directly into the family room. She caught sight of a glass case with pictures inside of it, so she walked a little closer. She saw Tonya and Pete's high school and college graduation pictures. Then she saw two pictures of Tonya dressed in a long gown. In one picture she was standing with a pale, blonde boy. In the other picture, she was standing with a slightly tanned boy with black hair. She assumed those were Tonya's junior and senior prom dates. Then Jada saw a picture of Pete dressed in a black suit, with a pale, brown-haired girl standing next to him. Jada knew that had to be his junior prom picture, because the picture with Monica was nowhere to be found.

Jada heard footsteps behind her and turned to see Pete.

"You can use the bathroom now," he said in a strained voice. He looked distraught. She wondered what he had been doing.

"I don't really need to go after all," Jada said. The sooner they got out of there the better. It was obvious to her that neither one of them were happy.

Pete took Jada by the hand, and walked her back into the dining room. Mr. McKnight stood up as they entered the room.

"I'll walk you two out," Mr. McKnight said.

Pete walked over to his mother. He leaned down, and kissed her on the cheek. "Bye, Mom." he said.

"Bye, sweetheart," she replied.

"Good-bye, Mrs. McKnight," Jada said as kindly as she could.

"Good-bye," Mrs. McKnight replied coldly without looking at Jada.

Jada walked with Pete toward the front door where Mr. McKnight waited.

He patted Pete on the back.

"I'll see you later, son," he said.

"Bye, Dad."

"Good-night, Mr. McKnight," Jada said. "It was nice meeting you."

"Same to you, dear," he replied.

As they walked to Pete's car, Jada began to conclude where Tonya and Pete had gotten their personalities. It must have been from Mr. McKnight. If he had a problem with her, at least he didn't show it, Jada thought.

Pete opened the car door for Jada and waited for her to get in. He walked around to the driver's side, got in, and started the car. Before he drove off, he turned and looked at Jada with sadness in his eyes. "Are you okay?" he asked.

Jada nodded. She didn't really feel like speaking. She didn't have anything good to say, so she figured she might as well stay quiet. The way Mrs. McKnight had thrown out stereotypes left and right had Jada fuming inside.

It was a quiet ride to the comedy show. The only sounds that could be heard were the instruments and voices from the car stereo. When they arrived at the comedy club, Pete put his arm around Jada and they walked inside. It could have been a great date, as it was a classy club, and they were seated at a small intimate table. But, Jada could hardly enjoy any of it after what Mrs. McKnight had put her through.

CHAPTER 19

Professions

JADA HAD BEEN UPSET ALL NIGHT over Mrs. McKnight, but today was a new day, so she decided to put it out of her mind. Jada walked over to her kidney shaped reading table and sat down, waiting for the students from her third grade tutoring group to arrive. The third grade reading tests were now complete, and she had been informed that all of her students had passed. Today was now the last day of tutoring and Jada had planned to let them play a reading board game. It would reinforce their reading strategies and allow them to have fun at the same time.

At eight o'clock sharp the students began to enter Jada's classroom one by one. They put their backpacks on the rug, and gathered around the reading table.

"Good morning, boys and girls!" Jada announced.

"Good morning, Miss Calloway," the three more vocal students replied.

The four quieter students simply responded with shy smiles. Jada looked at the faces that sat around her reading table. Three Hispanic students, two black students, and two white students sat facing her. Jada opened the box to the game and placed the pieces used to move around the board onto the table. Allowing the students to choose their own pieces, Jada quickly stepped over to the back counter to retrieve the list of rules.

Just then a voice said, "Here you go, blacky. This one's perfect for you."

Knowing the voices of all her students, Jada believed she knew who had uttered those words. It was the voice of her butterscotch toned student Latasha. Latasha may have been light-skinned, but she was still black. Latasha could be mean spirited at times by laughing at other students or calling them hurtful names. Jada's suspicions were confirmed when she looked up just in time to see Latasha hand a black playing piece to Desire, a cute little girl with a very smooth, dark skintone. The fact that Latasha had chosen to call Desire 'Blacky' was extremely disturbing to Jada. Jada was not about to allow a student to make someone else feel bad because of their skintone. She decided to calmly walk over to Latasha.

"Latasha, I need to see you at my desk please," Jada pleasantly said.

Latasha walked with Jada to the large teacher desk. Jada sat down so she would be eye level with Latasha.

"Do you think you may have called Desire a name that wasn't nice?" Jada asked.

Latasha looked down and nodded her head.

"Can you tell me what you called her?"

"Blacky," Latasha mumbled.

"Is that her name?" Jada softly asked.

Latasha looked up slowly. "No."

"So do you think that was a nice thing to call her?" Jada kept her tone sympathetic.

Latasha shook her head.

"Why did you call her that name?" Jada inquired gently.

Latasha shrugged.

"Have you heard someone else say that before?"

Latasha looked at Jada and nodded her head. Jada waited patiently for her to say something, but Latasha just stood there.

"Okay. Well you don't have to tell me who you've heard say that name before, but I want you to listen to me very carefully. Calling people names can be very hurtful. If you call someone a name that makes fun of the way they look, or act, it makes them feel bad about themselves. Do you understand?"

Latasha continued to look at Jada, and said, "Yes."

"So what do you think would be the right thing for you to do now?" Jada smiled slightly.

"Say I'm sorry?" Latasha asked with uncertainty in her voice.

Jada's smile widened. "You got it."

Jada walked with Latasha back over to the reading table. She watched Latasha sit down in her seat next to Desire. Then Latasha tapped Desire and looked at her.

"I'm sorry that I called you a name," Latasha said quietly.

Desire looked at Latasha and shrugged. "It's okay," she replied.

Desire was a very mild mannered child. She rarely complained about anything. Jada was glad that she had attempted to resolve the situation to avoid any hurt feelings that could have surfaced later on.

Jada sat back down in her seat at the reading table and quickly read over the rules to the game. She watched as the children smiled, laughed, and cooperatively played the game together. Jada could tell that Desire had genuinely forgiven Latasha. At that moment Jada wished for an ounce of the same strength that was in that little child.

Traces of the evening sun streamed through Jada's bedroom window as she sat at her desk checking e-mail. Hearing her cell phone ring, she picked it up and looked at the screen.

"Hi, Pete," she answered.

"Hey, doll," he replied.

"Doll?" questioned Jada. "What do you mean by that?"

Pete laughed softly. "When I look at you, you remind me of those little dolls my sister used to play with. What are they called?"

Jada paused for a moment. "Barbie dolls?" she asked.

"Yeah! That's what they're called! You remind me of a Barbie doll, Jada. So that's the nickname I gave you in my mind. Do you mind if that's what I call you sometimes?"

Jada thought for a moment, and then a smile came on her face. The name was kind of cute. "I guess not," she said.

"All right," Pete sighed. "So how was your day?"

Jada logged off of her computer to give Pete her full attention. "It was interesting."

"Why? What happened?" Pete's voice was inquisitive.

Jada told Pete about what happened in school between her students Latasha and Desire. When she had finished every detail, she waited for Pete to respond.

"I think you did a great job, Jada," he said. "Sounds like by the end of class they were acting like the best of friends."

Jada thought about how Pete was such a good listener. She loved that about him. "You always know how to encourage me."

"Isn't that what your man is supposed to do?"

"Oh, so you're my man?" Jada asked through a smile.

"Well that's up to you. But I'll let you know right now. I'm already claiming you as my woman."

Jada felt her heart skip a beat. She couldn't believe what she was hearing. "Are you sure about this, Pete?" she hesitantly asked.

"I've been sure since the day I met you."

Jada was speechless. Her heart said "yes", but her mind still said "Is he for real?"

"I know what you're thinking, Jada. I don't see black. I just see beautiful. But since you're black, I guess that means black is beautiful.

Jada placed her hand on her fluttering heart.

"Seriously, Jada. You're beautiful inside and out. I'd be honored to call you my woman."

Jada let out a long, deep breath. "Well I guess that makes us a couple then."

CHAPTER 20

House Hunting

JADA RANG THE DOORBELL OUTSIDE OF Tonya's apartment door and waited to be let in. Pete had agreed to go along with her today to check out some condos with her realtor. He had suggested that she stop by for breakfast before they took off for the day.

The door opened and Tonya stood on the other side. "Hey, Jada!" she greeted cheerfully. "Pete just told me you were coming by this morning."

Jada walked inside as Tonya closed the door behind her. "I guess I'm finally going to taste some of this great cooking you've been telling me about."

Tonya smiled and began to clip back the sides of her hair. "Pete's finishing up in the kitchen." She smoothed the back of her hair down and zipped up her hooded sweatshirt. "Make sure you guys save me some food."

"Oh you're not staying?" Jada sounded surprised.

Tonya shook her head. "I'm going to the gym. You're not fooling me, Jada. I know you two want to be alone anyway." A curious smirk came across her face. "So are you guys officially together yet?"

Jada nodded and grinned happily. "We just made it official yesterday."

"Aaahh!" Tonya screeched. "I knew it! I knew you two were falling for each other!"

Pete came around the corner with a smile on his face. "What's all this noise out here."

"Jada just told me that you two are officially together!" Tonya exclaimed. "That's great! You guys are going to work out. I know it."

Jada beamed as Pete put his arm around her and kissed her on the cheek. She wrapped her arm around his waist as they both stood looking at an excited Tonya.

"Well, I'm going to let you two have some time for yourselves." Tonya opened the front door. "I'll see you guys later," she said as she closed the door behind her.

Pete gave Jada another kiss on the cheek. "You ready to eat?" He smiled down at her.

Jada nodded. "I just need to wash my hands."

Pete gave her shoulder a squeeze. "I'll wait for you in the kitchen."

Jada washed her hands in the bathroom, and then walked into the small eat-in kitchen. She was surprised at what lay on the table in front of her. A bowl of fresh fruit salad, home made waffles, home fries, and fluffy scrambled eggs were all neatly arranged on the center of the glass, circular table.

"I don't know where to start." She stared at the table with her mouth open in shock.

Pete laughed and rose from his seat. "How about you start with sitting down," he said jokingly. He walked to the chair next to him, pulled it out, and waited until Jada was seated. Then he sat down, took Jada's hand, and blessed the food.

Jada lightly buttered her waffle, and drizzled syrup over it. She used her knife to cut off a small piece and placed it into her mouth. It was so good she had to close her eyes while she chewed.

"Mmm," Jada exhaled. "Where'd you learn to cook like this?" She opened her eyes and looked at Pete.

The side of Pete's mouth raised into a crooked little grin. "My mom loves to cook. When we were kids, Tonya and I would hang out in the kitchen with her. She started showing us how to cook when I was like seven. After a while we started to catch on."

Jada wiped her mouth with her napkin and picked up her glass of orange juice. "She definitely taught you well."

After taking a few sips of her juice, Jada placed her glass down thoughtfully. With the mention of Pete's mother, Jada was reminded of her visit with his parents the other night. Mrs. McKnight hadn't made any attempts to be pleasant towards her. Jada wondered how a man as nice as Pete could have a mother who had been so mean.

"I don't think your mother likes me very much," Jada sadly glanced up at Pete.

Pete placed his fork down and sighed. "I love my mother, but she's very ignorant."

"What do you mean?" inquired Jada.

"She grew up in a very small town in Vermont. The only people she was exposed to growing up were white. She stereotypes people of other races based on what she sees on the news." Pete looked at Jada very seriously. "She's ignorant, because most of what the news reports is negative. If she meets a person of another race who falls into her stereotype, then she starts judging everyone else from that race."

Jada gave Pete a confused look. "But I thought you and Tonya had black friends when you were growing up."

"We did, but we stopped bringing them to our house when we saw the way our mother would treat them." Pete took a sip of his orange juice.

"What would she do?" Jada looked at Pete intently.

"The same thing she did to you. She'd make them uncomfortable by asking them all sorts of inappropriate questions. She was rude and they could tell that she didn't want them around." Pete paused thoughtfully. "I always hoped that one day she'd understand that not everyone fits into her stereotypes."

Jada silently stared at Pete. She wished she didn't care so much about the way Pete's mother had treated her, but she wanted the woman to like her. Especially since she was now in a relationship with Pete.

Pete reached for Jada's hand and looked at her gently." "Let's stop worrying about my mother and enjoy the rest of this food." He squeezed Jada's hand and grinned slightly.

Jada tried to return Pete's smile. He was right. She needed to stop thinking about Mrs. McKnight. It was spoiling the mood. She released Pete's hand and began to finish her breakfast.

When they had finished eating, Jada helped Pete wrap the leftovers and load the dishes into the dishwasher. They then headed off to check out Jada's potential condos.

Pete started the car engine and began to drive away from the last of the three condos on Jada's list. Jada was gazing out of the passenger side window with a look of disappointment on her face.

"I'm sorry you didn't like any of them," Pete said sympathetically.

"It's okay," Jada calmly replied. "It's not your fault."

Pete quickly glanced at Jada. "Maybe the timing isn't right," He was trying to find something positive out of the situation.

Jada shrugged, "Maybe." She sighed as she continued to gaze out the window.

"I don't see why it's necessary for you to look for a place now that we're together." Pete casually added. "I'm planning to buy my own place really soon."

Jada quickly turned her head to look at him. "I thought we agreed that we want to do things God's way." There was confusion in her tone. "That means separate places and no premarital sex."

Pete focused his attention on Jada as he stopped at the red traffic light in front of him. "Well what if we get married?"

Jada's eyes widened. "We've only been together for a day, Pete. I'm really ready to move out and I want to buy something of my own. It's a buyer's market right now, so I know I can get a good deal." She looked at Pete with determined eyes.

Pete grinned and shook his head, "I'm going to have to find a way to talk some sense into that pretty little head of yours."

Pete turned onto a suburban side street lined with nearly identical single family homes. He stopped in front of a yellow, neatly maintained ranch style house. The grass was neatly cut, and various flowers had been planted throughout the front yard. As Pete turned off the engine, he noticed that Jada was staring at him with a bewildered look on her face.

"What's going on?" Jada's voice echoed the surprise her face showed.

Slightly amused by the look on her face, Pete couldn't help but smile. "Last week when you asked me to come house hunting with you today, I called your realtor and arranged for her to show us this house, too." His tone became serious. "If it's in good shape, I might consider purchasing it."

Jada quickly glanced at the house and then back at Pete. "Can you afford this by yourself?"

"The asking price is pretty cheep." Pete pulled the keys out of the ignition and opened his car door. "Let's go check it out." He stepped out of the car and walked around to the other side where Jada was standing.

The young realtor, Nancy Bell, stopped next to Pete and Jada. "What do you think so far?" She asked.

Pete nodded. "The outside looks great."

Nancy smiled. "The owners are a retired couple. They spend a lot of their time gardening which is why the house has so much curb appeal. They're the only people who have lived in this house. They purchased it right after it was built thirty years ago. The couple hasn't done any cosmetic updates, so the interior may not look as good as the exterior."

"That explains the low asking price," Pete said with raised brows.

"True," Nancy agreed. "Why don't we go inside and take a look."

Pete and Jada followed Nancy into the home. The front entrance put them directly into a medium sized living room with a fireplace. They followed Nancy through the living room into an eat-in kitchen. The cabinets were dark and outdated, and the appliances were old.

Pete looked around the spacious kitchen. "The kitchen has good space to it." He glanced at Jada and then at Nancy.

"Definitely," She stretched her hand out and touched the refrigerator. "You could consider purchasing new appliances whenever you're ready, and the cabinets and flooring can always be updated." Nancy paused while Pete and Jada continued to look around. "Would you like to go see the bedrooms?"

After taking a quick look out the window, Pete nodded in agreement. "Sure." With Jada beside him, he followed Nancy down a long hallway.

They stopped in front of the only bathroom located in the house. It was narrow, but didn't look as old as Pete had expected. It had double sinks and a vanity. Then they viewed a large master bedroom, and two smaller bedrooms. After looking inside each bedroom, they followed Nancy back into the kitchen where she opened the door to the garage.

"This garage is a little small, but it's designed to fit two cars ," Nancy stepped into the garage and looked back at Pete and Jada who were following behind. "It's unusual for this type of house to have a two car garage, so this is a nice bonus." Nancy briefly waited for Pete and Jada to glance around. "The only room you haven't seen is the basement."

Pete's eyes lit up. "Let's take a look." He had dreams of making a basement into an entertainment room.

Nancy led the way back into the kitchen. Then she opened a second door revealing a long set of stairs. They followed her down into the large basement. The floors were carpeted and the walls were covered in wood paneling.

"It's a little outdated, but it's heated and can be used as additional living space." Nancy smiled brightly. "The house is big enough for a family, and there's more than enough land in the back yard to build an addition if you outgrow the space."

Pete liked what he had seen so far. The basement was definitely one of his favorite rooms in the house. He could easily fit a large television, stereo, couches, and fitness equipment into the space.

After studying the room, he followed Nancy and Jada back up the stairs into the kitchen. When they entered the kitchen, a musical tone began to fill the air.

Nancy retrieved her phone from her handbag and looked at the screen. "I'm sorry. I have to take this," she stated. "I'll go outside and you two can continue looking around." Nancy headed for the front door as she answered her phone.

Pete glanced around the kitchen once more. His eyes stopped when they met Jada's. "So what do you think?"

"It's nice," Jada replied through a bright smile. She walked over to the back door and looked out the window. "There's so much you can do. The kitchen can be updated. You could add a deck with a sliding glass door. You could add onto the master bedroom and build a master bath. You could update the basement..." Jada's voice trailed off as she continued to stare out the window.

Pete folded his arms over his chest and smiled contently. He loved seeing how excited Jada was getting over all the possibilities the house contained. Peaceful silence engulfed the room as he stood there thinking about the joy that living in this house with the woman that he loved could bring.

Jada suddenly turned around and an embarrassed look came over her face. "What?" she asked through a nervous grin.

Pete walked behind Jada and wrapped his arms around her waist. He rested his chin on top of her head and looked out the window that had been occupying her view. Suddenly, a vision of children playing in the back yard began to flash though his mind. The little girl looked just like a younger version of Jada. The little boy resembled himself, only with darker skin and hair. As quickly as the vision had come, it was gone. What he had just seen in his mind surprised him, but brought a feeling of happiness at the same time.

Pete kissed the top of Jada's head and squeezed her a little tighter. "I just think this is the type of house that could make you happy."

CHAPTER 21

A Day of Remembrance

MIKE SAT ON THE COUCH WAITING for Mike Jr. to finish his snack in the kitchen. He had arrived to pick him up a little early today, because he wanted to make sure that he had time to talk to Brenda. Mike wanted to see if it was okay for him to keep his son an extra day this weekend. Monday was Memorial Day and he wanted to take Mike Jr. to the beach for the day. The beach had miles of open sand, a playground, and a small carnival was set up for the holiday. Mike hoped to spend the day there with his son.

Brenda entered the living room carrying Mike Jr.'s suitcase. She set it next to the front door and sat down on the other end of the sofa. Brenda picked up the remote and increased the volume on the TV. She focused her attention on the court show being broadcasted on the screen.

Mike draped his left arm over the back of the sofa and looked at her. "Would it be okay if I keep Junior until Monday? I want to take him to the beach carnival that's in town."

Brenda looked at Mike and hesitated. "Is Monday the only day that you can take him?"

"Technically no, but I want to take him to the arcade on Saturday, rest on Sunday, and the carnival on Monday." Mike studied Brenda's face. "Is that a problem?"

"Shawn is taking Mike Jr. and me to Playland on Monday," Brenda said casually.

Mike felt his body temperature go up. "I would appreciate it if next time you would tell me when someone offers to take my son somewhere."

Brenda looked at Mike calmly. "I'm sorry if you're upset that Shawn actually wants to spend quality time with us," Her look turned into a sharp glare. "You never do."

Mike's eyes grew wide. "How can you say that? I used to come down here and spend the weekends with you and Junior until you started seeing this dude."

"Playing video games all day, and trying to sweet talk me in between them is not my idea of quality time," Brenda folded her arms across her chest. "I'm sorry, but you have to bring Junior back on Sunday."

Mike Jr. rounded the corner with popsicle juice dripping down his chin. "I'm done with my snack, Mommy." He held out sticky hands.

Brenda stood up. "Let's go clean your hands and your face."

Mike walked to the door and picked up the small suitcase. He stood there waiting for Brenda to finish cleaning his son. When they returned to the room, Brenda kissed Mike Jr. goodbye. Mike then walked his son to the car and buckled him in.

"What are we gonna do today, Daddy?" Mike Jr.'s voice was full of curiosity.

"Today we're going to go home and relax." Mike looked at his sun in the rearview mirror. "Tomorrow we might go to an arcade, or a carnival."

"What's an arcade?" Mike Jr. asked enthusiastically.

"It's a place that has games," Mike explained.

"What's a carnival?" Excitement continued to ring in Mike Jr.'s voice.

"It's a place on the beach that has rides." Mike knew his son was at the age of asking multiple questions.

"I want to go to the carnival!" Mike Jr. exclaimed.

Mike glanced in the rearview mirror and smiled at his son. "If the weather's good, then that's where we'll go."

Within minutes of getting on the highway, Mike Jr. fell asleep. As Mike drove toward Connecticut, he began to feel annoyed that Brenda's new friend, Shawn was affecting his weekend plans. Mike had tried to find out more information about Shawn, but the only thing Brenda would tell him was that they worked together in the accounting department at the cable company. Mike didn't know if things were getting serious between the two of them, but it had now been six weeks since he had stopped staying at Brenda's. Those arrangements had ended when Brenda started making plans with Shawn. What was really upsetting Mike was the fact that Mike Jr. was now a part of those plans.

It wasn't until recently that Mike had really started making an effort to see Mike Jr. consistently. It had now been over two months since he had cancelled on his son. Lately he really had been trying to think of more interesting things that he could do with Mike Jr. That's why Mike had wanted to keep him an extra day this weekend. He couldn't believe that Brenda had agreed to plans with Shawn without telling him. Mike had to admit that Brenda was right about him not spending enough quality time with them. He hadn't made any efforts in the past and apparently now Brenda knew someone else who would.

Mike was beginning to realize that playing the field wasn't really getting him anywhere. Ever since Mike Jr. was born, Mike had been spending more time on dates than he had been spending with his own son. Now his son would be spending Memorial Day with Brenda and another man, and he would be spending the day alone.

Mike's mind began to travel back to his own childhood days. Although he had adjusted to his dad not being around for long periods of time, Mike remembered missing him when he was away on active duty. When his dad would come home, Mike remembered watching sports with him and playing basketball. Mike concluded that when he was a child, his dad would have spent a lot more time with him if he had a choice. Being in the army was his job. His father had to be away to provide for his family and serve his country, as he believed he had been called to do.

Mike began to wonder what his own excuse was. Why had he been wasting time playing the dating field when he had a son to raise? Why had he been spending time bouncing from woman to woman when he could have settled down with the mother of his child? He could see that Brenda was a strong woman with a good heart.

Mike thought about how his father had known a good woman when he'd seen one. His father had married his mother and did all he could for his family.

Mike wondered if his life would have turned out differently if his dad had been around to help him transition from boyhood to manhood. Maybe he wouldn't be in the situation he was in right now. His brother John had been eighteen when their dad died. Two years later John enlisted in the army, just like their dad. Within that same year John also got married and started a family. Mike thought about how different his own life had turned out. He had gotten a young woman pregnant and basically deserted her. To make the situation worse, he'd been neglecting spending time with his son ever since. Ultimately, Mike knew that the only person he had to blame right now was himself. It was time he started taking some responsibility for it.

Suddenly, Mike felt like he was beginning to see things clearly. He realized that when Mike Jr. was born, he had given up on a good woman. Now, four years later, he was starting to wish that there was a way to get her back.

CHAPTER 22

Summer Kick Off

JADA ANXIOUSLY PACED HER ROOM, WAITING for Pete to arrive. Today they had a full day ahead of them. She was going with Pete to a Massachusetts amusement park where they planned to meet up with two of Pete's cousins and their wives. They planned to enjoy a few rides before attending the park's Memorial Day concert featuring local gospel artists.

Jada hadn't met any of Pete's extended family, yet. What would they be like? From what Pete had told her, his cousins Josh and Aaron were the sons of Mr. McKnight's brother, Tom, and sister-in-law, Patty. Jada had been relieved when she found out that they were cousins from his dad's side of the family. As of right now, she was terrified of Mrs. McKnight. Jada didn't think she could deal with any more encounters with that lady.

When the doorbell finally rang, Jada turned off her stereo and began hustling down the stairs. As she neared the front door, her mother also approached, coming from the kitchen.

"Slow down!" Dana said. "Your man's not going anywhere."

Jada stopped to quickly hug her mom. "I'll see you later," she said as she opened the front door. A dimpled grin appeared on Pete's face as he stood on the front step waiting.

"Have fun you two," said Dana.

"Thanks, Mrs. Calloway." Pete gave her a quick wave.

When Jada's mom had closed the front door behind them, Pete pulled Jada close to him and kissed her on the cheek. "How's my beautiful baby doll doing today?" he asked.

Jada looked up at him and smiled, "Great now that you're here."

"Ooooh. Don't start nothin', won't be nothin'."

"Look at you, soundin' all gangsta." Jada raised her brows at him.

Pete laughed. "What can I say? I'm a white boy with soul."

Jada and Pete got into the cranberry Maxima, and Pete started the car. She agreed he was a white boy with soul all right. The voice of Robin Thicke singing Lost Without You came blasting through the stereo.

"You think you could turn that down a bit?" Jada asked.

"Sorry, doll. I was gettin' my groove on."

"Save all of that for the concert tonight," Jada said with her teasing grin.

"Oh, it's like that, huh?" Pete revealed the dimple that Jada had grown to love.

"Yeah, it's like that."

They both began to chuckle. They often amused themselves with the way they could go from sweet-talking each other, to playfully talking junk. But that was what Jada found so special about Pete. He was a friend who had surprisingly become her man. Sometimes she still had a hard time believing it.

Jada and Pete laughed, talked, and joked around all the way to the amusement park. They talked about things they could do together over the summer. The couple agreed to check out some state parks and go jogging on the trails. Jada teased Pete about his adventurous nature. She reminded him about their humorous adventure across the Golden Gate Bridge. Jada was amazed at how two people could have so much fun just riding together in a car. When they arrived at the amusement park, she couldn't believe how short the ninety minute trip had seemed.

As soon as Pete had pulled into a parking space and shut off the engine, he turned and looked at Jada with tenderness in his eyes. Then Jada saw him lean toward her as she next felt the gentleness of his lips on hers. It was the first intimate kiss he'd given her, and it was everything Jada had hoped it would be. It wasn't long, but it was soft and affectionate. Pete quickly pulled away and looked into her eyes. He looked as if he wanted to say something, but he only smiled instead. Jada returned his smile, and then Pete's cell phone began to ring.

"What's up, Josh?" Pete said into the receiver. "Yeah, we just got here, too. I think I see your car now. Are you driving your black Honda?...Then that's you. We're going to get out of the car so you'll see us after you park."

Jada was beginning to feel anxious again. She was a little concerned about what Pete's cousins would think of her. Jada concluded that she must just be traumatized by Mrs. McKnight. She reminded herself to relax and get out of the car. Jada walked over to Pete, and he took her hand.

They walked over to the parking space that Pete's cousins had just driven into. Jada watched an ivory-skinned, dark-haired man step out of the driver's side of the vehicle. A woman with a similar complexion stepped out of the front seat passenger side. Her blonde hair was cut into a shoulder length asymmetrical bob. Behind her stood another ivory-toned woman with very short hair. Strands of brown hair covered her forehead in a long, wispy bang. Jada saw a second dark haired ivory man exit the backseat of the vehicle.

Jada smiled as Pete introduced her to his cousin Josh, and his wife Leah, who was definitely rocking her blonde bob. Pete then introduced his other cousin Aaron and his wife Rebekah. Jada couldn't help but beam when Pete introduced her as his girlfriend. His cousins were immediately pleasant to Jada. Josh and Aaron hugged Jada and kissed her on the cheek. Then Leah and Rebekah both hugged Jada as well. After the greetings, they all walked toward the amusement park entrance.

A line had already formed by the time they reached the gate. As they waited, Pete's cousins took advantage of the opportunity to get to know Jada a little better.

"So, Jada," began Josh. "What do you see in this guy?" He playfully elbowed Pete. "I mean really. He's not all that, is he?"

Jada looked from Josh to Pete with a smile. "He's one of the nicest guys I've ever met."

Jada heard Leah and Rebekah emerge into a duet of "awwws."

Pete grinned and took Jada by the hand. "See. She knows a good man when she has one," he said cheerfully. "And I know a good woman when I have one, too," Pete added, looking at Jada as if they were the only two people standing outside of the park.

Just then, Rebekah broke their moment. "Jada, I love your hair!" she said looking at Jada's shiny, dark locks.

That past Saturday, Nicole had given Jada a new asymmetrical bang, and a fresh blow-out. Jada's hair was pulled back into a shiny low ponytail while her right eye played hide and seek behind her asymmetrical bang.

"Thanks," Jada replied somewhat surprised by the compliment. "I was noticing your haircuts, too," she said, looking at Rebekah and Leah. "Those styles look really good on you two."

The three women began a conversation about hair and fashion, while Pete and his cousins did some talking of their own. Before they knew it, they had handed the attendants their tickets and were on their way to the first agreed upon ride.

Jada was feeling like they were all in high school again on a triple date. They went on roller coasters and walked around the park holding hands. Jada really liked Pete's cousins and their wives. She was having a lot more fun than she expected.

After a few hours of riding thrilling roller coasters, they decided to get some fried dough to eat before the concert began. They all walked through a crowd of people and found a table big enough for their group. Jada sat down to hold the table while Pete and his cousins went to get the food. Rebekah and Leah took a bathroom break.

Jada was happily watching Pete from a distance, when she heard a voice from off to the side.

"Jada?" the male voice said with uncertainty.

Jada turned her head and looked up. She couldn't believe who was standing next to her after not having seen him in seven years. "Oh," she said somewhat surprised, but without much emotion. "Hi, Tony." He still looked the same as he did when she last saw him in college. He was still tall and slender. Only the hazel eyes that she used to find appealing no longer impressed her. "What are you doing here?"

"I came with some family that were visiting from out of town." Tony replied. He sat down in one of the empty chairs. "So how have you been?"

Jada looked across the table at him blankly. "Fine and you?"

"I've been okay." Tony looked at Jada thoughtfully. "So, are you a teacher now?"

"Yep." Tony looked as if her were waiting for her to say more, but Jada's lips were tightly sealed adding to the lack of emotion on her face.

Tony nodded. "I'm a manager at a health club."

"That's nice," Jada replied almost robotically.

As Tony looked at Jada, she started to see a dreamy look come over him. He began to smile. "Wow! You look really good, Jada. Do you ever wonder what would have happened to us if we didn't break up?"

"Not really," Jada quickly answered.

"Oh!" Tony's eyes widened. "That's cold, Jada."

Not caring a bit about her blunt response, Jada felt a wave of relief come over her when she saw Pete approaching the table. "Anyway. I'm here with someone."

Pete placed the tray of food he'd been carrying on the table, and looked at Tony with confusion on his face.

"Tony, this is my boyfriend, Pete," Jada said with a smile.

The confusion on Pete's face was replaced with a look of pride as he firmly shook Tony's hand. Tony on the other hand looked from Pete to Jada with raised brows. Jada didn't care what Tony thought about her man.

"Well, it was nice seeing you again, Jada," Tony stammered. He looked at Pete. "Nice meeting you," he said before turning to walk away.

Pete sat down next to Jada. "Was he over here trying to steal my woman?" he asked playfully.

"Something like that," Jada replied. "But I kicked him to the curb."

Pete grinned, leaning in to give Jada a kiss on the cheek. "That's my girl," he said.

Just then, Josh and Aaron both arrived at the table with a tray in hand. As soon as they had finished setting up the food, Rebekah and Leah returned to the table as well. They all filled their mouths with fried dough and bottled water. When they had finished eating, they walked over to the concert area of the amusement park. They found a spot on the grass where they had a good view of the stage and talked about music until the show began.

As various gospel acts took their turn on the stage, Jada stole a few glances at Pete's cousins. She could tell by the lack of expression on their faces that they weren't really into gospel. But as his cousins relaxed on the grass, they didn't seem too bothered by it. The way they cuddled with their wives, they seemed to be making the most of the moment. It seemed as if the McKnight men knew how to treat their women.

Jada felt Pete put his arm around her, and she rested her head on his shoulder. She couldn't think of a better way to start off her summer. At that moment, Jada believed that she had finally found true love.

CHAPTER 23

Fireworks

SCHOOL HAD BEEN OUT FOR WEEKS now, and Pete and Jada had been loving every minute of it. Pete was excited about almost being done with his summer accelerated route to certification program. By the end of the month, he would officially have his Connecticut teaching certification. Jada was so proud of him. They had been sitting together in every Sunday service and Wednesday night Bible class at church. They were inseparable. So it was no surprise when they arrived at Fernando's Fourth of July cookout wearing huge smiles and walking hand in hand.

Nicole hurried over to Jada and Pete and greeted them with hugs. "There's plenty of food. Fernando's working the grill, so go help yourselves."

Jada and Pete smiled as Nicole made her way to the cooler to dump in the bag of ice she had been holding in her hand. They scanned the backyard crowd as they walked over to the grill.

"What can I get for you two?" Fernando asked while flipping burgers on the large gas grill. "Burger, hot dog, hot sausage?"

Jada took a plate and Fernando put two hot sausages on her hot dog buns. Pete took two cheeseburgers.

Fernando gave Pete a curious look. "Tonya couldn't make it?"

Pete picked up the ketchup and squirted it on his burgers. "She's visiting our cousins up in Massachusetts."

Fernando nodded thoughtfully before looking down to take more sausages off the grill. "Why didn't you do the summer bowling league, man?"

"Since they changed the day to Tuesdays for the summer, Joe and Tyrese were able to come back. That put Sasha and me out of the game," Pete answered.

Speaking of Sasha, the only available place to sit was at a half-full table where Jada saw her seated. The rest of the people at the table were unrecognizable to her. She decided to go sit down and eat while Fernando continued to fill Pete in on the details of the summer bowling league. Jada smiled as she passed a table full of Nicole and Fernando's family that were visiting from New York and the Dominican Republic. She heard some talking Spanish and some talking English as she walked by. She said a quick hello to Gene, Joe, Tyrese and a relative of Fernando's that she didn't know. They were sitting around a card table playing spades. Finally, she made it to the table where Sasha was eating a burger and potato chips. Jada smiled and sat down across from her.

"How's it going?" Jada asked.

"Girl, I'm tearing this food up," Sasha said, holding a chip in one hand and a burger in the other. "Those sausages are good! I already had two."

Jada continued to smile as she took a small bite of her sausage and began to chew. "You're right. It is good."

"So are you and Pete together now?" Sasha inquired as she glanced toward the grill and then back at Jada.

Jada nodded as she chewed. "Yep."

Sasha looked at Jada curiously. "How long have you two been a couple?"

"We started seeing each other in April," Jada answered, smiling.

"I saw you guys when you walked in." A girlish grin appeared on Sasha's face. "You look so cute together."

"We do?" Jada responded. She had always wondered what people thought when they saw her with Pete. "Thanks."

Sasha finished the last bite of her cheeseburger and wiped her mouth on her napkin. "Tell me some of the things you guys do together."

Jada beamed as she thought of the time she and Pete had been spending together. "Sometimes we jog together on the trails. We go out to eat, to the movies. Anything fun, we'll do it, whether it's mini-golf, amusement parks, concerts, whatever."

Sasha was now looking at Jada with a smile and a dreamy look in her eye. "If you guys get married and you need another bridesmaid, don't forget about me."

Jada smiled. Maybe she had been wrong about Sasha. When she had hung out with her for the first time at the bowling alley, she thought Sasha was nothing but a huge flirt who threw herself at men. Now she felt guilty about judging her. Sasha was nice after all. It became evident to Jada that she was slowly overcoming a problem that was bigger than she had realized. Not only had she been guilty of judging white people, she had also been judging people she barely even knew.

Pete finally made his way to the table with one of his burgers gone, and one left to be eaten. Fernando joined them too, taking a break from the grill to eat a burger and a sausage. When they had finished eating, Jada, Pete, Sasha and Fernando played crazy eights while instrumental Merengue music blared from stereo speakers.

Eventually, a few of Fernando's family members got up and started dancing. Jada saw Nicole grab Gene and begin to show him a few dance steps. Gene picked it up quickly and began to dance with Nicole. Then Nicole reached over and grabbed Jada's hand, pulling her to her feet. Nicole then pointed to her own feet, signaling Jada to watch. Jada began to mimic Nicole's moves, and Nicole left Jada to dance with Gene while she moved to pull Pete to his feet. Jada watched as Pete alternated between watching Gene and Nicole, as he tried to pick up the steps. Then, before Jada knew what was happening, Pete was pulling her away from Gene to dance with her. Jada had never imagined that they would learn how to dance Merengue together, but it had now become another fun thing that they had managed to learn how to do.

In no time, there were couples all over the backyard dancing to the music, laughing, and having a good time until the sun had begun to retire from the sky.

After enjoying six hours of food and fun, Jada and Pete said their good-byes and left Fernando and Nicole to enjoy their vibrant family. Fernando lived very close to the beach, so Jada and Pete decided to take a drive over to catch the fireworks display. They managed to find an unpopulated section of the beach where they laid out two towels. Jada leaned into Pete as they sat in front of the ocean and waited for the fireworks to begin. She listened to the low ripple of the waves that were barely visible due to the darkening sky. As she felt Pete begin to gently rub her arm, she could still faintly smell the scent of his cologne.

She inhaled deeply. "You always smell so good."

"I do? After all that foot action we were doing at Fernando's, I still smell good?"

"Mmm hmm." The sound of the lively Merengue music began to replay in Jada's head. "That was fun wasn't it?"

"Yeah, it was," Pete cheerfully agreed.

Jada turned to glance at him. "I didn't know you could dance. You have rhythm."

A playful grin appeared on Pete's face. "I told you I'm a white boy with soul."

Jada chuckled. Pete was just full of surprises. Her mind began to recall all of the things that they had done together lately. She felt so blessed to be with someone who loves God first, treated her with so much respect, and loved to do so many of the same things that she enjoyed doing.

Jada turned her head and looked at Pete. "I have so much fun when I'm with you."

Tenderness filled Pete's eyes as he began to gently stroke Jada's face with his hand. Then he leaned in until his lips met hers. Time stopped for Jada as she and Pete made their own fireworks. She allowed herself to feel the strength of Pete's hand on her face, yet the gentleness of his touch.

Pulling himself away to look into her eyes, Pete said, "I love you, Jada."

Jada felt as if her heart stopped. She looked up at Pete in awe. Out of the three months they'd been dating each other this was the first time Jada had heard Pete say those words.

Pete looked deep into Jada's eyes. "I love you more than words can say right now." His eyes seemed to deepen with intensity. "My heart is filled with love for you."

Jada gazed into Pete's tender eyes. Her own emotions were awakened by his sincerity. She reached up and touched his face. "I love you too," she whispered.

Pete smiled and gave her another short gentle kiss as a burst of red and orange light emanated over their heads. Then Jada leaned her head on Pete's shoulder as they continued to watch huge flashes of random, bright colors illuminate the sky.

CHAPTER 24

An Honorable Request

"GOOD GAME," SAID PETE AS HE looked across the card table at Uncle Jack.

Pete had been sitting at the card table playing dominoes since the traditional Calloway Sunday dinner had ended an hour ago. He and Jada had just lost to Uncle Jack and Gene. Pete had enjoyed playing, but he wanted to sit out the next game. He looked over to the couch where Aunt Tina was seated.

"Tina?" Pete called from his seated position. "Do you want to take over for me?"

Aunt Tina looked up from her magazine. "Okay." She walked over to the table and smiled at Jada. "I guess it'll be ladies against the fellas."

Pete rose from his seat so that Aunt Tina could sit down. He then walked over to where Jada's dad was seated. Charles and Uncle Bob were both relaxing in matching leather recliners.

"Mr. Calloway, can I talk to you in private for a minute?" Pete whispered. "With your wife?"

Charles gave Pete a surprised look. "Sure." He stood to his feet and began to walk in the direction of the living room.

Pete stood outside the living room, and waited for Charles to get his wife. She was sitting and talking with Aunt Linda, Grandma, and Aunt Ira. When Charles had gotten Dana's attention, the two walked back over to Pete.

"We can talk downstairs," Charles suggested.

Pete followed Charles and Dana down into a lower level family room. He was impressed by the organized space. Exercise equipment was neatly arranged on one side of the room. Two comfortable couches and a large television occupied the seating area. Charles motioned to a small sofa as he and Dana sat down on the longer couch.

"So what would you like to talk about?" Charles calmly looked across the coffee table at Pete.

Pete leaned forward and nervously folded his hands. His hands felt clammy and he could feel beads of sweat beginning to emerge on his forehead. He quickly cleared his throat. "Mr. and Mrs. Calloway, I wanted to let you know that I love your daughter. I know I've only known her for six months, but we've been spending a lot of time together lately. I think she's a beautiful person, and I would like to ask her to marry me."

Pete stared across the coffee table feeling relieved that he had been able to get the words out. However his anxiety level was still high as he waited to hear Charles and Dana's response. He could see that Dana's face was beginning to light up, but Charles appeared stoic.

Charles looked Pete directly in the eyes. "Are you sure you can take care of my daughter?"

Pete's confidence level rose a little as he nodded. "Yes sir. I have my teaching certification now, so my job is secure. I just closed on a house, and I'm moving in next week. Jada's seen the house and she loves it." Pete's tone was passionate. "I want to make your daughter happy."

A slight smile appeared on Charles' face. "I think you're the type of man my daughter needs in her life."

"I agree." Dana beamed with enthusiasm.

A wave of relief rushed over Pete. He couldn't be happier with the way the conversation had just gone. Pete's face broke into a full grin as he rose to shake Charles and Dana's hands. He couldn't wait to find out what Jada would say.

Pete drove along I-84 deep in thought. He was still happy about having the approval of Jada's parents, but he knew that he couldn't get too excited yet. Pete had left Jada's parents' house a little earlier than usual so that he could take the ninety minute drive to his own parents' house. He needed to let them know that he intended to ask Jada to marry him. He knew if he didn't tell them in advance, it would make an already awkward situation worse.

Pete exited the highway and navigated toward his childhood home. He was happy with the man that he had become and the direction that his life was now headed. Although he still respected his parents, he did not agree with the way his mother had treated Jada. Pete thought that Jada was a kind, respectable woman who he couldn't wait to marry. If his mother would just give Jada a chance, he knew that she would like her. Somehow, he had to make his mother understand that.

Pete parked his car in his parents' driveway and walked to the front door. He had a key to the home, but always rang the doorbell out of respect. His dad opened the door with a slight smile.

"Hey, son," Mr. McKnight greeted. "Come on in." He stepped to the side to let Pete pass through. "Your mother's in the family room."

Pete walked with his dad through the kitchen into the family room. His mother was lying down on the couch watching Lifetime. Pete chuckled to himself. It never failed that whenever his mother had time to watch TV, Lifetime was the first channel she always turned to. Sometimes he'd catch her holding a box of tissues as she sat watching a mushy love story.

"Hey, Mom," Pete said as he walked over to her and gave her a kiss on the cheek.

"Hi, sweetheart." Mrs. McKnight sat up and smiled at her son.

Pete sat down on the love seat while Mr. McKnight sat next to his wife. He had told his parents earlier that he needed to talk to them and he wanted to get right down to business. A serious look came over Pete's face as he prepared himself for what he had to say.

"I have something important to tell you." Pete looked at his parents with determined eyes. "I'm in love with Jada, and I want to ask her to marry me."

Pete saw the shock appear on both of his parents' faces. Mr. McKnight's mouth was open slightly, and Mrs. McKnight's eyes were wide with surprise. The room filled with silence as Pete sat staring at their nearly frozen faces.

"Don't you think it's a little soon?" Mr. McKnight asked with raised brows. "She seems like a nice young lady, but are you sure you know her well enough?"

"Of course he doesn't," Mrs. McKnight snapped. She rolled her eyes and folded her arms across her chest. With wide eyes, she looked at her son. "I don't know what kind of crazy phase you're going through, but what you're feeling can't possibly be love."

Pete confidently looked at his mother, "I'm sorry, Mom, but you're wrong. Jada and I love each other, and I'm going to ask her to marry me." He looked his father in the eyes. "I know that she would make a good wife. She's smart, kind"

"I can't listen to this," Mrs. McKnight interrupted. She shook her head, stood up and walked out of the room.

Pete couldn't believe that his mother had just walked out on him. He thought that she had enough respect for him to at least hear what he had to say.

"I can't believe she just did that," Pete said in shock. "What is her problem?"

"This is not easy for her," Mr. McKnight said sympathetically. "She was a very sheltered child. When I met her at Vermont University, she told me the only time she had ever left the state was for family vacations to Maine. If we hadn't started dating, she'd probably still be living there like her parents and her sister. It wasn't until your mom and I got married that I realized how badly her lack of exposure was affecting her."

Pete rested his elbow on his knee and rubbed his forehead in agitation. "Why can't she just get over it? Lots of people marry outside their race these days."

Mr. McKnight leaned forward and clasped his hands together. "I'll talk to her. Call me and let me know what Jada says when you ask her. Your mother's having some pride and anger issues right now, but underneath all that there's a sweet woman. Eventually Jada will get to see that."

Pete sighed and leaned back against the sofa. He wanted to believe that his mother would grow to accept Jada, but he was starting to have doubts after what he had just seen tonight.

CHAPTER 25

A Birthday Surprise

PETE WOKE UP THINKING ABOUT HOW good it felt to finally be in his own house. Yesterday, Jada, Gene and Tonya had helped him move in. The house still wasn't fully furnished, but at least the bedroom was complete.

As Pete lay in bed, thoughts of the talk he had with his parents earlier that week tried to make their way into his mind. He had been battling feelings of discouragement since he left his parents' house on Sunday. He was disappointed that his mother had refused to listen to his point of view. After spending the last few days in prayer, Pete had faith that God had brought him and Jada together for a purpose. They both loved God and had been obedient in their relationship. He was sure that God would work all things together for the good.

With his mind again at peace, Pete sat up, and looked out the window. The sun was already taking its position in the sky. It looked like it was going to be a nice, dry day. Pete stood up, stretched, and prepared to make the next step toward his future.

Jada sat up in her bed, pulled open her nightstand drawer, and took out the photo album she had created after returning from California. Initially, it contained only photos from her trip, but now it was full of pictures of her and Pete. It seemed to tell a story of their relationship. It was hard to believe, but they had been a couple for four months now. To Jada the time had flown by. But time flies when you're having fun, and that's exactly what the pictures showed.

The album began with a picture of Jada, Tonya, and Nicole standing outside of the San Francisco airport. Then there was a picture of Pete and

Gene standing in front of the Envoy they had rented. Jada touched the picture, running her hands down Pete's face. She looked at the next picture and smiled when she saw her, Tonya, and Nicole standing in the cold San Francisco water. A laugh escaped Jada's lips when she looked at the photo of Pete and Gene flexing their muscles amongst the waves.

Jada turned the page and saw pictures of them all eating at the Cliff House restaurant with the Pacific Ocean in the background. Then there were pictures of them touring Alcatraz and eating sandwiches on Angel Island. She was reminded of all the shopping they did when she saw the photo of her, Tonya, and Nicole standing on Pier 39 with their shopping bags. She could almost taste the shrimp again when she came to the image of them all eating at the Franciscan.

Jada chuckled when she saw the photo of Tonya hanging onto the arms of her and Nicole as they stood on the Golden Gate Bridge. She admired the next picture of Pete and Gene standing on the bridge with the boats in the background. Jada thought about how good Pete looked with his eyes squinted because of the sunlight, and his dimples complementing his smile. She was so in love with him. She didn't care that he was white. The way that he treated her made her feel loved, and respected. Jada remembered the day she and Pete first went out. She had asked God for a husband who gave her love, laughter, kindness, and was devoted to God. Pete definitely met all of those requests, and in her heart she believed he was the one that God had for her.

Jada looked at the picture that a stranger had offered to take of her and Pete at the comedy show. It had been taken after Jada had finally managed to get out a laugh. Then she looked at the photo of the two of them in front of a fountain at the amusement park. Her mind went back to how well she had gotten along with Pete's cousins when she saw the picture of her, Rebekah, and Leah. Jada then looked at the photo of Pete standing with his cousins, Josh and Aaron. Jada thought about how loving Pete and his cousins were toward their women when she saw the picture of Josh holding Leah, and Aaron cuddled with Rebekah.

Jada turned the page to find the image of her and Pete dancing Merengue at Fernando's Fourth of July cookout. They were looking at each other and grinning from ear to ear. It was obvious they were having a great time.

Finally, Jada saw the photo taken just a few days ago when Pete came over again for Sunday dinner. Pete was sitting on the couch with his arm around Jada. Jada remembered how Pete had disappeared suddenly that day. She had walked from the family room, to the kitchen, and then to the dining room and living room, but had no clue where he was. After following that same route a couple times, she saw Pete emerge from the basement with her parents. Sure there was a second family room, bathroom, and two offices down there, but it still didn't make any sense to her why Pete was down there with her parents. When she had asked Pete about it, he had told her to hold that thought while he went to the bathroom. She had forgotten all about it. Now she was curious all over again.

Jada began to wonder if it all had something to do with her birthday today. Pete had said that he had something very special planned. Knowing how much she was into fashion, he said she could still look cute, but she had to where comfortable shoes. Jada's mind immediately went back to their walk across the Golden Gate Bridge. She wondered what adventurous surprise Pete had in store this time.

Jada closed the photo album and returned it to its drawer. Then she got up to prepare herself for the special birthday that Pete had planned for her. She washed up and dressed in denim capri pants with a white short-sleeved shirt, and white sneakers. She pulled her hair back into a low ponytail, and put on her large silver hoop earrings. By the time she was ready it was nine 9:55 a.m.. Pete had said he would pick her up at ten.

With both of her parents out running errands, Jada decided to go ahead and lock up the house and wait outside. It was a beautiful August day. She sat down on the front step of the house and gazed around the quiet upscale neighborhood. Jada felt like she had come full circle. She had grown up as the only little black girl in her classes at school, and allowed herself to develop bitterness, which she carried around for many years. Then, she had gotten accepted to a regional magnet high school where she was no longer the only black student, and she was introduced to young, black men. She had met many other black men since then, some of them extremely nice and good looking, but they weren't the ones for her. Surprisingly, Jada had found love in the color she least expected. Now the color that at one time had made her feel disgust was the same color that made her feel love. Jada was feeling the same way she did as a little girl sitting on the step for the first time at five-years-old, waiting for the school bus. She was excited. She was confident. There was no bitterness in her heart.

Jada stood up and walked toward Pete's car that had just backed into the driveway. He quickly got out to open her door. After a brief hug, they both got in the car and buckled their seatbelts. Then they leaned into each other for a short kiss.

Jada pulled back and looked at Pete. "I love you," she said.

Pete smiled. "And you know I love you too. Happy Birthday."

"Thank you," Jada replied before receiving another kiss on her lips. "It's hard to believe our birthdays are only a week apart."

"I know," Pete said as he started the car. "Only, you're twenty-eight now, and I'll be twenty-nine."

"I never realized how close in age you are to Tonya."

"Yeah, we're only eleven months apart. But that still makes me Big Brother."

Jada leaned back and smiled. She relished in the thought that Tonya's brother had become her man.

Pete drove them to a popular breakfast restaurant where they both feasted on ham and cheese omelets and fluffy buttermilk pancakes. As they ate, they noticed an interracial family in one of the booths across from them. A caramel colored boy with a low haircut sat next to his brown-skinned dad, and a little girl with two very curly ponytails sat next to her ivory-skinned mom.

"That may be us one day," Pete said, looking into Jada' eyes.

Jada felt her eyes widen as she looked back at Pete. She had suspected that the thought may have crossed Pete's mind at some point. To Jada, the comment about marriage he had made when they were house hunting was an indication of that. But to actually hear Pete say it was surprising. It made her feel good to know that Pete saw her as someone he could start a family with.

After finishing up their breakfast, Pete drove them to a nearby state park.

"So this is why you told me to wear comfortable shoes," concluded Jada. "You're going to have me hiking on my birthday," she said with a hint of sarcasm.

"But you're going to like this hike," Pete replied.

Pete was actually right. The park contained a beautiful scenic path lined with trees, blooming shrubs, and exotic flowers. Pete gently caressed Jada's hand as they walked up the winding path.

"It feels like we're getting higher up," Jada said.

Pete just looked over at her and smiled. He was unusually quiet. He wasn't making silly comments like he usually did. He continued to caress her hand and periodically glance at her from time to time.

"So what do you think of this trail so far?" he finally asked.

"It's beautiful! I haven't seen this many plants and flowers since we went to the Japanese tea garden in California."

"You know, that trip was when I first started falling for you, Jada. By the end of the trip, I knew you were the one for me."

Jada felt a tingle all over as a smile came to her face. The extra tingling in her legs told her that they were definitely walking up hill. Jada looked ahead and saw some type of monument surrounded by blooming flower bushes. It looked as if they had walked as far as they could go. There were two benches on either side of the monument. Pete led Jada to a bench where they turned their bodies around to sit.

When Jada turned around, her breath was taken away by what she saw. From where they were sitting, she could actually see the Connecticut shoreline beyond the bushy tops of trees.

"This is amazing, Pete," Jada exhaled, turning to look at him.

"You're amazing," he replied with the most intent look Jada had ever seen. Her eyes were now locked with his and she couldn't look away. Pete took her left hand and began to stroke it gently. "I love you, Jada. You're the only woman I want or need. You're beautiful, fun, smart, caring. My life would not be the same if I hadn't met you."

Jada saw Pete begin to fidget a little. He continued to talk, and she continued to look at him with eyes filled with wonder.

"You make me so happy, Jada." Pete's voice was tender. "But you would make me even happier…if you would marry me."

Jada looked at Pete. He was now on one knee holding an open ring box in his hand. A single solitaire diamond set in platinum looked up at Jada from inside the box. Pete was still caressing Jada's left hand. His light brown eyes looked up at her with intensity.

"Will you marry me, Jada?" he asked.

Jada's left hand was now shaking. Her right hand was covering her mouth. Slowly, she lowered her right hand and exhaled, "Yes."

Pete licked his lips and smiled as his dimples began to appear. He took the ring out of the box and slipped it onto Jada's finger. Leaning up, he gave her the longest kiss of their lip-locking history. Jada threw her arms around him. They hugged each other not wanting to escape one another's embrace.

After they had released each other, Pete took Jada's hand, and they began their walk back down the scenic trail. They now felt closer to one another than they ever had before.

"We should go tell your parents the good news," Pete said when they reached his car.

At that moment Jada felt like it was about to rain on her parade. She knew her parents would be ecstatic, but they weren't the only ones that needed to hear the news. "What about your parents?" she hesitantly asked.

"We can call them now actually," Pete replied.

Jada watched Pete take out his cell phone, retrieve the number from his electronic phone book, and press send. He put his phone on speaker and laid it on the dashboard. A female voice answered the phone.

"Mom," began Pete.

"Hey, sweetheart?" answered Mrs. McKnight.

"I have you on speaker phone. Can you get Dad and put me on speaker too?"

She hesitated. "Okay."

There was a brief rustling before a husky voice joined the line. "We're here."

"Jada's here too." Pete glanced at Jada.

"Hello, Mr. and Mrs. McKnight," Jada tried her best to offer a polite greeting.

"Hello, dear," a male voice replied.

"We have some big news," continued Pete.

"What is it, son?" Mr. McKnight inquired.

"Jada and I are engaged."

CHAPTER 26

Out of Control

SINCE RECEIVING THE NEWS ABOUT PETE and Jada's engagement, Mrs. McKnight had been angry all week. She roughly flipped through the pages of *Populace* magazine, as her husband lay next to her watching late night reruns.

As the show went to commercial, Mr. McKnight began to gently rub his wife's arm. "You're not still angry are you?"

"Yes," Mrs. McKnight answered shortly.

"Honey, this isn't healthy."

Mrs. McKnight put the magazine down into her lap and glared at her husband. "You congratulated them, Paul. How could you?"

Mr. McKnight sighed heavily. "What else was I supposed to do? He is a grown man."

"Well he's acting like a child," she sneered.

"Are you sure he's the one acting like a child?" Mr. McKnight looked at his wife sternly.

She gasped and looked at him with raised brows. "What's that supposed to mean?"

Mr. McKnight turned off the TV, and rolled over. "I'm going to sleep."

"Fine." Mrs. McKnight was too worked up to sleep. She decided to get up and start wrapping gifts.

Tomorrow Pete and Tonya were supposed to be coming over so that they could all go out to eat for Pete's birthday. Turning the bedroom light out behind her, Mrs. McKnight headed down the foyer stairs in her silk pajama pantsuit toward the basement door. She had left the bag of dress slacks and khaki pants that she had purchased for Pete next to the wrapping paper she stored in the basement. As she opened the door, she turned on the basement light and proceeded down the stairs.

Mrs. McKnight sifted through the decorative wrapping and selected a roll of striped blue paper. Then she opened the large shopping bag. As she looked through the stacks of neatly folded pants, she realized she had forgotten to ask for boxes. Sighing in frustration, she placed the roll of paper into the shopping bag, and slipped the bag onto her arm. She opened the storage closet and took out the stepladder she would need to get some boxes down from the pull down attic.

Managing to climb the stairs with both the shopping bag and stepladder, Mrs. McKnight closed the basement door, and placed the bag down in front of it. She began to carry the stepladder up another flight of stairs toward the pull down attic. *Hopefully Pete won't bring that Jada tomorrow,* she thought to herself as she reached the top of the stairs.

Mrs. McKnight turned on the upstairs hallway light and placed the ladder under the attic door. She stood on the first step and used the latch to pull the door down. With the attic door fully open, she could see a stack of boxes to the right of the door, but she couldn't reach them. Mrs. McKnight climbed to the top step of the ladder, and used her right arm to slide a large box off of the pile.

As she began to carefully step down the ladder, her left foot got caught up in the hem of her silk pajama pant. She felt herself lose her balance as the caught foot skipped two steps completely and began to touch the floor. As the weight of her body came down, it forced her left ankle to roll to the side with a loud cracking sound. Her ankle gave out beneath her and she crashed down onto her left elbow. With her right foot now resting on the last step of the ladder, the box made a hollow sound as it hit the floor next to her. Mrs. McKnight immediately felt a sharp pain begin to go through her left ankle.

"Paul!" she cried, wincing in pain.

The bedroom door immediately opened, and Mr. McKnight emerged in his pajama bottoms. "What happened?" he asked wide-eyed, kneeling next to his wife.

"I fell." Mrs. McKnight's face was in agony.

"Where does it hurt?" Mr. McKnight's hands were out in front of him ready to touch his wife, but frozen from fear that he'd hurt her if he did.

"My ankle. My arm." Her face was twisted and her breathing was quick.

"Which ankle? Which arm?"

"The left!"

Mr. McKnight lifted the bottom of his wife's pants to examine her left ankle. It was already starting to swell. He looked at her arm but didn't see anything unusual. "Can you stand up?"

"I don't think so. It really hurts."

"All right. I'm going to have to take you to the emergency room. Just let me put some clothes on."

Mr. McKnight disappeared into the bedroom, and appeared a minute later wearing jeans and a white T-shirt. He scooped his wife into his arms. Then he carried her down the stairs and into the garage. He gently laid her on the backseat of the car and climbed into the driver's side. He drove as safely, but as quickly as he could to the emergency room.

***

Mrs. McKnight lay back on the hospital bed, and her husband sat beside her. He was leaned forward and rubbing her arm gently in an attempt to calm her nerves. She had already been at the hospital for almost an hour, but she still didn't know if she was okay. She was nervous, irritable, but most of all still in pain.

Suddenly the curtain surrounding her bed was pulled back, and the doctor entered with x-rays in his hand. He rolled a stool next to Mrs. McKnight's bed, and sat in front of her. "How are you feeling, Mrs. McKnight?"

"I'm still in pain."

"Well, I have good news and bad news." He looked from her to Mr. McKnight with a stoic expression on his face. "The good news is your arm is only bruised. The bad news is your ankle is broken."

"Broken?" Mrs. McKnight exclaimed. Her mind immediately saw images of her hobbling around the university campus in the fall trying to get to the English classes she had to teach. "How long will it take to heal?"

"Most likely, the weight put on your ankle during the fall was too much pressure for the bone," explained the doctor. "We're going to have to operate in the morning. We can discharge you as early as a day after the surgery, but it will be at least six weeks before you reach a full recovery."

Mrs. McKnight felt her eyes tear up. She leaned her head back against the pillows of the hospital bed. She felt her husband take her hand and give it a tight squeeze.

The doctor looked down and began jotting a few notes on his clipboard. "Considering the time it is now, we'll begin prepping you for your surgery in just a few hours. I'll give you something for the pain in the time being."

"Thank you, Dr. Smith," Mrs. McKnight said in relief.

She was given a pain medication and then transported into a small hospital room while Mr. McKnight sat in the waiting room filling out paperwork.

With all of her family gone, all there was left for Mrs. McKnight to do was think. She couldn't understand how her life had begun to spiral out of control. She was lying in a hospital bed facing surgery and at least six weeks of limited mobility. Pete had gone against her wishes by dating a black girl, and now they were engaged!

To Mrs. McKnight, black people seemed lazy and irresponsible. The news was always showing black men getting arrested. To her that said a lot about the way they must be raised. Mrs. McKnight shuddered to think of the type of people that could be in Jada's family. She could not let Jada become the mother of Pete's children. Mrs. McKnight couldn't see herself being the grandmother of kids that were half black.

Jada is not welcome in this family, Mrs. McKnight thought to herself. There was no way she was going to support this engagement. Then Jada would see that she was not welcome and there would be no wedding. But if there was a wedding, Mrs. McKnight concluded that she wouldn't go.

At that moment the throbbing in Mrs. McKnight's ankle became so intense that she clutched the sheets on either side of the bed. She wished that the pain would stop so that she could finally get some sleep.

CHAPTER 27

A Rude Awakening

MRS. MCKNIGHT WAS JARRED OUT OF her sleep by the sound of an electric drill. She opened her eyes and scanned the small room for the source of the sound. Then she felt it again. The sharp pain had returned to her ankle. As her eyes came to the doorway, she saw a young black woman reading an electronic file at a mobile workstation just outside the door.

"Excuse me," Mrs. McKnight called out. "I need to see my nurse, please. I'm having pain."

The young woman quickly entered the room, and stood by Mrs. McKnight's bed. "I'm your nurse, ma'm. I'll be taking care of you this morning."

"Oh," Mrs. McKnight replied with an instant frown.

The young nurse stared at Mrs. McKnight for a moment. The young woman's expression indicated that something was painfully familiar about her patient's frowning face. "Aren't you Pete McKnight's mother?" she finally asked.

Mrs. McKnight looked up at the young woman in awe. "Yes?"

"It's me, Monica White. I went to the senior prom with your son."

Mrs. McKnight felt her heart skip a beat as she stared at the young nurse. She didn't look like the same girl. She had a honey brown short haircut, which was much different from the long, dark hair Mrs. McKnight remembered seeing on her years before. "You look so different," she slowly replied.

Monica smiled. "I know. I get that a lot from people I haven't seen in a while."

Mrs. McKnight squirmed uncomfortably on the white linen. "And you're my nurse?"

"Yes, ma'm." Monica grinned and pointed to her name badge.

Mrs. McKnight's frown deepened. Can things get any worse? she thought.

Monica moved to the end of the hospital bed. "Let me adjust the pillows under your foot to give you a little more elevation." She began to gently raise the pillows that supported Mrs. McKnight's injured ankle. "This should help with your pain."

"Can't I get some more pain medication?"

"I'm afraid that's not possible. You're going to be prepped for your surgery soon, and it would interfere with the anesthetics you're going to receive."

"Where is that drilling coming from?" Mrs. McKnight held one hand to her head and one to her ear. The harsh, high-pitched sound seemed to be going straight through her eardrum to her temple.

"They're working on the hospital addition. Don't worry, the noise usually stops around lunch time." Monica continued to watch Mrs. McKnight rub her head. "Would you like me to turn on the TV to drown out the noise?"

"Sure," Mrs. McKnight said flatly.

Monica pressed a button on the front of the television and the ivory face of a popular minister appeared on the screen. She took the remote from the holder that attached it to the TV and handed it to Mrs. McKnight. "My fiancé and I love this minister. He's a lot different from our pastor, but his messages are so deep."

Mrs. McKnight leaned her head against the elevated pillows and closed her eyes. She was already tired of the hospital. Having Monica as her nurse wasn't helping one bit. Right now she wished she had one of two things. A mute button that would turn off Monica's mouth, or a fast forward button that would get her out of this place.

"The doctor will be coming in soon to take you to surgery," Monica said with a smile that Mrs. McKnight still did not find pleasant.

Mrs. McKnight let out a relieved sigh when Monica finally proceeded to leave. As the pain began to dull a little, her ears tuned in to the minister's voice coming from the television screen.

"I'm going to begin this sermon by reading from Proverbs 16:18," the minister said. *"Pride goes before destruction, a haughty spirit before a fall.* So I'm titling this message 'Pride Before A Fall'."

Mrs. McKnight opened her eyes and began to watch the minister deliver his message.

"Now I'm going to share with you the story of King Nebuchadnezzar who was stripped of all of his honor and splendor because of the arrogance and pride in his heart, until he acknowledged that God is the true King with all power and control."

There's nothing wrong with having a little pride, Mrs. McKnight arrogantly thought to herself as she picked up the remote and changed the channel. As she flipped through the channels, a middle-aged doctor and two nurses entered the room with her husband.

The hospital workers stopped next to Mrs. McKnight's bed as her husband leaned over and kissed her. They exchanged pleasantries.

"Mrs. McKnight, I'm Dr. Daniels. Are you ready to get that ankle taken care of?"

"Yes, I am," Mrs. McKnight answered with certainty.

Dr. Daniels gestured to his right, "These two lovely nurses are going to escort you to the operating room, and then I'll be performing your surgery."

"Okay." Mrs. McKnight felt relieved that the two nurses resembled herself.

"I'll be in the waiting room, honey." Mr. McKnight hesitantly turned to leave the room.

As her husband exited the room with Dr. Daniels, the nurses began to roll Mrs. McKnight down a corridor and into the operating room. Mrs. McKnight was introduced to the anesthesiologist who began hooking her up to monitoring machines. Mrs. McKnight felt her body relax as she began to drift out of full consciousness.

With the surgery complete, Mrs. McKnight awoke to find her husband, Tonya, and Pete sitting in her hospital room.

"When did you all get here?" she asked still groggy.

"We've only been here for about ten minutes," Tonya replied.

"Happy birthday, sweetheart," Mrs. McKnight said looking over at Pete. "I'm sorry that it's not turning out quite the way we planned."

Pete walked over and kissed his mother on the cheek. "That's okay, Mom."

"Pete was already at the restaurant when I finally got a hold of him." Mr. McKnight explained. "So I had him order take-out and bring it here."

"Why were you at the restaurant?" Mrs. McKnight asked.

"We were in church this morning when Dad was trying to call us, so Tonya and I both had our cell phones turned off," began Pete. "We drove to your house. Since you guys weren't there, we figured you were already at the restaurant. That's when Jada reminded us to turn on our cell phones, and"

"Jada?" Mrs. McKnight interrupted.

"Yeah," continued Pete. "She's in the waiting room."

Mrs. McKnight became furious. "I'm in the worst physical pain in my life since giving birth and you bring that girl to cause me emotional pain too! Aaaah!" Mrs. McKnight reached toward her ankle, grimacing in pain.

"Can I get you something, Mom?" Tonya's face was full of worry.

"Just some water, sweetie," Mrs. McKnight replied.

Pete's tone became serious. "Jada's in the waiting room, because she didn't know if you wanted to see her." He opened his mouth to continue, but his mother's voice interrupted.

"Good." Mrs. McKnight took the cup of water from Tonya and took a short sip. Then she leaned back against the pillows. "I just want my family."

Pete looked at his mother with sadness all over his face. In his eyes, she was making herself miserable with the pride she was harboring. If she thought her behavior was going to keep him from marrying Jada, she had another thing coming. What was she going to do when Jada officially became family?

"Mom," Pete gave his mother a stern look, "Jada is my fiance now. The way you treat her is unacceptable. She's sitting out there worried about you. If you're not going to allow her to come in, then there's no reason for me to stay in here."

His mother frowned and looked away. Pete couldn't believe she was being so stubborn.

He sighed and shook his head. "I'll be in the waiting room."

Pete walked out of the small hospital room, and down the hall to the room where Jada waited. She stood up when she saw him coming,

"How is she?" she asked with concern in her voice and eyes.

"She's still in a lot of pain." Pete stood with one hand in his pocket, and the other agitatedly rubbing his face.

"Are you okay?" Jada gently took Pete's hand from his face and held it.

"I don't know, Jada." Pete's heart was heavy. "Let's just sit out here for a while."

Pete sat down next to Jada on the stiff couch. He leaned his head back against the wall wondering how his mother could be so cold to someone he found so kind. He didn't know how long they sat there with Jada quietly reading a magazine as he gently stroked her arm, but Tonya and his dad were now approaching them.

"She's sleeping again," Mr. McKnight said. "They say she'll be in and out like that until tomorrow. You guys can probably head home."

"All right." Pete rose to his feet. "I'll call you tomorrow to find out how she is."

Pete stood next to Jada and watched Tonya and his dad head back to the hospital room. With the way that his mother's attitude had been, he was glad to be able to leave.

Jada wrapped her arm around Pete's waist. She looked up at him. "My gifts for you are still in the car." Her eyes searched his face. "Do you want to take them back to your house and celebrate your birthday there?"

Pete put his arm around Jada's shoulder and gave her a slight smile. "Sounds good to me."

Mrs. McKnight slowly opened her eyes when she heard footsteps approaching her. The dim light of dusk had now settled into the room.

Monica quietly walked over to the hospital bed with a cup in each hand. "It's time for your medication, Mrs. McKnight."

Mrs. McKnight blinked a few times before taking the small cup from Monica's hand. She put a pill in her mouth and then took a sip of water from the larger cup. Then she repeated the process one more time.

"How are you feeling?" Monica asked sympathetically.

Mrs. McKnight glanced at the cast on her leg. "A little better."

"That's good." Monica took the empty cup that held the pills from Mrs. McKnight's hand. "So how's Pete?"

"Fine." Mrs. McKnight neither smiled nor frowned with her response.

"He was always such a nice guy. Now I'm engaged to an extremely nice guy. He's a minister of music." Monica began to check Mrs. McKnight's blood pressure and heart rate as she continued to engage in small talk. "Do you still work in the English department at the university?"

"Yes."

Monica jotted a few notes on a clipboard. "For the past two years I've been writing spiritual poems. My fiancé writes music, so he's been thinking that we can write songs together by putting my poems to music. So maybe one day"

"Maybe one day you'll stop talking so I can get some peace and quiet!"

Monica froze with her hand still on the clipboard. Mrs. McKnight stared at her, waiting to see her response. For a second, Monica looked angry enough to slap her. If Monica touched her or cursed at her, Mrs. McKnight was prepared to file a complaint.

Eyes wide with surprise, Monica opened her mouth and then closed it again. She calmly replied, "Sure, Mrs. McKnight. You have a good night." Monica rolled her cart into the hallway, and stopped to enter data into her patient log at the mobile workstation.

Mrs. McKnight tried to ignore the sad expression she saw on Monica's face. She leaned her head back and closed her eyes. Mrs. McKnight felt that Monica needed to know that she was there to be a nurse, not to socialize.

How could she pay attention to what she was doing if she was busy running her mouth. All Mrs. McKnight wanted was for her leg to be taken care of. She wasn't interested in what Monica had to say.

When she thought that Monica was gone, Mrs. McKnight opened her eyes and looked in the direction of the hallway. Monica's head was lowered as if she were saying some type of prayer. Mrs. McKnight stared at her, bewildered. What on earth could she be praying for?

CHAPTER 28

Hostility vs. Hospitality

FOR SIX WEEKS NOW, MRS. MCKNIGHT had done nothing but sit, read, and hobble around the house when she needed something. She was itching to get her cast off. Thankfully, her appointment was next week.

Mr. McKnight had been spoiling her left and right. From helping her bathe, to gently rubbing lotion all over her body, and then showering her with kisses in all the places she loved it most. With the weather still warm, he had been grilling chicken, shrimp, and steak for their dinners. Basically, he had been treating her like a queen.

"Smells good, Tonya," Mrs. McKnight called out from the kitchen table where she was watching her daughter prepare lasagna for dinner.

When Tonya came over, she would cook and clean. Mrs. McKnight was grateful to Tonya for helping, and happy to see her when she came. However, Tonya always rambled on about Pete and Jada's wedding plans, and how excited she was to be a bridesmaid. Mrs. McKnight had told Tonya multiple times that she didn't want to talk about the wedding, but Tonya seemed obsessed or something. It was all she wanted to talk about lately.

Mrs. McKnight wasn't happy that she'd broken her ankle, but she was happy that she had used it as an excuse to why she couldn't accept Dana and Charles Calloway's dinner invitation. Accepting the dinner invitation would be like accepting the wedding, which she wasn't intending to do. From what Tonya had told her, Pete and Jada had set their wedding date for February twenty-first because it was almost a year to the day that they met. That meant that there was only four months left for Pete to come to his senses. Mrs. McKnight still believed that Pete's relationship with Jada was some kind of ridiculous phase that he had yet to grow out of. She was sure that somehow, someway, they would not go through with the wedding. If they did, Mrs. McKnight was sure it would be more than she could bare.

Mrs. McKnight continued to read the latest edition of *Populace*, her favorite magazine, while Tonya began to work on the salad.

"The bridesmaid dresses Jada picked are beautiful," Tonya suddenly blurted. "The dresses are crimson. Her colors are crimson and gold."

The slight smile on Mrs. McKnight's face quickly turned upside down. She felt a throbbing pain begin to return to her ankle.

Suddenly, a ringing sound filled the house.

Tonya began to walk toward the phone, but before she could pick it up, the ringing stopped. She shrugged as she headed back toward the counter.

While Tonya continued to cut the vegetables for the salad, Mrs. McKnight attempted to continue to read. Then her husband walked in.

Mr. McKnight leaned against the doorframe and looked at her intently. "That was Pete. He was calling to see if it would be okay for Jada to come with him to dinner. I told him it would be fine."

"Paul?" Mrs. McKnight wailed. "How could you do this to me?"

"Honey," Mr. McKnight said with firmness in his voice. "Pete loves that girl. She's going to be family soon whether you like it or not. You're going to have to learn to accept that."

Mrs. McKnight folded her arms and looked straight ahead, refusing to make eye contact with her husband.

"Why can't you just be happy for our son?" Mr. McKnight rubbed his hands through his hair before turning and walking out of the room.

Tonya shook her head and rolled her eyes as she turned back toward the counter. Mrs. McKnight sat at the table, no longer able to read.

Jada sat in the passenger side of Pete's car, wondering why she had put herself in this uncomfortable situation. When Pete told her he was going to visit his mother this evening, Jada decided she was ready to go along. Pete had already visited his mother two other times since she had been home from the hospital, but this was the first time Jada had offered to go.

When they started their premarital classes three weeks ago, Jada and Pete told Pastor John that Mrs. McKnight was having a hard time accepting their interracial relationship. Pastor John had suggested that they give Mrs. McKnight time to get to know Jada a little better. Jada was taking Pastor John's advice by deciding to take this trip with Pete.

The closer they got to Pete's parents' house, the more nervous Jada began to feel. "I don't know if I'm ready for this," Jada said as they got off the exit.

"I've told you, doll. We've just got to keep having hope that my mother's heart will be changed. She may be having a hard time accepting our relationship, but I love you no matter what, and I have faith that God's going to work this out."

"I'm only doing this, because I love you too. But honestly, Pete I think your mother hates me."

"She doesn't hate you, Jada. She may have some messed up points of view, but she doesn't hate you."

Jada didn't respond. She didn't want to get into an argument, so she decided to stay positive and try her best to be polite and patient no matter what kind of nonsense Mrs. McKnight might try to put her through this time.

Pete parked his Maxima in the driveway and rushed over to open Jada's door. She held onto the box of pumpkin pie as she stepped out of the car. They walked up to the front door, and Pete rang the bell.

Jada was relieved when Tonya opened the door. Only Tonya's face didn't look as cheerful as it normally did. She greeted them almost robotically.

"Hi, Tonya," Jada said as she stepped inside with Pete. She gave Tonya a hug. "Is everything okay?" Jada was feeling more and more anxious by the minute.

Tonya gave Jada a sympathetic look. "To be honest, Mom wasn't happy when she found out you were coming. She's in the kitchen, and Dad's in the family room."

Jada reluctantly walked with Pete toward the kitchen. When they entered, Mrs. McKnight had her arms folded. She was facing the television in the family room where Mr. McKnight was seated in a recliner.

"Hi, Mom and Dad," Pete said calmly.

"Hi, Mr. and Mrs. McKnight." Jada felt like it was taking every last muscle in her jaw to get a smile to come on her face.

Mrs. McKnight only looked at Pete. "Hi, sweetheart."

Mr. McKnight stood up and began to walk toward them.

"Pete told me that you both love pumpkin pie, so I brought one for dessert." Jada nervously looked at Mrs. McKnight who still had not even glanced at her.

"Thanks, dear," Mr. McKnight said as he took the pie from Jada and gave her a kiss on the cheek.

"The food's ready, so everyone can have a seat," Tonya announced deciding to take charge.

Jada and Pete quickly washed their hands in the bathroom and returned to the kitchen where they helped themselves to lasagna, salad, and lemonade.

"Do you mind if I bless the food?" Pete asked.

"Go ahead, son," Mr. McKnight replied.

Pete waited for everyone to bow their heads. "Lord, we thank you for this opportunity to gather together as a family. We thank you for this food we are about to eat, and we ask you to bless it, Father. In Jesus' name, Amen."

After a small chorus of 'Amens', everyone began to eat. For a while only the sound of clinking silverware could be heard in the kitchen.

Mr. McKnight cleared his throat. "So how are the marriage classes going?"

Jada saw Mrs. McKnight shoot a fierce glare over to her husband. He seemed to completely ignore her as he looked over at Pete.

"They're going okay," Pete replied. "Pastor John has us spending extra time on the extended family section, but everything else is going fine."

Mr. McKnight nodded and returned to eating his food. They all continued to eat mostly in silence.

Jada couldn't believe that this was the type of family that she was going to be marrying into. They actually wouldn't be so bad if it weren't for her future mother-in-law. She hated that Mrs. McKnight treated her like she wasn't good enough for Pete. What was it about her that Mrs. McKnight couldn't stand? Was the color of her skin the only thing that Mrs. McKnight could see? Jada had a responsible career and she believed that she carried herself with poise. Didn't her personality and character count for anything?

When everyone was just about done eating, they began to stare at one another awkwardly.

"Do you need me to help you clean up?" Jada politely asked Tonya.

"No thanks, Jada," Tonya replied with a smile. "There isn't really anything to clean up. I'll just put plastic wrap over the leftovers and stick them in the fridge."

"Well I can at least help you put the dishes in the dishwasher," Jada insisted. She was eager to escape the awkward silence.

"All right," Tonya agreed. She stood up and stacked a few plates in her arms.

"Pete, why don't you come downstairs with me?" Mr. McKnight beckoned. "I want you to check out my new golf clubs." He calmly rose to his feet.

Pete followed his dad down to the basement, while Jada began to place each dish into the dishwasher after Tonya had rinsed it. Jada had felt closeness between her and Tonya for some time now. The trip to California had allowed them to become better friends. She could tell that once she and Pete were married, the bond between them would be even greater. It would be like getting the sister she never had.

"Why don't we go sit in the family room?" Tonya suggested. "I'll help you, Mom," she added when she saw her mother reaching for her crutches.

As Tonya helped her mother stand up, Jada rushed over and pushed in Mrs. McKnight's chair. Tonya helped her mother sit down on the couch, and place her injured foot on the ottoman. Jada sat down on the love seat, and Tonya sat down next to her mother. Tonya began to flip through the TV channels with the remote. Eventually she stopped at a movie on the Lifetime network. Ironically, the movie featured a black woman in a relationship with a white man. Jada glanced at Mrs. McKnight and saw that she actually seemed to be watching the movie. She began to wonder if Pete was right about this whole situation working out. Then Tonya interrupted her thoughts.

"I got fitted for my bridesmaid dress yesterday," she said excitedly.

Jada began to get excited too, until she saw Mrs. McKnight. The evil look she could give returned again as Mrs. McKnight now glared at Tonya.

"I just wanted to let you know that it's really cute." Tonya looked from Jada to her mother with a determination in her eyes. "They have beautiful mother's dresses there too, Mom."

Mrs. McKnight totally disregarded her daughter's comment. "Can you bring me my pills and a glass of water, please, Tonya. The pain in my leg is getting shaper by the second."

As Tonya stood up to fulfill her mother's request, Jada kept her eyes glued to the TV. She wanted to try to talk to Mrs. McKnight, but the woman was acting like she wasn't even there. She, Tonya, and Mrs. McKnight ended up watching the entire movie in silence.

Finally, Pete and Mr. McKnight entered the family room. They both looked around curiously.

"Is everything going okay up here?" Pete asked. He had a worried look on his face.

Tonya uncurled herself from her pretzel position and stretched. "We were just watching a movie. What were you guys doing down there all that time?"

"Well, Dad showed me his new golf clubs. Then we played a quick game of pool." The worry on Pete's face reappeared. "We figured it would give you all a chance to talk."

Jada exchanged a look with Tonya that told her they were thinking the same thing. A pin drop could have been heard in the family room earlier if they had turned off the TV. Awkward silence was putting it lightly.

"We'd better get going, Jada," Pete said.

Jada stood up to say her good-byes. She hugged Tonya. While Pete was kissing Mrs. McKnight's right cheek, Jada managed to sneak a kiss in on her left. Jada noticed the shock on Mrs. McKnight's face from the corner of her eye. As she and Pete followed Mr. McKnight through the kitchen en route to the front door, Jada noticed that the pie was still sitting in its box unserved.

After she'd put her light jacket on and received a kiss on the cheek by Mr. McKnight, Jada turned around as Pete opened the front door. She saw Mrs. McKnight hobble into the kitchen and throw the pie away.

Jada got into Pete's car with her spirit again crushed. She had tried so hard to be nice to that lady, but she was still as cold as ice. None of her kindness seemed to matter to Mrs. McKnight.

As Pete started the car and began to drive down the street, Jada leaned her head back and closed her eyes.

"Tired, doll?" Pete asked with concern.

"Yeah," Jada's voice was weary. She didn't want to disappoint Pete, but she had to tell him the truth. "I'm getting very tired of being disrespected by your mother."

Pete gave Jada a worried look. "What did she do?"

"She didn't say one word to me the entire night. She wouldn't look at me or talk to me." Jada sighed heavily. "When we were leaving, I saw her throw away the pie that I brought for her."

Pete released a long, deep breath. "I'm sorry, Jada." He shook his head. "I had really hoped things would improve this time."

"Me too," Jada whispered.

A sad look came over Pete's face. "I don't know why my mother's being so stubborn." He reached over and grabbed Jada's hand. "Please try not to take it personally."

Every time Jada was around Mrs. McKnight she felt insecure and unaccepted. She really loved Pete, but his mother wasn't the type of person that she wanted to be around. Jada came from a loving family that supported each other. She always hoped that when she got married, her in-laws would be the same way.

Jada sighed in frustration. "I don't know what it's going to take for your mother to like me."

CHAPTER 29

Giving Thanks

JADA COULDN'T BELIEVE THAT IT WAS Thanksgiving already, but she definitely had a lot to be thankful for. She and Pete had completed their pre-marital counseling sessions. Pastor John told them that he could see that God was at the center of their relationship. He also said that their determination to persevere through their extended family issues, was an example of God's unconditional love. He said that their union would be a testimony to that.

So Jada had forged ahead with the wedding planning. The church had been booked, and they'd made a deposit for the reception hall. She signed contracts for a photographer, videographer, and a DJ. The invitations had been ordered, and she planned to mail them after Christmas. All of her bridesmaids had received their dresses. She had begun to purchase decorations for the church with the help of Nicole, her maid of honor. Jada's order for bouquets of red and white roses with gold ribbon had been placed. She and Pete had also spent many sentimental evenings selecting wedding music. Jada felt like the wedding plans were running smoothly, and she was really enjoying it all.

As Jada began to dress for the local Thanksgiving Day Parade, she thought about how well things had been going at school too. Her new bunch of first graders had now settled into their daily routines nicely. From morning message, to morning math, reading groups, and literacy centers, they worked as busy little bees all day. Her class was racially diverse and getting along well with one another. That was something Jada really loved to see.

Some of her former students often stopped by her classroom in the mornings to say hello and ask if they could help out. Jada would often find some papers for them to pass into student mailboxes while chatting with them about how they liked their new grade. Even Latasha and Desire, her two former tutoring students regularly stopped by. And just as Pete had predicted, they were now the best of friends.

Jada and Pete had decided to go to the parade today before Thanksgiving dinner. They knew that they both had students who were going to be in the parade. It had now become a habit for Jada to wait on her front step for Pete to pick her up. She often used the time to quietly talk to God. As Jada sat there dressed in dark blue jeans, flat brown boots, a brown v-neck sweater, and a suede jacket, she continued to silently give thanks until Pete finally arrived.

"Good morning!" Jada greeted as she entered the car.

Pete leaned over and gave Jada a short kiss. "Happy Thanksgiving."

Pete navigated the ten-minute drive to the city hall parking lot. He and Jada took a spot along the sidewalk, waiting for the festivities to begin. Pete stood behind Jada, rubbing her shoulders as the participants began to make their way up the city street. The high school marching band led the way, playing various upbeat tunes.

"I have some of those girls playing the flute in my Geometry class," Pete said into Jada's ear.

Jada nodded in acknowledgement. The girls appeared focused and professional dressed up in their band uniforms. As the wind instrumentalists passed by, the students playing horn instruments approached with the percussion section behind them.

"See the boy playing the tuba?" Pete continued. "He's in my pre-calculus class. And like half those boys on the drums are in my Algebra class."

The band continued to march up the street past the curious onlookers lining each side of the wide street. Jada saw a group of young students approaching wearing martial arts uniforms. The young students were doing martial arts movements as they walked. As the performers came closer, Jada noticed that in the front row was her former student, Mya. Mya was now in second grade. She had often talked a lot about karate when Jada had her in first grade that past school year. Mya was a child of mixed heritage. Her mother was Japanese, and her father was black. Jada began to remember how excited Mya had been when Jada returned to school from spring break with the box of Japanese items she had purchased in San Francisco's Japantown.

"Let's all sit in a circle on the rug," she had told her first grade class.

Jada had taken a seat in the rocking chair and waited patiently as the students cooperatively squeezed themselves into a circle.

"I've brought some things that I'm going to share with you for our mini-unit on Japan," Jada had informed her students. "First I'm going to read a Japanese story to you, so I want you to be good listeners."

The students had listened attentively as Jada had read aloud the Japanese fairy tale titled The Spider Weaver, which told the story of a man who saved a spider from a snake. In the story, a young girl offers to weave cloth for the man and weaves eight kimonos for him. When the man secretly goes to watch the girl weave for him one day, he sees that the girl weaving is really the same spider that he saved from the snake. The students had listened, completely engrossed in the Japanese fairy tale.

"Why did the spider weave for the man?" Jada had asked when she finished reading the fairy tale to the class.

A well-spoken student had raised his hand and answered, "To thank the man for saving her from the snake."

"And what did the spider weave?" Jada had then asked.

Mya was the first to raise her hand. After Jada called on her, Mya confidently said, "Eight kimonos."

At that point, Jada had shown the class the kimono that she had purchased. The students had observed and touched the garment with wonder.

Next Jada had showed the class the educational Japanese DVD. When the video showed children doing karate, Mya had been on the edge of her seat. Jada had instructed the students to make a poster showing what they'd learned about Japan. Mya had turned her poster into a card, which she bashfully handed to Jada at the end of the day with a quick hug. The colorfully decorated card had read, *Thank you MiSS CaLLoway. Your tHe Best!*

Jada smiled and waved at Mya who was now standing in front of her with the other performers from the group. They all bowed, and Mya managed to flash Jada a big toothy grin. The young martial arts performers continued to move forward with their routine.

Jada and Pete continued to watch the rest of the parade while pointing out their various students. Some of the other groups that marched by were junior cheerleaders, the high school drill team, Irish step dancers, local dance teams, and a few special floats. When the last float had rolled by, the crowd began to separate as everyone headed back to their cars and homes.

Pete looked at Jada curiously, "We've still got an hour before we have to be at your folk's for dinner. Do you want to take a walk?"

Jada smiled slightly. "Sure."

They began to head for the town green, which contained various walkways and a peripheral trim of red, orange, and yellow leafy trees. Pete put his arm around Jada and pulled her close as to protect her from the brisk November air.

"What does your family usually do for Christmas?" Pete asked.

"The same thing we do on Sundays." Jada answered casually. "Just with more food."

Pete chuckled. "Your family does love to eat." He paused for a moment. "My family usually has dinner and then we exchange gifts. Josh and Aaron usually stay in Massachusetts, but their parents, Tim and Patty always come down and celebrate with us. Aunt Patty is the nicest woman. Everyone she meets loves her. She's gone on mission trips to Africa and the Dominican Republic. Her missionary crew would bring food and supplies to the schools there. She would always come back with pictures, souvenirs, and music."

"Wow," Jada said thoughtfully. "I wish I could travel like that. I like learning about other cultures."

"I'd love for you to meet my aunt." Pete smiled. "I think you'd like her."

"I would like to meet her, but I don't think I can handle being around your mother again." Jada shook her head. "She can't stand me."

Pete gave Jada an assuring look. "I understand, doll. I'm just as disgusted with my mother's behavior as you are. I've told her the way she treats you is unacceptable."

Jada looked at Pete in desperation. "Why won't she listen to you?"

"I don't know, Jada. You've done everything you could to be pleasant toward her. I don't want her around you anymore if she's going to disrespect you." Pete's tone was certain. "We can spend Christmas with our own families and then hook up with each other later."

Jada looked down sadly. "They say when you marry someone, you marry their whole family. If your mother can't stand me now, what's she going to do if we get married?"

Pete's steps suddenly slowed. "If we get married?" He looked at Jada with squinted eyes and a furrowed brow.

"I really love you, Pete. But I'm starting to wonder if I can go through with this."

Pete stopped completely. "Because of my mother?" He looked at Jada deep in her eyes. "Remember what Pastor John said. We just have to keep hoping and praying for her." He embraced Jada in a hug. "We can't just give up on each other."

CHAPTER 30

The Night before Christmas

`

THE SPAN BETWEEN THANKSGIVING AND CHRISTMAS seems all too short when one's as busy as Jada had been. She had been busy working on report cards and preparing files for parent teacher conferences.

Ever since Thanksgiving, Pete and Jada had been having dinner together every night. Sometimes he and Jada would eat alone, or sometimes they would eat with her parents. Anytime Jada and Pete spent time with her parents, or her whole family even, everything felt so right to her. But today, the Calloways and the McKnights were finally going to meet each other. Jada sat in the back seat of her parents' Audi nervous about how this meeting would turn out.

Due to having their own Christmas day traditions, the parents had agreed to get together for a Christmas Eve lunch. They had all decided that it would be easier to meet at The Basil Patch.

"So we're finally going to meet Pete's parents," Charles cheerfully said from the driver's side of the vehicle.

Jada didn't feel one bit as cheerful as her father sounded. "Pete's dad is nice, but I can't say the same about his mother."

Dana glanced at Jada from the passenger side of the car. "Has she been rude to you?"

"She's been very rude to me." Jada's tone was certain. "Most of the time she doesn't talk to me or acknowledge me at all. When she does talk to me, she makes inappropriate racial comments. I'm sure she doesn't want Pete to marry me."

Charles looked at Jada through the rear view mirror with a furrowed brow. "This is something we're going to discuss tonight. You and Pete are going to be married in two months. His mother needs to start respecting you."

The restaurant parking lot was sparse when they pulled in. Charles parked the car. Jada and her parents entered the front of the restaurant and sat down in the waiting area. They had only been sitting down for about a minute when Jada saw Pete approaching the front doors. He pulled the door open, but it was only his dad who walked in behind him. Pete smiled and walked over to give Jada a hug while their parents began introducing themselves.

"Hello, I'm Paul, Pete's dad." Mr. McKnight said in a deep voice as he extended his hand to Jada's parents.

"I'm Charles," Jada's dad replied shaking Mr. McKnight's hand.

"I'm Dana," Jada's mom shook his hand and smiled.

"I'm sorry my wife couldn't make it." Mr. McKnight stuck his hands into his pant pockets. "Her ankle started bothering her again."

"Oh. I'm sorry to hear that," Dana sympathetically replied.

After being escorted to a large, round table, the waitress promptly came and took their orders. They began to engage in conversation as they waited for the food to arrive.

Mr. McKnight talked about his job as a professor at the University School of Pharmacy, and Charles and Dana opened up about their ophthalmology practice. As she watched the parents talk, Jada realized even more how much Pete was like his dad. Mr. McKnight warmed up to both of Jada's parents. By the the time the food arrived, they were all laughing and having a wonderful time. Mr. McKnight even offered to take Jada's dad to play golf sometime. Golf had never really interested Jada's dad in the past, but he accepted the offer.

Suddenly, Charles' face turned serious. "There is something we had hoped to discuss tonight."

The table grew quiet as everyone stopped eating. All eyes were on Jada's dad.

Charles looked at Mr. McKnight. "We've heard that your wife doesn't approve of Jada and Pete getting married. Jada says she is very disrespectful toward her and has made inappropriate racial comments."

Mr. McKnight looked like a dear caught in headlights. Jada could tell that the topic was making him uncomfortable.

Pete released a frustrated sigh. "I've been trying to tell my mother that she's wrong, but she refuses to listen."

Mr. McKnight began to recollect himself. "I don't approve of the way my wife's been treating Jada." A sincere look came over his face. "Part of it is my fault. In the past I noticed she had a prejudiced attitude, but I never confronted her on it. I've been trying to get her to see that her attitude toward Jada is unacceptable. I'm going to keep trying to get through to her." He looked at Charles and Dana genuinely. "I'm in support of Pete and Jada getting married."

Charles nodded thoughtfully. "I appreciate your honesty. We think Pete is a wonderful young man, but the way your wife treats our daughter really disturbs us. I hope the situation gets resolved before the wedding. If it doesn't, it's definitely going to add tension."

Jada knew that her dad was right . The mood always changed whenever Mrs. McKnight was around. The joyous tone surrounding the table had been diminished just by talking about her. Thankfully they had all finished eating and were ready to leave.

The waitress returned to the table with their tab. They divided the amount equally and walked out of the restaurant.

"It was nice meeting you," Mr. McKnight smiled at Charles and Dana.

"Same to you," Charles said shaking his hand.

"We'll see you at the rehearsal dinner," Dana added. "Hopefully your wife will be ready to join us by then."

After hugging their parents, Jada began walking with Pete toward his car. She was excited about going back to his house to spend some one-on-one holiday time together.

Jada and Pete sat cuddled together on the floor of Pete's living room. Jada looked around the newly decorated space. Early in the month, they had picked out a hunter green living room furniture set with a matching area rug. The décor went perfectly with the artificial tree they had decorated together. Mary Mary's Christmas album was playing softly in the background. They had decided to exchange their gifts tonight since they wouldn't be spending Christmas day together. They had agreed to spend Christmas day with their own families.

Jada turned around and smiled at Pete. "I want you to open your gift first."

Pete grinned. "If you insist."

Jada retrieved a rectangular box from underneath the tree. She handed it to Pete and sat with her legs crossed in front of him. He smiled at her as he began to remove the wrapping.

Pete's eyes lit up when all the paper was removed. "Curve Soul! My favorite fragrance." He stared for a moment at the box full of cologne and aftershave. With tender eyes, he leaned over and placed a gentle kiss on Jada's lips. "Thank you, doll."

Jada smiled at him lovingly, "You're welcome, baby."

Pete reached underneath the tree and handed Jada a small rectangular box. It was wrapped neatly with a ribbon tied around.

Jada grinned and began to remove the wrapping. Underneath the paper was a black box. Jada's eyes widened when she lifted the top. Staring up at her was a shiny white gold and diamond chipped tennis bracelet.

"It's beautiful," Jada whispered.

"I know you like jewelry, so I thought you'd like it." Pete's dimples appeared on the sides of his face.

Jada reached out and stroked his cheek. "I love it. I'm going to wear it on our wedding day as my something new." She leaned in and placed a soft kiss on his lips. "Thank you."

"You're welcome, doll." Pete pushed himself up onto the couch and pulled Jada up with him. He wrapped his arm around her shoulder. "What time is your family having dinner tomorrow?"

Jada gave Pete a curious look. "Two o'clock."

Pete grinned at Jada. "I'll stop by your folks place for an hour. Then I'll go up to my parents' house,"

Jada looked at Pete thoughtfully. She hesitated. "I'll go with you."

Pete's eyebrows shot up. "What?" He shook his head firmly. "I don't want you being disrespected by my mother anymore."

Jada's eyes softened. "I want to spend the day with you tomorrow. I'd also like to meet your aunt." Her tone became unsure. "I can't avoid your mother forever. If we're going to get married, I'm going to have to get used to her."

CHAPTER 31

A White Christmas

IT HAD BEEN A LONG TIME since Jada remembered having a white Christmas. It would always snow a week before or a week after Christmas, but never almost the same day. Overnight, a light snowfall had swept across the state. Now, as Jada sat in the passenger side of Pete's Maxima gazing out the window, she admired how the branches, leaves, and grass were still hidden beneath the fluffy white substance though the roads were perfectly clear. Pete pulled into his parents' driveway, and Jada got out of the car wondering what this Christmas would bring.

As they stood on the doorstep with food and gifts in hand, Pete rang the bell, and turned to Jada. "Don't worry. Everything's going to be okay," he said.

"Hi, dear," Mr. McKnight said to Jada after he opened the door. He leaned over and gave her a kiss on the cheek, which was now becoming very familiar for him to do.

Pete and Jada placed the food and gifts down on the console table and hung their coats on the coat rack.

"Let me get a picture of the happy couple," Mr. McKnight said suddenly holding up a camera.

When the flash had gone off, Jada looked through the foyer into the dining room where she saw Mrs. McKnight and Tonya setting the table for dinner. Mrs. McKnight looked up toward them.

"Hi, sweetheart," she called out.

"Merry Christmas," Jada said, straining to sound cheerfully polite.

"Merry Christmas to you guys too!" Tonya answered enthusiastically.

Pete picked up the gifts and walked toward the living room to put them under the tree.

Jada picked up the food she had brought and hesitantly walked into the dining room. "I brought macaroni and cheese."

"You did?" Tonya exclaimed. "Mom, Jada's macaroni and cheese is so good." Tonya took the tin from Jada's hands. "I'll put it in the kitchen."

Jada now had a genuine smile on her face, feeling uplifted by Tonya's comment. "I also brought some double chocolate chip cookies," she said, looking at Mrs. McKnight.

Mrs. McKnight walked over to Jada. "Don't we have enough chocolate around here?" She snatched the plate from Jada's hand and walked off toward the kitchen.

Jada stood there alone, flustered with embarrassment. She didn't have to wonder who Mrs. McKnight was referring to when she said 'chocolate'. Jada was still standing there frozen when a cheerful voice commanded her attention.

"I thought I heard a voice that didn't sound familiar."

Jada turned to see a full figured dark haired woman enter the dining room. Her straight, almost black hair barely touched her shoulders, and she reached up to pull it away from her face as she looked at Jada.

"Hello," Jada smiled slightly at the woman. "I'm Jada."

"So you're my nephew's fiance," the woman said through a smile. "It's so nice to meet you." She placed a hand on her chest. "I'm his Aunt, Patty. I'm married to Paul's brother."

Jada's smile grew. "Pete talks really highly of you." Jada could see why. The woman emanated warmth and friendliness.

"He does?"

"Yes." Jada's eyes widened as she looked at Aunt Patty's pleasant face. "He says everybody loves you."

"See, that's why he's my favorite nephew." The woman grinned and winked at Jada. "Then again, he is my only nephew. I'm an only child myself."

Jada's eyebrows rose. "So am I."

Aunt Patty's smile widened. "See. We've got something in common already. Let me introduce you to my husband."

They walked through the foyer and living room into the family room. Mr. McKnight, and a dark-haired man that had a strong resemblance to Mr. McKnight were sitting down watching TV.

"Pete?" Aunt Patty looked into the living room where Pete was finishing up with the gifts. "Aren't you going to introduce this beautiful young lady?"

Pete walked into the family room. He went over to Jada and put his arm around her. "Aunt Patty, this is my fiancé, Jada."

Aunt Patty silently nodded and smiled.

Pete continued. "And that's my Uncle Tim."

Uncle Tim stood up, shook Jada's hand, and kissed her on the cheek. "It's a pleasure." He looked directly at Pete. "This young lady sure is pretty. Do you model?" he asked, now looking at Jada.

Jada was sure that if she were lighter, her face would be completely red. She smiled and shook her head.

"It's time to eat!" Mrs. McKnight announced from the kitchen with her hands on her hips. "I'm sure this food is a lot prettier than whatever it is you all are looking at over there."

Jada was sure they could have gotten frostbite from the ice that now filled the room. As she looked around, she could tell she wasn't the only one who felt it. Everyone gaped at Mrs. McKnight.

"What's gotten into her?" Uncle Tim mumbled.

"If she doesn't check her attitude, I'm putting her in time out," Mr. McKnight murmured.

"Well are you all just going to stand there, or are you going to come eat?" Mrs. McKnight asked flipping her clipped back hair over her shoulder.

Everyone slowly began to walk into the kitchen. They headed toward the dining room to get their plates off the neatly set table. Jada saw Pete walk over to his mother.

"Mom," he began in a firm tone. "That comment you made a minute ago was uncalled for. You're disrespecting my future wife. You know you're wrong, and you need to apologize."

Mrs. McKnight turned her head and looked away.

A disappointed look came over Pete's face. He shook his head and glanced around at the family members who were all roaming the kitchen with plates in their hands. "I'm just going to bless the food first," he suddenly announced.

Everyone froze in their tracks. The authority in Pete's voice dared them to protest. They all stood in the kitchen and bowed their heads.

"Lord," Pete began. "We just want to thank you for this time to gather together as a family." Jada cracked her eye open, and saw Pete glance at his mom who was looking down with her arms folded. Pete continued to pray. "Help us not to forget the true reason that we celebrate this time of year. We thank you for your Son, Jesus, who you sent to us as a gift of love. We thank you that we can be saved and receive forgiveness, because he died for us. Lord, we ask that you'd bless this food, and help us to remember to love each other as you love us. In Jesus' name, Amen."

Jada felt calmness return to the room as she lifted her head, but Mrs. McKnight looked anything but calm. Something definitely wasn't right about that woman; the way she was yanking serving spoons out of the drawers and ramming them into the dishes. Mrs. McKnight stood to the side with her arms folded as everyone began to fill their plates. Jada filled hers with roast chicken, cranberry sauce, string beans, and rice pilaf. Then Jada stopped. Her eyes surveyed the kitchen. Her macaroni and cheese was nowhere to be found. As Jada made her way through the kitchen toward the long dining room table, she purposely glanced into the garbage can. She didn't see any macaroni, but she still wondered where it could be.

Jada sat between Pete and Tonya and tried her best to enjoy the meal. But her mind just wasn't there. She could have been eating stale bread, and everyone could have been speaking Martian, and she wouldn't have known the difference. She just ate silently, and smiled when everyone else smiled though she never had a clue of what had been said.

Suddenly, Mrs. McKnight began to push herself away from the table. "Excuse me," she said.

"Are you alright, honey?" Mr. McKnight asked.

"I need to elevate my ankle," she replied. "It's starting to throb again."

"We'll clean up for you, Trisha," Patty called out as she watched Mrs. McKnight leave the room.

"I'll help too," Jada offered. She stood up and began to help Aunt Patty and Tonya collect empty plates, as the men continued to sit and talk about sports.

They stacked plates and glasses into the dishwasher, covered leftover food, and placed it into the refrigerator. As Aunt Patty and Tonya wiped down the counter tops, Jada took a wet paper towel and began to wipe down the stove. As she cleaned the stove, a few rice kernels fell on the floor. Jada kneeled down to grab them with the paper towel. As her eyes raised, she saw through the oven window that there on an oven rack sat her tin of macaroni and cheese. Jada frowned. Pete's mother must have thought it wasn't good enough to be served. Just then, Mr. McKnight entered the kitchen. "Trisha says you can come into the living room to open gifts when you're done."

"We're coming now," said Tonya.

The three women followed Mr. McKnight into the living room.

"I'll pass out the gifts," Tonya announced. She held up a package and read the label, "To: Mom and Dad. From: Pete and Jada."

Mr. McKnight accepted the package as Mrs. McKnight looked at it with a frown. Mr. McKnight opened the package of his and her watches and thanked Pete and Jada.

"To: Tim and Patty. From: Paul and Trisha," Tonya read.

Patty reached for the package. "You didn't have to get us anything."

"We wanted to," Mrs. McKnight replied with a smile.

Patty opened the box of plush purple towels. "Thank you. These are just what we needed."

"I saw that you changed your shower curtain the last time I was over there and figured these would look nice with it," Mrs. McKnight explained.

"To: Tonya. From: Pete and Jada." Tonya opened the large box. "A new toaster! Thanks guys."

"You're welcome," Jada responded with Pete.

"Now I won't be burning my toast anymore," said Tonya. "My old toaster would get stuck and burn my toast all the time." She looked at the box and smiled. "Anyway. To: Pete. From: Mom and Dad," she read, and then handed Pete the package.

Pete opened the box. "A laptop? I don't believe it. This is just what I needed." He looked at his parents and smiled. "Thanks."

"You're welcome, sweetheart," Mrs. McKnight replied as her husband smiled.

Tonya picked up another package. "To: Tonya. From: Mom and Dad." She ripped off the wrapping. "A GPS navigation system! This is great! Now I won't get lost anymore when I'm going on road trips to visit friends." She smiled at her parents. "Thank you."

"You're welcome, sweetie," they replied almost in unison. Then they opened the gift Tonya had just given them to find a set of dinnerware glasses. They smiled and thanked her.

Tonya picked up the last package. "To: Pete. From: Tonya." She handed the package to Pete, but then looked back at the Christmas tree with a disturbed look on her face.

Pete opened the gift. "A bowling ball! Thanks, sis," he said, smiling.

"You're welcome. You said you needed one…" Tonya's voice trailed off as she now stood, walked over to the foyer, and then back to the tree. "I'm sorry, Jada, but I could have sworn I brought up a gift for you." Tonya scratched her head while looking at Jada with concern and confusion in her eyes. "Could I have left it at home?"

"It's okay, Tonya. Don't worry about it," Jada replied. After seeing where her pumpkin pie and macaroni and cheese had gone, Jada had a suspicion that Mrs. McKnight had now conveniently discarded the gift Tonya had brought for her. She wouldn't put it past her.

Jada watched as Mr. McKnight began to pick up wrapping paper and stuff it into a garbage bag with a concerned look on his face. "Why don't all of you go into the family room where you can get more comfortable?" he suggested.

As Jada and the rest of the family obliged, she saw Mr. McKnight begin to quietly talk to his wife. Jada's curious nature wondered what he might be saying. She was curious, but not nosy. She sat down in the family room, and decided to mind her own business by watching the movie, Home Alone, that was on TV.

Pete sat down on the edge of the couch and looked at Jada. "You can come with us downstairs if you want. I'm going to play Uncle Tim in a game of pool."

Jada forced a smile. "All right. I might go down in a little bit." At the moment, she wasn't interested in watching them play pool.

Jada watched Pete and Uncle Tim disappear down the basement door. Tonya was across the room stretched out on the loveseat. Aunt Patty came over and sat next to Jada as she sipped on some punch.

"How you doing, honey?" she asked pleasantly.

"Okay." Jada forced a smile. "How are your sons Josh and Aaron doing? I met them this summer."

Aunt Patty smiled warmly. "They're good. Their wives are doing well too. No babies yet, but both of them say they're working on it."

Jada smiled weakly. "So they stayed in Massachusetts for Christmas?"

"Yeah. They only come down for Thanksgiving." Aunt Patty took another sip of her punch. "Pete and my sons are very close. They're looking forward to your wedding."

Jada felt her weak smile begin to fade. Right before Aunt Patty came over, Jada had been sitting there wondering if there should even be a wedding. She'd had it with Mrs. McKnight's abuse and was feeling ready to call it quits. "Why can't Pete's mom be more like you?" Jada asked. Her eyes widened and she froze when she realized she had actually said that out loud. "I'm sorry. I shouldn't have said that," she stammered, looking at Aunt Patty.

Aunt Patty put her arm around Jada and whispered, "It's okay. Sometimes I wonder the same thing myself." She kept her voice low. "Trisha looks down on people in a really arrogant way. Heck, she looks down on me, because I'm a full figured woman." Aunt Patty's tone became serious. "If Trisha doesn't start watching her attitude, she's going to end up being a lonely woman one day."

Even though it was now just her and Pete in the car, Jada couldn't wait to get home. This had officially been the most unpleasant Christmas gathering she had ever been to. She wanted to go straight home. She couldn't understand why Pete had just turned down the dark street leading to the apartment he used to share with Tonya.

"Why are we going to Tonya's place?" Jada asked.

Pete pulled into the apartment complex and parked the car. "Tonya suggested we check to see if your gift is here," he said turning off the ignition.

Jada looked down silently and began to twist her platinum engagement ring. "I don't want to go inside, Pete. Can you just take me home?"

Pete looked over at Jada for a while and she sensed that he was confused. "Okay," he finally replied as he turned the key in the ignition and started the car.

The radio filled the silence for the ten-minute drive, until Pete backed his car into Jada's driveway.

Pete turned off the car and stared at Jada. "You've been awfully quiet," He said with concern in his voice. "What's wrong?"

Jada looked up at Pete. The only light that could be seen in the car was the light from the garage lamp on the house. Though everything on Pete's face appeared much darker, Jada could still see the worry in his eyes. She took a deep breath. "I didn't have a good time tonight, Pete. Your mother doesn't want me to marry you, and she's going to do everything she can to try to make me miserable."

Pete's lips were tight, and his brow was furrowed. The concern in his eyes grew.

Jada began to slowly twist her engagement ring farther up toward the tip of her finger. Tears filled her eyes. "If being a part of your family means being treated like I was today, then I don't want to be a part of it." Jada's lip began to tremble as she took Pete's hand and placed the ring in his palm.

"So you're giving up just like that?" Pete asked in a shaky voice with his palm still holding the ring.

"I'm sorry." Jada sniffed as she opened the door and rushed out of the car.

CHAPTER 32

Letting Go

FOR NINE DAYS STRAIGHT, JADA'S PHONE had continued to ring. Pastor John had returned her phone call yesterday and listened to her reasons for not wanting to go through with the wedding. She'd explained that she could no longer deal with the racial tension. At one point Jada had thought that she could handle being a part of a family that was white. She thought they could all blend together and make it work. But Jada just couldn't see herself being disrespected for the rest of her life. She had been down that road, and didn't want to go down it again. Pete's number continued to appear on her cell phone at least three times every day. Just the thought of not being with Pete made Jada want to cry. It was tearing her up inside. The only people who new about her cancelled engagement right now was her family. She was still too distraught to talk about it with anyone else. Since breaking up with Pete, she'd been an emotional mess. She was desperately trying to pull herself back together.

On New Year's Eve, Uncle Jack and Aunt Tina had a small family get together. Jada, Gene, Joe and Tyrese were the only family members who had attended. That night, Jada had made the resolution to get on with her life. But the messages that Pete had been leaving on her voice mail were making it hard for Jada to do that. Each day that she listened to her voice mail, Jada would here Pete's voice saying, "I love you, Jada." Or the message would say, "I miss you, Jada." Sometimes he would say, "Call me, Jada." Yet, she would never call.

Jada picked up her purse just as Alicia Keys' No One began to play from her cell phone. She immediately knew that it was Pete. Jada hit the reject button. She figured if she kept rejecting his calls, he would get the message that she wanted to move on.

When the song playing from her cell phone stopped, Jada stuffed the phone back into her purse and left her room to head to the Teacher Appreciation Breakfast they were having at church for the children's ministry workers. As she walked into the kitchen to grab a bottle of water from the refrigerator, she saw her mother standing at the counter fixing her usual Saturday morning bacon sandwich.

"Hi, Mom," Jada said flatly.

"Hi, honey," Dana answered with a concerned smile. "How are you feeling today?"

Jada plucked a strip of bacon off of the pile sitting on the counter, took a bottle of water out of the refrigerator, and sat down at the table. "I'm okay." She took a small bite of the bacon and looked out the window as she began to chew.

"Why are you eating now when you're about to go to the breakfast?" Dana placed her sandwich and a glass of orange juice at the head of the table and sat down.

"I don't know." Jada shrugged and continued to look out of the window. "I don't really want to go. I'm just going because I signed up."

"It'll be good for you to go. You haven't gotten out much this week."

"I know." Jada popped the last bite of bacon into her mouth.

"When are you going to start telling people that there isn't going to be a wedding?" Dana stared at her daughter, waiting for a response.

Jada felt her body stiffen. "I don't know, Mom." She heard the impatience in her own voice.

"You can't avoid it forever, Jada." Dana's tone was sympathetic.

"I know, Mom, but it's just…" Jada sighed deeply.

"I can see it on your face, Jada, that you still love him."

Jada looked down and closed her eyes. "I have to go, Mom," she said as she stood up to leave.

Once in her car, Jada blinked back tears as she drove to the church. Her mother had definitely struck a nerve. One that she had been trying to tell herself she didn't have. In her attempts to get over Pete, Jada had been trying to ignore the love that she still felt for him.

"Get a hold of yourself, Jada," she said aloud as she pulled into the church parking lot. She looked in the rear view mirror, quickly checked her face and hair, and exited the car to go inside.

As Jada walked into the already crowded fellowship area, she saw Greg vigorously waving at her. Jada tried to smile as she walked over to the table. She stopped in front of the empty chair.

"Sit down," said Greg. "I saved a seat for you when I realized you were going to be late."

"Thanks," Jada replied. "I was having a hard time getting out of the house this morning. Did they start yet?"

"No. They had some problems with the microphone, but they're about to start now."

Jada saw Pastor George, the children's pastor, take the microphone out of the podium at the front of the room.

"Good morning everyone!" Pastor George eagerly extended his greeting. "I'm so glad all of you could join us today. This is a day where you get to sit back, relax, and let us serve you." Pastor George spoke with his usual high energy. "You all work so hard to serve the children in this ministry. Today the parents of the children you work with are going to be serving delicious food to show how much we appreciate all of you. We're going to let you all enjoy a great breakfast, and then we'll move on to some awards and raffles in a little bit."

The crowd burst into applause as Pastor George turned off the microphone, and parent servers began to bring carafs of juice to each table. Then they were all directed by table to the buffet of fresh breakfast food. Jada returned to her seat with a bowl of fruit salad, a slice of French toast, fluffy scrambled eggs, and two sausage links. Talk of the joys and occasional challenges of teaching the children filled the conversation at Jada's table.

When the hungry teachers had begun to finish up their breakfast, Pastor George started to announce a series of awards. Some of the awards given were Teacher of Patience, Teacher of Persistence, Teacher of Creativity, Teacher of Enthusiasm, and so on. To their surprise, Jada and Greg received the award for "Teaching Team of the Year." Both humbly walked to the front and accepted their award. They each returned to their seats with framed certificates acknowledging their efforts.

Following the awards, there were two raffle prizes of restaurant gift cards given. Afterward, Pastor George dismissed the crowd to enjoy the rest of their afternoon. Everyone began to stand up, and a low roar of conversation started to fill the large open area.

"What a way to end our year of teaching together," Greg said, looking at Jada with a smile.

"This was certainly unexpected." She looked down at her framed certificate with a grin.

"I'm going to miss working with you, Jada," Greg said with sincerity in his voice. "Now I have to get used to working with somebody new all over again."

"I know. New year, new partner."

"Well, the three month break should give you the time you need to focus on your wedding."

Jada's eyes widened as she realized this was the first person besides her parents who had now forced her to address the wedding. "I haven't told anyone yet, but Pete and I broke off our engagement."

Greg's neck jerked forward and his eyebrows rose. "For real?"

Jada nodded. "I'm going to be sending out cancellation notices soon."

"I'm sorry to hear that, Jada." Greg's eyes were full of sympathy.

"It's okay." Jada managed to smile slightly.

"I hope I'm not being too forward, but would you like to get some dinner and talk?"

Jada looked compassionately at Greg. They had become good friends over the past year. But friendship was all Jada saw in him, though she sometimes sensed he could be interested in more. "You're a nice guy, Greg. But I don't know if I'm ready for that yet."

The hope in Greg's face faded, but it was replaced by an understanding smile. "You still love him, don't you?"

"Now you sound like my mother, Greg," Jada replied, suddenly irritated.

Greg held up his hands in retreat. "Hey, it was just a question."

"I'm sorry," Jada apologized. "I guess I'm still having a hard time with all this."

"It's understandable," Greg assured her. "I'm sure that with time you'll get through it."

Jada froze when she heard her cell phone ringing, but she sighed in relief when she recognized the tune.

"Hi, Nicole," she said into the receiver.

"What are you up to?" Nicole asked.

Jada took a deep breath. "I just got back from the Teacher Appreciation Breakfast. Now I'm trying to finish addressing my wedding cancellation notices."

"Your what?" Nicole's voice rose in shock.

Now that the holidays were over, Jada had planned to get her bridesmaids together all at once and tell them that the wedding was cancelled. But Jada could never keep anything from Nicole. She would be fuming if she found out she wasn't the first to know.

"Pete and I broke up." There was no emotion in Jada's voice. Jada heard Nicole gasp into the phone.

"Okay, listen," Nicole began. "I was going to ask you if you wanted to go see this new movie with me today, but I'm coming over there right now and we're going to talk."

As she disconnected the phone, Jada continued to sit on the floor and robotically write names and street numbers onto the small envelopes containing the sad announcement. She felt like she was operating on autopilot. Jada continued to function that way until Nicole appeared in her bedroom doorway. Her parents must have let Nicole in, because Jada hadn't even heard the doorbell ring.

As Jada looked up at her friend, instant moisture filled her eyes.

Nicole sat down on the floor between Jada and the scattered paper that covered the floor. "What happened?" she asked sympathetically, blinking back moisture from her own eyes as well.

"I just couldn't do it." Jada's voice shook with emotion.

"Why not?"

"If you saw the way his mother treated me, you would understand why I'm not marrying Pete. She's a monster." Jada wiped a few tears that had escaped from her eyes away from her face. Then as she looked at Nicole, her cry turned into a short laugh as they both realized the intensity of her statement.

"I'm sure she can't be that bad, Jada." Nicole handed a tissue to her friend.

"Where should I begin?" Jada wiped her face and nose. "She thinks all black women are baby machines who end up as single mothers with wild kids who all have different fathers." Jada sniffed. "I brought the woman her favorite pie after she broke her ankle, and she threw it away. On Christmas day she snatched the cookies I made out of my hands, and I never saw them again after that. She also refused to serve the macaroni and cheese that I made. She's compared me to food. And I think she had the nerve to secretly steal the present that her own daughter bought for me just so that I wouldn't have it."

Nicole continued to look at Jada with sincerity. Jada could see that she was trying to understand her point of view.

Jada shook her head. "She's just a cold, heartless person, and every time I see her she gets worse."

"So you don't think that you're strong enough to stay with Pete and deal with his mother?"

Jada looked at Nicole and shook her head no.

"I just can't believe that you called off the wedding." Nicole looked wide-eyed at Jada.

"Please don't tell anyone else yet," Jada pleaded to her friend.

"You don't have to worry about that. This isn't the kind of news I like to tell." Nicole looked around at the paper crowded floor. "Anyway, it looks like you have it covered."

"Yeah, I only have two more to address," Jada said sadly.

Nicole looked at Jada compassionately. "Well why don't you do one, and I'll do the other. Then I'm getting you out of this house."

"Why?" Jada asked curiously.

"This is just straight depressing." Nicole looked at the notices and then back at Jada. "We need to do something fun."

Jada's face turned into a pout as she thought about all the fun times she and Pete had shared. She'd had some of the best times of her life with him. How would anything or anyone else ever compare?

CHAPTER 33

Rebound

"WHAT DOES PETE THINK ABOUT THE way his mother treats you?" Nicole asked Jada as they stood in line at the movie theater waiting to pay for their tickets.

Jada looked at Nicole sadly. "He doesn't like it either. He's told her that, but she won't listen." Jada shook her head. "I just can't deal with all of Mrs. McKnight's drama. I've dealt with enough of that in my past."

They each paid for their ticket and began walking to the center of the lobby.

Nicole stopped next to the concession stand. "I'm going to get some popcorn. I haven't eaten anything all day. Are you getting anything?"

"No. I'm going to go wait for you on that bench." Jada pointed to the backless seat closest to where the attendants would collect their tickets.

Jada walked over to the bench and sat down. She probably could have used a snack too since she hadn't eaten since the appreciation breakfast five hours ago, but she just wasn't in the mood to eat. As she sat and watched strangers walk by, her heart ached every time she noticed a couple. Jada took numerous deep breaths as she tried to keep herself together.

As she looked toward the theater entrance, she noticed a familiar tall figure coming her way. As the figure came closer, Jada recognized that it was Mike holding the hand of a little boy. His eyes met hers, and he smiled slightly.

"Long time no see," Mike said, stopping in front of Jada.

Jada stood up. "I know." She was actually glad to see Mike again. It surprised her to see him with a little boy. "How have you been?"

"I've been good. This is my son, Mike Jr." Mike looked down at his son. "We call him Junior."

Jada smiled at the boy who barely reached Mike's hip. "Hi, Junior. I'm Jada."

The boy looked up at her with big, brown, deer like eyes. "Hi," he said in a small voice.

"I'm taking him to see this new animated movie that's out," Mike explained with a proud smile.

"That's nice," Jada replied, touched by the image that stood in front of her. It was a wonderful thing to see a father holding the hand of his son.

"So what have you been up to?" Mike asked.

"Not much. I'm just hanging out with Nicole. She's getting popcorn."

Mike nodded thoughtfully. He squinted at Jada. "Do you think we could get together this week or something? Maybe get a cup of coffee?" Mike went on in response to Jada's confused look. "I didn't like the way things left off between us, Jada. I just want to talk and have the chance to explain some things to you."

Jada thought for a moment. She figured she could go to make sure there were no hard feelings between them. "Well, when are you free?"

"I'm bringing Junior back to New York tomorrow, and I'll be back no later than two." Mike looked at Jada, waiting for a response.

"Do you want to meet at Sunset Cafe?" She asked casually.

"Sure." Mike grinned. "You want to go for four o'clock?"

"That's fine." Jada caught sight of Nicole walking toward her with a disapproving look on her face.

"Hello, Mike," Nicole said in a motherly tone when she approached them.

Mike turned around. "Hey, Nicole. How's your brother doing?"

"Fernando's fine." Nicole's eyes traveled from Mike's arm to the little person who joined him by the hand.

"This is my son, Junior," Mike said proudly.

"He looks just like you," Nicole's tone softened. "How old is he?"

"He just turned five actually," Mike replied through a grin.

"He's so cute," Jada cooed, smiling down at Mike Jr.

"Well he's going to get kind of impatient soon, so I guess we'd better go." Mike smiled. "It was nice seeing you both again."

Jada watched Mike walk away, still moved by the bonding between father and son.

"I haven't seen him in a while," Nicole remarked.

Jada thought a moment. "Oh, that's right. He doesn't bowl in the league anymore, because of his coaching schedule." She looked down at her bare left hand. "So he probably doesn't even know that I was engaged."

CHAPTER 34

Broken Hearts

"WHY IS JADA SITTING ALL THE way over there?" Tonya whispered to Pete. She was looking over at the other side of the congregation.

"Just listen to the sermon," Pete whispered in reply.

Pete still hadn't told Tonya about what had happened between him and Jada. He wasn't ready to accept the fact that their engagement was over. He didn't want to accept it until he had talked to Jada at least one more time. He had to know that she was sure.

Pete kept his head forward and listened to Pastor John teach on the peace of Christ. Throughout the sermon, he kept silently praying that his mother would really come to know Christ the way he had so that they could truly live in peace with one another. He knew in his heart that she did not have peace. She was dealing with a very proud spirit that was making herself miserable as well as everyone around her. He prayed that she would come to know humility so that her mind, heart, and family could be at peace.

As the pastor read from Colossians 3: 1-17, verse 11 jumped out at Pete from the page. *Here there is no Greek or Jew, circumcised or uncircumcised, barbarian, Scythian, slave or free, but Christ is all, and is in all.* Pete knew that this was exactly what his mother needed to understand. He knew that to God, it didn't matter what race you were, because he created every one of us. So if it doesn't matter to him, it shouldn't matter to us either. He silently prayed that the Lord would use someone to help his mother see this.

As Pastor John dismissed the congregation, Pete's heart was still a little heavy, but his hope had been renewed by the sermon he had just heard.

"Mom needed to hear this message," Tonya said as she gathered her purse and Bible in preparation to leave. "She's been angry and rude all the time lately. I don't think she knows how to be nice anymore. Dad's getting fed up with her."

"Is that why you didn't stay up there all weekend?" Pete asked.

"Yeah. I just didn't want to be around her."

"We've just got to keep praying, Tonya. That's all we can do at this point. Dad and I have already told her how we feel." Pete looked at his sister who was now vigorously scanning the church lobby.

"Where'd Jada go? she asked as she continued to look around.

Pete had been trying not to be obvious, but he was looking for her too. Then he saw Jada push open one of the glass exit doors and begin to walk across the parking lot.

"Wasn't that her who just left?" Tonya asked.

"Yeah," Pete answered as he quickened his steps toward the exit.

"Why is she walking so fast?" Tonya asked as she clunked across the parking lot in her four-inch heels, trying to keep up with Pete.

Pete watched Jada open her car door and get in. He had to stop in the middle of the parking lot as a line of exiting cars came between him and the woman he didn't want to get away. He watched a patient driver let Jada's car enter the exiting line which was now turning onto the main road car by car. The load in Pete's heart increased as he watched Jada's Civic turn onto the main road and drive away. Pete turned around to see Tonya staring at him thoughtfully.

"I'll just call her when I get home." Pete said, sadly as he began to walk in the direction of his car.

Jada hit the reject button on her cell phone for the second time today. She had completely ignored Pete in church. His two recent phone calls were making it obvious that he didn't want to be ignored. Now Jada was getting nervous about how she was going to avoid Tonya when she went back to school tomorrow. She knew that the whole situation with Pete could change things between her and Tonya. She was afraid that Tonya would be upset with her for breaking her brother's heart. She wasn't sure that Tonya would understand her point of view. And she also worried that Tonya could try to talk her into sticking it out with Pete. She already knew that that's what Pete would try to do. So she just chose to avoid them both for a while.

Jada secured her purse to her shoulder, left her room, and walked down the upstairs hall. With her car keys in her hand, she ran into her mother at the bottom of the stairs.

"Where are you off to?" Dana curiously asked.

"I'm going to Sunset Café," Jada replied casually.

"You're going by yourself?" inquired Dana.

"No. I'm meeting up with Mike."

Dana's brows lowered until her face now had a disapproving look. Somewhat like the look Nicole had given Jada when she walked up to her and Mike at the movie theater.

"I ran into him yesterday at the movies," Jada explained. "We're just going to talk." Jada opened the front door. "Don't worry. I'll be right back."

Dana held the door open as Jada walked to her car. While walking Jada could still feel her mother's disapproving eyes following her. Jada had told her mother about Mike's dishonesty as soon as she'd found out. Her mother now saw Mike as being irresponsible. Jada quickly got in her car without looking back, and began driving toward the café.

Ten minutes later, she parked directly in front of the Sunset Café entrance. As she exited the car, she was glad to have found such a close parking slot, because it was getting dark outside, which made the January air even colder. Jada opened the café door and was engulfed by the warm smells of coffee, vanilla, and chocolate.

She looked around and saw Mike sitting at a small, round window table to her right. He was looking down at his cell phone. Jada figured he was probably calling or texting Junior's mom, Brenda. She began to walk toward him anyway.

Mike didn't notice her approaching him. As Jada neared the table, her eyes traveled directly to his open cell phone. It was obvious she didn't trust him. But to Jada's surprise, Mike wasn't calling or texting anyone. He was playing Who Wants To Be A Millionaire. The moment reminded Jada of Pete. He loved to play those types of games on his cell phone.

"What's up?" Jada asked stopping next to Mike.

Mike looked up at her. "I didn't even see you standing there."

"I know." Jada sat down in the chair across from Mike. "You're too into Who Wants To Be A Millionaire. I didn't know you like cell phone games."

"I didn't until Pete put me on."

She was right. She knew her...Jada stopped. She was going to say she knew her man, but Pete wasn't her man anymore. The thought of it made her feel sad inside.

"When's the last time you've seen him?" she asked.

"Probably when the regular bowling league finished in May." Mike closed his cell phone.

Jada thought for a moment. That was the same month that she and Pete had officially become a couple. "Do you still talk to Gene a lot?"

"No." Mike shook his head. "I don't work at his school anymore."

"Oh." Jada sounded surprised. "You stopped teaching?"

"No, I still teach physical education and coach varsity basketball, but I transferred to another school to be head coach." Mike's face beamed. "I'm trying to build up my resume so that maybe I can get a job coaching at the college level."

Jada nodded and began to add up Mike's details in her head. If he hadn't seen Pete since May, and didn't work with Gene anymore, then he most likely hadn't heard that she and Pete had been engaged. She decided that since the wedding was off, he didn't need to know.

"Why don't we go order something hot to drink," suggested Mike.

Jada walked with Mike to the counter where she ordered a large hot chocolate with whipped cream. She moved to the side and waited for Mike to order his double expresso.

As Jada watched Mike pay for the drinks and step to the side to add his condiments, she thought about how awkwardly things had ended between her and Mike. Now as Jada observed Mike carefully add sugar and cream into his beverage, she noticed that the attraction she had felt toward him almost a year ago seemed to be gone.

Jada walked with Mike back to the table and lowered herself into her chair. "So how did your son like the movie?" she asked.

A proud grin appeared on Mike's face. "Oh he loved it. His eyes were glued to the screen the whole time."

Jada smiled. "I think that's really nice the way you're spending time with him. I can see you really care about him."

A serious look replaced Mike's grin. "Jada, I really am sorry for trying to hide the fact that I had a son. I should have told you about the situation with him and his mother sooner."

"What situation?" Jada asked with friendly concern.

"Well, I was a bit of a player in my past. I loved women, but didn't want a commitment. That's why things didn't work out between his mother and me."

"So were you embarrassed about having a son?"

"There's a little more to it than that." Mike continued to seriously look at Jada.

"Do you want to tell me about it?" she asked.

"Okay I'll try to keep this story brief." Mike took a short sip of his expresso. "I met Brenda when I was taking graduate classes and she was still an undergrad. I was twenty-five and she was twenty-one." Mike took a deep breath. "There was something so special about Brenda that I would be kickin' it with another girl and still be thinking about her. Things got a little too serious between Brenda and me, and she got pregnant with Junior right before she was about to graduate."

Jada looked at Mike. He was now looking down. She was quietly waiting for him to continue.

Mike sighed deeply. "Her parents flipped out. Brenda started telling me that we had to get married, and I wasn't ready for all that. I was still kickin' it with other girls. Her parents said that I was a jerk. They said she shouldn't keep seeing me, and they didn't want me around their house."

Jada hesitated, but then decided to speak her mind. "If you were still seeing other women, they probably thought they were doing you and Brenda a favor by saying that."

Mike looked at Jada with sadness in his eyes. "I know. Brenda's a good woman. I don't know what she was thinking getting involved with me. I wasn't ready to treat a woman right. I started thinking that she deserved better than me, so I let her go."

"You think you needed to grow up?" asked Jada.

"Definitely. Everything that happened with you really showed me that. You were right, Jada. I was neglecting my son and running away from my responsibility. And Brenda had always tried to tell me that. She would always say, 'You may have let go of me, but you're not letting go of our son.' That was why I started going to New York on weekends to see him."

Jada smiled slightly. "I'm sure he appreciated it."

Mike looked directly at Jada. "You're a very wise woman, Jada."

Jada tilted her head to the side, a little thrown off by Mike's statement. "Why do you say that?"

"Because you saw right through me. You knew I was trying to have my cake and eat it too."

Jada suspected that she knew where Mike was going with that, but she wanted him to continue. "What do you mean?"

Mike looked at Jada genuinely. "I used to stay at Brenda's house, because deep down I always hoped that things could be the way they used to be. I wanted to be able to date other women, but still have her. But she always resisted me. She wasn't having it."

Jada decided to be blunt. "That must have been hard with you staying in her house. She probably still wanted you, but she wasn't willing to share you."

Mike looked Jada straight in the eyes. "You know when you broke things off with me, you actually did me a favor. I mean, you're a beautiful woman Jada and any man would be blessed to be with you, but you made me ask myself some hard questions."

"Like what?" Jada's voice was full of curiosity.

A sincere look came over Mike's face. "Well, I asked myself if I was a good example to my son. And Junior may only be five, but I realized that one day he's going to be looking at me to see what it means to be a man and how to treat women. So I decided to grow up. No more games. I pick my son up when I say I'm going to now, and I try to spend quality time with him. I spend so much time with him that I haven't been on a date in months."

"How's it workin' for ya?" Jada asked with a grin.

Mike smiled. "Great actually. Brenda says that Junior talks about me all the time, and can't wait to come back to Connecticut with me on weekends. I didn't even go down to Virginia to spend Christmas with my family. She invited me to spend Christmas with hers."

Jada watched the emotion that she saw creep into Mike's eyes. "Did you have a nice time?"

Mike's smile grew. "I did. It was the best Christmas I've ever had. I got to see how good Brenda is with Junior. We played the Candyland game we bought him for Christmas, and then we played Hungry Hippos with him." Mike's smile suddenly weakened. "But her parents still don't like me. So I'll probably stay clear of being around them from now on."

Jada thought about the things Mike had told her. "Maybe they don't know that you've changed."

Mike began to rub his hand back and forth across his head. "Maybe. I know I hurt their daughter, but I wish they could see that I'm not the same man."

"Mike, it sounds like Brenda's starting to see that you've changed. If you want to be with her and your son, you shouldn't let what her parents think of you keep you from being where your heart is. Keep showing her the new you, and eventually her parents will forgive you and see it too."

Jada thought about what she had just told Mike. She knew that her heart was still with Pete. Yet, she had put an end to their relationship because of the tension between her and Mrs. McKnight. Suddenly, Jada wondered if she should be taking the same advice she had just given Mike.

CHAPTER 35

Back on Track

JADA DROVE DOWN THE DESERTED HIGHWAY toward Jordan Baptist Church. She was on her way to her old childhood church to see Grandma get honored as a mother of the church. Today they would be showing appreciation to elderly church mothers for their service, dedication, and inspiration to the church family. Jada planned to sneak in and leave. That way there wouldn't be any wedding questions from her grandmother's friends.

Jada ended up having to drive by herself to the church. Her parents had brought her grandmother there early for pictures and preparations. At times, Jada had a hard time getting up early on Sunday mornings, so she passed up the offer to ride with her parents. Today, she didn't mind driving by herself, because it gave her time to think.

As she drove, Jada thought about how she had managed to get through a full week at school without anyone asking why she didn't have on her engagement ring. Had they not noticed? Maybe they didn't want to be nosy.

Jada had avoided Tonya completely by saying that she wasn't going to be eating in the teachers' lounge because she had to catch up on paperwork. The teacher's lounge was the place where talk always became more personal. As long as she didn't go down there, she pretty much didn't have to worry about personal questions being asked.

She still hadn't sent out her wedding cancellation notices. They were already addressed, stamped, and ready to go, so she didn't know what she was waiting for. Jada knew she should send them, but something inside of her was keeping her from doing it. Her heart still wanted things to work between her and Pete. Only her mind was filled with too much doubt. The wedding date was now six weeks away, so she knew she had to send the notices soon. The cancellation notices weren't the only things she had been procrastinating on. She still hadn't told any bridesmaids, except for Nicole, and she still hadn't contacted any of her wedding service providers. She'd probably take care of everything tomorrow.

Jada parked her car in the already crowded parking lot. After exiting her vehicle, Jada quietly entered the church. She accepted the bulletin handed to her by the middle-aged hostess dressed in white and followed another hostess to a pew. She didn't object when the hostess seated her toward the back. It was late and the front rows looked to be full already. Sitting toward the back would make it easier for her to get to the lobby without being stopped to answer questions. The church was singing What A Friend We Have In Jesus. Jada opened her hymnal and began to sing along.

After the hymn was completed, the congregation was seated and the church gospel choir remained standing to sing a selection. Jada listened as the harmonic voices lifted praises to God by singing Richard Smallwood's Total Praise. By the end of the song, her heart was open to receive the word of God.

"Amen!" Pastor Rivers shouted as he took the microphone. "Are you ready for the word?"

"Yes!" the congregation replied.

Pastor River's energy level increased. "I said are you ready for the word?"

"Yes!" the congregation's response matched the Pastor's passion.

"Today I'm going to title this message Living a Life of Love."

"Amen!" a voice replied.

Pastor Rivers continued. "Today we're going to be honoring four very special ladies. These ladies have been wonderful examples to us here at Jordan Baptist Church. They have shown what it means to live a life of love."

Jada's eyes traveled to her grandmother who was seated in the front row next to three other elderly women. Grandma was dressed in gold with a matching hat and the other ladies to be honored were dressed to impress as well. She noticed her parents, Uncle Jack and Aunt Tina, and her cousins' parents Uncle Bob and Aunt Linda sitting in the row behind her grandmother. Jada returned her attention to the pastor.

"But how many of you know living a life of love ain't always easy?"

"Well!" a voice sang out.

"Some people just ain't easy to love."

"Talk about it!" a female voice replied.

Thoughts of Pete and his mother began to enter Jada's mind. As much as she had loved Pete, she just couldn't see herself loving that mother of his.

"There's two verses that I'm going to have you turn to today," Pastor Rivers spoke calmly into the microphone. "First turn to Matthew 5:44." He paused to allow the congregation to find the scripture before he began to read. "*But I tell you: Love your enemies and pray for those who persecute you.* Did ya'll here that one?"

The congregation joined Pastor Rivers in a chuckle. Jada stared at the passage. At that moment she felt like the words were meant just for her. Following the instructions of Pastor Rivers, she flipped to Matthew 6:14 and listened to him read.

"*For if you forgive men when they sin against you, your heavenly Father will also forgive you,*" Pastor Rivers looked out over the faces that filled the church.

Something in Jada's spirit confirmed to her that she was supposed to hear that message today. Jada knew she had to forgive Mrs. McKnight for being rude and disrespectful to her, or she would become bitter all over again. She continued to listen to Pastor Rivers' words of wisdom. Jada concluded that hating Mrs. McKnight in return for how she had treated her wasn't an option. She had to love her, and do what she had yet to do. She needed to pray for her.

As Pastor Rivers asked the congregation to bow their heads in prayer, Jada silently prayed that one day Mrs. McKnight's heart would be softened so that she could learn how to love with God's love.

Associate Pastor Frank then honored Jada's grandmother and the other dedicated ladies by reading a short passage about their involvement in the church and community. He then presented them each with a plaque. Jada's grandmother had run the hospitality committee for the past forty years, cooking and organizing the food for all church events, and served as a Deaconess for the past thirty years.

After collecting an offering, the congregation was dismissed. Jada immediately began her quick exit toward the lobby. As she walked out of the sanctuary, she felt a light tap on her shoulder. She turned around and saw Mike walking behind her with a very attractive young woman.

Jada stepped to the side, out of the way of the sanctuary exit doors. "Hi," she said sounding somewhat surprised.

"How you doin', Jada?" Mike asked.

"I'm good." Jada smiled and looked from Mike to the young brown skinned woman beside him. "How about yourself?"

"I'm great." Mike's enormous smile revealed the straight line of teeth in his mouth. "This is Brenda, Junior's mom. Brenda, this is Jada. We used to go to Sunday school here together way back."

"Nice to meet you." Jada extended her hand with a smile.

Brenda revealed a beautiful pearly white smile and took Jada's hand. "Same to you."

Suddenly, a young looking man lightly grabbed Mike's shoulder and pulled him into a manly embrace. Mike and the man began smiling, and talking as if they had just seen each other again after being disconnected for years.

Brenda looked at Jada with emotion in her eyes. "Thank you," she said now placing her left hand on top of Jada's hand.

Confusion filled Jada's eyes. "For?"

"Mike told me that God used you to open his heart back up to me." Brenda released Jada's hand and tucked her shoulder length brown hair behind her ears. "He said you've been a good friend who showed him he needed to grow up."

"I could tell that he still had feelings for you," Jada replied.

"Well thanks to you, we're going to start going to church together and spend time with each other again." Brenda smiled at Jada.

"Suddenly Mike turned around. "Have ya'll been talking about me over here?" he interrupted.

Jada exchanged a smile with Brenda. "Only good things."

"Oh, okay," Mike replied with a grin. "Well we have to go get Junior out of children's church."

Jada watched Mike walk with Brenda toward the multipurpose room to pick up their son. It seems like they're headed in the right direction, Jada thought. But was she?

Standing to the side to wait for her grandmother to pass by, Jada began thinking about her relationship with Pete. Could she be with Pete, have children with him, and still manage to be happy, despite Mrs. McKnight?

"What ya thinkin' bout so hard, baby?" Grandma stood next to Jada looking at her through the glasses framing her eyes.

"I just ran into Mike," Jada replied. "Do you remember him?"

"Sure, I remember him. You reminded me who he was at Tim's house a while back." A thoughtful look came over Grandma's face. "I ain't seen him in church since his family moved to Virginia 'bout ten years ago now. I thought he moved with them."

"No, he still lives here." Jada said casually. "He just introduced me to the mother of his son."

"He has a son?" Grandma sounded surprised.

"Yeah. He and his son's mother are trying to work things out." Jada paused thoughtfully. "They seemed really happy."

"A woman should be happy when she finds a good man." Grandma's eyes began to search Jada's face. "Pete's a good man, baby. He loves God, and he loves you."

Jada's mind filled with doubt. "But, Grandma I don't know if we can make it with Mrs. McKnight…"

Grandma put her hand gently, but firmly on Jada's arm. "Jada, God's word says, *what God has joined together, let man not separate.*" She looked at Jada with eyes that seemed to see straight through her.

Jada reached out and hugged her grandmother. "Congratulations, Grandma." She released her grandmother and looked her in the eyes. "Tell the rest of the family that I'll see them at the house later. There's something that I need to go do first."

CHAPTER 36

Reconciliation

JADA SAT IN HER CAR OUTSIDE of Jordan Baptist Church wondering if she should call Pete. Jada realized that in a few days it would be three weeks since she'd last talked to him. He had continued to leave messages every day asking her to call him, but she never did. She knew he had too much respect for her parents to show up at their house unannounced. Jada reached into her purse and took out her cell phone. As she scrolled down to his name, a familiar song suddenly began to play from her phone. It was Pete.

Jada took a deep breath and pressed okay. "Hi," she said softly.

There was a short pause. "I can't believe you answered your phone," Pete replied. "I've missed you."

"I was about to call you." Jada hesitated. "I wanted to see you so we can talk."

"I've been wanting to talk to you too. Are you home?"

Jada noticed that her heart was skipping beats from the sound of Pete's voice. "Not yet. I went to my grandmother's church today. I was about to leave now."

"Well call me when you get home. I can come over or something."

Jada paused thoughtfully. "My family's going to be over there. We might not get much privacy."

"You can come here if you want?"

Jada was moved by the patience in Pete's tone. She missed hearing his voice. "Okay. I'll be there in thirty minutes or so." Jada couldn't wait to get there. She now realized how much she missed him too.

Pete anxiously sat waiting in his living room. What was it that Jada wanted to say? Had she changed her mind about breaking things off with him? Or did she want to tell him once and for all to leave her alone. The suspense was getting to him. He needed some air.

Pete grabbed his leather jacket and walked outside the front door. He sat down on the step and tried to wait. The air was chilly and the neighborhood was quiet. With his hands stuffed in his pockets, he watched the deserted street, waiting for Jada's Civic to come into view.

When he saw the silver of her car approaching his driveway, he took his hands out of his pockets and began to nervously rub them together. He took a deep breath as he watched her step out of her car. Her hands were in the pockets of her short, black leather jacket, and she approached him slowly.

"What are you doing out here?" she timidly asked.

"I needed some air," he replied. Pete looked deeply into Jada's dark brown eyes. He was looking for indications of what she might be feeling.

Jada sat down next to him and looked straight ahead. She looked like she was far away somewhere, lost in her own thoughts.

"So what's going on with us, Jada?" Pete finally asked. "I thought we both really loved each other and were committed to making our relationship work."

"Pete, I'm really sorry for breaking things off between us. I still want things to work out for us just as much as you do. But they say when you marry someone you don't just marry that person, you marry their whole family." Jada sighed deeply. "I don't mean to disrespect your mother, but I know she hates me. If we have kids, she'll probably hate them too." Jada turned her head to look at him.

Pete stared at Jada for a moment before speaking. He saw the sadness in her beautiful eyes. "Jada, I still love you, and I know you love me too. I'm still confident that you're the wife that God has for me regardless of what my mother thinks. If we get married, we're going to be starting a family of our own. This will be our house, and we can start our own family traditions. We can decide who we want to invite into our home. If my mother continues to disrespect you, then she won't be allowed in our home. But I have faith that one day my mother's going to love you just as much as I do." Pete reached out to wipe away the tear that ran down Jada's face. He put his arm around her and pulled her closer, rubbing her arm to console her.

Jada rested her head on Pete's shoulder. "Do you really think we can make this work?"

Pete gently lifted Jada's face and looked down into her wet eyes. "I know we can."

Jada smiled faintly as Pete leaned in and placed a gentle kiss on her lips. "So, will you be my fiancé again?" He looked into her face with anticipation. When she nodded, Pete gave her another kiss and smiled. "Now I can give you back your ring."

Jada leaned into him closer, and he held her tight. "I love you," she said softly.

Though it was cold, at the sound of those words, Pete felt warmth run through his body. He kissed the top of Jada's head. "I love you too."

Pete thought about how good it felt to have Jada in his life again. He felt like he was made to love that woman. He also thought about how glad he was that he hadn't told anyone the wedding was off. It had been a hard couple of weeks, but as he had hoped, he and Jada had managed to work things out.

"Come on," Pete said grabbing Jada's hand. "It's cold out here. Let's go inside, so I can put that ring back on your finger."

Jada thought about what Pete had said as she sat on the living room couch, waiting for him to return with her engagement ring. There were many people in both of their families who were accepting of their relationship. If they wanted to spend time with those family members, they could always go to the Sunday dinners at Jada's parents' house, or they could invite Pete's accepting family members into their home. Their future children would have two parents, an aunt, and three grandparents who loved them. It would be Mrs. McKnight's choice as to whether she wanted to be included or not.

Pete entered the living room, sat next to Jada and slipped the ring back onto her finger. Jada took a deep breath and sighed as a feeling of peace came over her. She knew she was making the right decision. Her mind was no longer filled with doubt.

CHAPTER 37

Behold, I Stand At The Door and Knock

MRS. MCKNIGHT'S LIDS FLUTTERED OPEN SLOWLY. The space in bed beside her was empty. The bedroom was still pretty dark for it to be morning. She turned her head and looked at the bedside clock. It was 7:00 am, and she wondered if Paul had already gone to his office. Though the university was still on winter recess, he had been going into his office almost every day. He said that he wanted to get some things ready for the spring semester. But Mrs. McKnight didn't remember him ever spending this much time working during winter recess before. With him off working, lately she was left alone in the house all day. So she had decided to tackle her New Year's Resolution of reorganizing the house and throwing away the things she no longer needed. Today she planned to work on her craft room.

Not wanting to waste any time lying around, Mrs. McKnight sat up and swung her legs over the side of the bed. As she placed her feet on the floor and began to stand up, the dull pain began to throb in her left ankle. It was going to be another rough day. Ever since her fall, her ankle hadn't been the same. Looking over to the window, Mrs. McKnight saw the rain pouring down outside. Rainy weather seemed to always intensify the pain. The doctor had said that the bones in her ankle were all aligned correctly, but the throbbing feeling just wouldn't go away.

Mrs. McKnight leaned down and gently rubbed her ankle. She slowly stood up, despite the pain that she felt.

She quickly freshened up in the bathroom and put on windbreaker pants and a T-shirt. Then she went down to the kitchen and poured a cup of coffee from the pot that her husband always brewed first thing in the morning. She carried her cup down the hallway off of the kitchen and into the room at the end of the hall. She placed her coffee mug down and began to scan the room. She was trying to decide where she should begin. Her eyes stopped at the large bookshelf full of boxes. Each of the boxes were labeled, and she knew they were probably full of pictures that still needed to be put into albums, things that could be displayed, or things that should be thrown away.

Mrs. McKnight began to read the letters written in bold black marker to label each box. Some of the words read Tonya, Pete, Vacations, Christmas, Thanksgiving, Trophies, Awards, and Birthdays. On the bottom shelf next to the box labeled "Birthdays," she saw a small red, wrapped box. Though Mrs. McKnight hadn't thought twice about removing Tonya's gift for Jada from underneath the Christmas tree a month ago, she'd never gotten the nerve to open it or throw it away. She'd been so angry about Jada spending Christmas with her family that she'd decided to remove the gift from under the tree. She didn't want Jada feeling welcome in her home. Not wanting to be reminded of Jada, she quickly looked away from the gift.

Mrs. McKnight walked over to the box labeled "Pete" and slid it off of the shelf. She placed it on the round coffee table and sat down on the couch. As she opened the box, she saw two graduation caps lying inside. She lifted the caps and placed them next to her on the couch. She then saw two graduation gowns neatly folded inside of the box. She made a mental note to bag them and give them to Pete so that he could decide what he wanted to do with them.

After neatly placing the caps and gowns on the couch beside her, Mrs. McKnight's eyes returned to Pete's box. She saw piles of pictures lying on top of each other. She must have either forgotten to put those pictures in an album, or just not gotten around to it. On top of the pile was an extra copy of Pete's college graduation picture.

This is already framed in the display case, Mrs. McKnight thought as she added it to the pile of things to give to her son.

As she returned her eyes to the open box, her face became rigid at the sight of the next picture that lay inside. She saw Pete, dressed in a black suit and golden yellow tie. His hands were linked with the hands of a girl dressed in a long, shiny yellow and gold gown. Long, dark, curly tendrils framed her light brown smiling face.

Mrs. McKnight looked at the image of Monica in her teenage days. She was a nice girl then, and she was still nice now. Mrs. McKnight's mind went back to when she had first met Monica. Pete had brought her by the house so that he could show her the suit and tie that he planned to wear to the prom. He had brought Monica into the kitchen for a drink, while Mrs. McKnight had been making dinner.

"Mom, this is Monica," a smiling Pete had said.

"Hello," Monica had replied through a smile.

Mrs. McKnight had stared back at her silently.

"Remember how I said I was taking a girl from my Physics class to the prom?" Pete had asked.

"Yes?" Mrs. McKnight had looked wide-eyed at her son.

"This is the girl I was talking about." Pete was still smiling. "Monica and I have been lab partners all year."

Monica had cheerfully joined in the conversation. "Yeah. We help each other out. He likes Math and I like Science, but neither one of us really like Physics."

"Pete has an A in Physics, so why would he need your help?" Mrs. McKnight had snobbishly remarked. She remembered seeing the smile on Monica's face fade away.

"We both have A's, Mom, because we work so well together," Pete had explained. "We have so much fun when we're working together, that we decided it would probably be fun to be each other's date to the prom."

Mrs McKnight had just stared at Monica in disdain.

"We're going to go downstairs, and I'm going to show Monica my suit," Pete had said.

Mrs. McKnight sat on the couch, and thought about how she really had absolutely no reason not to like Monica at that time. Even as a teenager, Monica was polite and hardworking. Pete told her that she had gotten a full academic scholarship to an Ivy League university.

Thoughts of the kindness that Monica had shown to her in the hospital began to flood Mrs. McKnight's mind. Monica had always greeted her with a smile, and asked if she was comfortable or in pain. She seemed to genuinely care about how she was feeling. Mrs. McKnight felt a twinge of guilt inside when she remembered the way she rebuked Monica for making small talk when it was only her way of being kind.

Suddenly, Mrs. McKnight remembered that Monica wasn't the only person she had reproached despite their attempts to show kindness. Mrs. McKnight pushed Pete's box to the side and walked over to the shelf that held the photo albums. She took the Christmas album she had just begun to work on off the shelf and walked back to the couch. Placing the album on the coffee table in front of her, Mrs. McKnight opened to the first page. The first five pictures had all been taken in the foyer. She saw Tim and Patty standing next to each other when they had first arrived. Mrs. McKnight saw a picture of her and Paul smiling and standing next to each other. Then she saw Tonya and Paul in one picture, her and Tonya in another picture, and her, Tonya, and Paul standing together with the Christmas tree in the background.

As she began flipping through pictures of them all opening gifts, Mrs. McKnight noticed that there weren't any pictures of Jada on display. She knew that her husband had taken pictures with Jada in them, because she remembered angrily separating them from the pile after she had picked up the developed photos from the store. She just couldn't remember what she had done with them after that.

Mrs. McKnight closed the album and picked it up to bring it back to the shelf. As she lifted it, she saw a photo envelope fall on the floor. She picked it up and slid the photos out. They were the missing pictures containing images of Jada. Mrs. McKnight saw a picture of Jada sitting on the living room couch next to Pete, and also a picture of the two of them eating dinner next to each other. Then she saw a picture of Jada sitting by herself on the family room couch. Mrs. McKnight noticed that in each picture, Jada's face was consumed with sadness. The only photo in which Jada had a bright smile on her face was the one she now held of Jada coming through the door with Pete's arm around her.

She sat there gazing at the photo. A part of her heart was softened as she thought about her encounters with Jada. She seemed like a genuinely nice person, and Pete seemed to sincerely love her. For a moment, Mrs. McKnight wondered if she should accept the marriage, and stop causing her son and his fiancé pain. Then she thought about how Pete would be marrying Jada, having kids with her, and starting a mixed family. Her son would have a black wife, and kids that were half black. An image of Monica's niece and nephew began to flow into her mind. Those kids always seemed wild and undisciplined. She frowned and tucked the photos back into the envelope. Then she forcibly stuffed the envelope in the back of the album. Mrs. McKnight didn't want a black daughter-in-law, and she didn't want black grandchildren. Even if they were mixed.

CHAPTER 38

Parting the Waters

"ARE YOU SURE YOUR MOTHER HASN'T changed her mind about coming to the wedding?" Jada looked across the dress rack at Tonya.

"She hasn't said a thing about the wedding," answered Tonya. "I guess if she doesn't come to the rehearsal tonight, we'll know for sure."

Jada's heart sunk. She had thought she wouldn't care whether Mrs. McKnight came to the wedding or not, but time had told otherwise. That was why Jada had asked Tonya to come with her to the dress shop. She had planned to pick out a dress with Tonya that her soon-to-be mother-in-law could wear to the wedding. Seeing as Mrs. McKnight had elected not to purchase a dress, Jada decided to purchase one as a gift for her. Then Tonya could bring the dress to Mrs. McKnight in hopes that she'd change her mind about not coming to the wedding.

Everyone, besides Mrs. McKnight, was excited about the wedding. Nicole said she was glad to see Jada finally happy again. Jada's family said they fully supported her and Pete's decision to go through with the wedding, and they would continue to pray for Mrs. McKnight.

"Ever since Pete moved out, my apartment seems so much bigger." Tonya held up a long champagne colored dress and then looked at Jada. "You still haven't moved into the house yet, right?"

"Nope." Jada shook her head. "Not until after the wedding." Jada looked at a shiny gold colored dress. "Most of my things are there already; I just haven't stayed there yet."

"Wow. I've got to hand it to you two. A lot of people wouldn't have been able to hold out as long as you guys did." Tonya walked with Jada to a rack of dresses that lined the wall. "So all of those days that you two had my apartment to yourself, nothing ever happened?"

Jada smiled slightly while shaking her head. "Nothing happened. I always went home before it did, and I never stayed there too late." Jada felt her smile grow a little bit wider. "But a lot's going to be happening at our house tomorrow night."

Tonya broke her gaze at Jada to begin scanning the dress rack. "That was just too much information, Jada. He is my brother, you know. I can only take but so much."

"Hey. You asked."

Tonya's hand dropped from the rack and she turned to look at Jada. "I like the gold dress you picked out. Why don't you just get that one?"

Jada walked back to the circular rack and searched for a size eight. "So you're sure this one will fit her?"

"Everything always fits my mother perfectly. She's a Pilates fanatic, and it pays."

Jada quickly remembered how her own mother was also into Pilates. If only Mrs. McKnight would give her and her family a chance, Jada thought she could actually realize that their families have some things in common. Maybe Mrs. McKnight and her mother could become friends just as Mr. McKnight and her father planned to do. One day, she thought to herself as she laid the dress on the checkout counter. She paid for the dress and waited for the clerk to cover it in plastic wrapping. Then she smiled as the woman handed the covered dress to her.

Jada walked with Tonya to her black Nissan Sentra. She handed the dress to her and waited for Tonya to neatly lay it on the back seat of her car.

Tonya closed the car door and turned around. "I'm going to drive this up to my mother now, and then I'll see you at the rehearsal."

Jada sat on the plush green chair and watched Pete take his place next to Pastor John. Then Josh, the best man, stood next to Pete. Jada couldn't believe it. Tomorrow she'd be crossing over to become a married woman.

Who would've thought she'd be marrying a white man? Jada chuckled to herself as the rest of the bridal party began to take their places at the front of the church. They had timed their entrances correctly this time, so Jada knew that this would be the final run through.

Jada looked at Pete. He was dressed in black pants and her favorite brown crew neck sweater that he sometimes wore when they would go out to eat in the evening. She loved seeing him in that sweater. It showed off the broadness of his chest so well. It also brought out the copper tone of his hair. Pete was wearing his hair different now in preparation for the wedding. He'd let it grow some, and he often added mouse and gel to make it stand up a bit. He looked so sexy today, that Jada began wishing that the rehearsal was the actual ceremony so that she and Pete could get up out of there and head to their new home.

Jada let out a long, deep breath to calm herself down and patiently waited for her cousin Joe to finish his solo. It was the first time he'd sang that night. As Jada allowed herself to listen to the silkiness of his voice, she was in awe. Give My All to You, by Myron, was the song she and Pete had selected for Joe to sing. It really captured their feelings about their relationship. Jada couldn't wait to be standing in front of Pete tomorrow as Joe sang that song.

Finally, with the solo completed, Pastor John briefly summarized the events of the ceremony in order, and the bridal party practiced their exit from the front of the church one last time. Then Jada stood in a circle next to Pete as Pastor John closed them out in prayer. She held Pete's hand and listened as the pastor thanked God for bringing Pete and Jada together. He also thanked God for bringing their families together and asked that God would bless each family member that was there, as well as the ones who were not there.

When Pastor John had said "Amen," Pete still held onto Jada's hand. As the bridal party and family members prepared to head over to the restaurant for the rehearsal dinner, they both began to walk out of the sanctuary together. They walked out into the February darkness toward the parking lot. When they had reached Jada's car, Pete stopped and turned to face Jada.

"This is where we first met," Pete looked at her with loving eyes.

Jada smiled. "I was wondering who the handsome guy was that was following Tonya and me. I had no idea you were her brother. I thought you were some cute guy trying to get her attention."

Pete grinned, allowing Jada to admire the dimples that she loved. "I'm just glad I got your attention." He reached out and ran his thumb down Jada's cheek to her chin. "I can't wait to make you my wife tomorrow." Pete leaned down and planted his lips right on the corner where Jada's lips met her cheek.

"Hey!" a familiar female voice shouted. "Break it up, you two. You're not married yet!"

Jada turned and saw Nicole walking toward them with Sasha and Tonya closely behind. Pete stepped away from Jada now that they had an audience.

"Pete, your guys are looking for you." Tonya said. "They're ready to go eat just like we are."

"All right," Jada surrendered. "I get the idea." She unlocked her car doors so the ladies could get in. "I'll see you at the restaurant," she said, looking at Pete.

Jada drove toward Mimi's Mediterranean Restaurant where her family had reserved a room for the rehearsal dinner. The ladies teased Jada all the way to the restaurant so much to the point where Jada threatened to pull over so that they could walk. She was only kidding though. Jada loved every minute of it. She didn't care if the whole world could see her and Pete's love.

At the restaurant, the families and wedding participants indulged in a magnificent buffet of food. There was salad, pasta, chicken marsala, pork tenderloin, and richly seasoned mashed potatoes. Jada sat next to her husband-to-be with a little of everything on her plate. He too had filled his plate with a healthy portion of each food. Jada looked around the private room to the tables full of friends and members of each family that were now enjoying the food. Even Pastor John and his wife Mary were there seated next to Jada's parents. Everything seemed almost perfect. But one person was still missing. Mrs. McKnight had not shown up at the rehearsal, and now she wasn't at the dinner either. Mr. McKnight sat there next to Jada's dad, alone. The hope Jada had that Mrs. McKnight would change her mind was slowly beginning to fade.

Right before the wedding rehearsal began, Tonya said that her mother had snatched the dress out of her hand and said, "I'm not coming and that's final." But Tonya also said that when she had left, she saw sadness in her mother's eyes. She told Jada that her mother may be having second thoughts. Now that Mrs. McKnight still hadn't joined them, Jada was finding it hard to keep the faith.

One thing that was no longer hard for her to do was to admit how much she loved Pete. Jada couldn't imagine why she had ever considered not marrying him. He was patient and he was kind. She had so much fun when she was with him. He had been nothing but loving toward her, and he had been trying hard to protect her from his mother's evil schemes. Most importantly, they both had learned to put God first in their lives and be obedient to his ways. Jada knew that Pete was going to make a great husband no matter what trials may come their way.

CHAPTER 39

Ribbon of Love

JADA WATCHED HER MOTHER PUT HER hand on the doorknob in response to the light tap they had heard on the door. Jada, her mother, and Nicole were using the church nursery as Jada's bridal dressing room. As Jada's mother carefully turned the knob, Nicole continued to smooth bronze color onto Jada's lips. Rebekah, the wife of Pete's cousin Aaron, slid through the crack Dana had provided through the door. She stood there wearing a brown sweater dress that stopped just at her knees and gold high healed shoes.

"The guests have started arriving!" she said excitedly. "Leah's already started passing out programs."

Nicole stood back away from Jada and capped the lipstick.

"Oh, Jada," Rebekah began. "You look beautiful!"

Jada reached for the hand held mirror Nicole was extending to her and put it in front of her face. The woman looking back at her looked like she belonged on the cover of a bridal magazine. Her light brown skin was glowing, her eyelashes looked full and long, her eyebrows were delicately arched, and her lips looked rich and shiny. "Wow, Nicole. I can't believe this is me!" Jada looked at her friend while already trying to blink back tears.

"No tears, Jada," Nicole said. "I just finished your make up, and we can't have you messing it up."

Dana walked up to her daughter, attempting to blink back tears as well. "I need to give my baby one last hug," she said.

Jada stood up and embraced her mother. "I love you, Mom. Thanks for everything you've done for me." She felt her mother squeeze her tighter.

"I love you too and always will. I'm so happy for you." Dana pulled back and looked at her daughter. "Would you like me to put your veil on for you?"

"Sure, Mom." Jada turned her back to her mother as Nicole handed Dana the veil.

Dana attached the veil to the middle of Jada's head using the short clear comb attachment. The veil covered the neat bun of hair delicately placed at the back of her head. Jada looked down at the white gold and diamond tennis bracelet that looped her wrist. It was still visible due to the unique gloves she had found that covered her arms but opened at the hands.

"Well I have my something new, and I have on a blue garter. I just don't have anything old or burrowed. Is that okay?" Jada asked. She seemed concerned.

Just then there was a knock on the door. Rebekah cracked the door, and then opened it wider to let the person on the other side through. A smiling Aunt Patty entered the room.

Aunt Patty gasped and put her hand to her chest. "Jada, you look lovely!"

Jada felt her face beam at the compliment.

Aunt Patty walked up to Jada holding a small blue box. "I thought you might like to wear these today." She handed the box to Jada.

Jada opened the box and gasped at the flashing jewels that lay inside. They looked like long, dangling icicles. "Are these real?"

Aunt Patty nodded. "They're white gold and diamond."

"She let Leah and I wear them on our wedding day too." Rebekah chimed in. "That way you'll have your something old and something burrowed as a two in one."

Jada removed the cosmetic earrings that hung in her ears, and carefully hooked each spiral, diamond earring to her ear. Filled with emotion, she smiled and stood to hug Aunt Patty. "Thank you."

"You're welcome, honey." Aunt Patty embraced Jada in a warm hug. "I'd better go get myself seated."

As Rebekah opened the door to let Aunt Patty through, the sound of instrumental music entered the small room. She looked back at Jada. "I think they're about to get started."

Dana motioned to Nicole. "We'd better get lined up so we'll be ready." Dana smiled at Jada one last time as she and Nicole followed Rebekah out the door.

Before the door could close, Jada's dad slipped in. He was dressed in a black tuxedo with a dark red vest and necktie. He looked very distinguished with his black hair closely shaven, and thin mustache. Scattered strands of gray could be seen around his hairline.

"So my little girl's getting married." He looked down at his daughter through a grin. "Are you ready?"

"Yes." Jada smiled at her dad. "How about you?"

"I'm feeling proud to walk my beautiful daughter down the aisle." He leaned in and kissed Jada's cheek. "I love you."

Jada wrapped her arms around her father. "I love you too, Dad." She heard the voice of CeCe Winans singing I Promise flow through the speakers. That meant that her bridesmaids were now walking down the aisle. "I think it's almost time." Jada looked excitedly and nervously at her dad.

Charles helped Jada pull her veil over her face, and then linked his arm with hers. She heard CeCe Winans' track come to an end. That was her cue to begin her walk toward her groom. They exited the room arm and arm. The melodic tune of Luther Vadross' Here and Now started to play. Just as the words began, Jada prepared to take her first step down the aisle next to her father. Her gaze was fixed on Pete. He stood next to Pastor John dressed in a black tuxedo, crimson vest, and matching necktie. His hair was spiked to perfection and his eyes seemed to lock with hers from her very first step.

Jada's eyes never left his until she reached the stage and realized that it wasn't a track from Luther Vandross' CD that was playing. It was Joe singing to a blank track of the song. That was a surprise to Jada, because she didn't think that Joe was supposed to sing until later in the ceremony. But Joe sounded good, and Pete looked good, so she could care less how the song was sung. She continued to smile as Pete grinned at her until the song was complete.

Pastor John welcomed the guests and opened up with an introduction and brief prayer of thanks for the couple, guests, and special occasion. Then Pastor John asked, "Who gives this woman to be married to this man?"

Charles and Dana answered in unison, "We do."

Jada looked at her mother who was seated on the front row of the left side. Then she glanced to the front row of the right side. Sadly, Mr. McKnight sat there without his wife. However, Tim and Patty were seated there next to him, smiling. Jada returned her eyes back to her very soon-to-be husband. She heard Pastor John direct them to take each other's hands.

Pastor John then directed his attention to Pete. "Peter Jordan McKnight, do you take Jada Journey Calloway for your lawful wedded wife, to live in the holy estate of matrimony? Will you love, honor, comfort, and cherish her from this day forward, forsaking all others, keeping only unto her for as long as you both shall live?"

Pete looked at Jada intently. "I do."

After being addressed the same question, with her eyes still lost in Pete's, Jada answered, "I do."

"At this time there will be a reading from first Corinthians thirteen that the couple have planned to recite to one another alternately," Pastor John announced.

Jada squeezed Pete's hand, and began, "Love is patient,"

Pete continued where she left off, "love is kind."

"It does not envy,"

"it does not boast,"

"it is not proud."

"It is not rude,"

"it is not self-seeking,"

"it is not easily angered,"

"it keeps no record of wrongs."

"Love does not delight in evil"

"but rejoices with the truth."

"It always protects,"

"always trusts,"

"always hopes,"

"always perseveres."

"Love never fails."

Jada was now sniffing and blinking rapidly to keep back her tears. She heard a few sniffles coming from the audience and people around her as well. This was now the point where Joe was supposed to begin singing Give My All To You by Myron. But as the track began to play, Joe was still not on stage, and Pastor John was handing the microphone to Pete.

Jada didn't have a clue as to what was going on, but then she stood there in awe as Pete began serenading her. She knew that he could be full of surprises, but never had she imagined that he would sing to her on their wedding day. She had heard him singing in church and singing along to songs while they rode together in the car, but she never knew that he could sing the way he was singing at that moment. She watched him as he gazed at her, and she listened as he put his heart and soul into the song. She continued to blink furiously as he stroked her left hand and concluded the selection.

Pete handed the microphone back to Pastor John and took Jada's other hand. Then the pastor directed them in the exchanging of traditional wedding vows. With their vows complete, Pete placed a platinum and diamond wedding band around Jada's finger. She slid the matching band on his in the exchanging of rings. Pastor John placed his hand on theirs and prayed over them. After the prayer, he pronounced them husband and wife with the permission to kiss.

Jada watched Pete lift her veil and lean toward her. She wrapped her arms around him and their lips met in a tender, passionate kiss.

Mrs. McKnight lay in bed staring at the dress her husband had hung on the bedroom door. It was after three o' clock in the afternoon and she still hadn't gotten out of bed. She was in pain from top to bottom. Her head was throbbing and she felt dull pain radiating through her ankle. She had told Paul that she wasn't getting out of bed today, yet he had the nerve to hang that dress she was supposed to wear to the wedding right where she could see it. She had never been one to get headaches, but today her head was in immense pain. Every time she turned her head it hurt.

She gently massaged her temples and stared at the muted television. Why was this happening to her? Her forehead crinkled in frustration. Why was she in so much pain? She wanted to cry. Then she remembered what Tonya had said to her yesterday when she dropped off the dress.

She had said, "Mom, just let go of your pride and come. Everyone's happy for Pete, except you."

It was true that she wasn't happy. She was miserable. Her son and daughter no longer wanted to be around her, and neither did her husband. She knew it was because she had been angry and irritable for months now. It saddened Mrs. McKnight that her children now barely came around. She missed spending time with her husband. By the time Paul came home for dinner, Mrs. McKnight had already eaten, so he would take his food into the basement. He wouldn't come back up until it was time for bed. Sometimes he wouldn't even come upstairs to bed. She would find him sleeping in the family room. She couldn't remember the last time they had been intimate. Over the past six months her health and her marriage had taken turns for the worse.

As the throbbing in both her head and ankle increased, Mrs. McKnight decided to get up to take something for her pain. She slowly walked down the stairs and into the foyer. Just as she was passing the front door, the doorbell rang. Feeling surprised and curious, Mrs. McKnight looked through the side window at the young man standing on her front step with a bouquet of colorful roses in a glass vase.

She cracked open the door. "May I help you?"

"I have a special delivery for Mrs. Trisha McKnight," replied the young man.

"I'm Trisha McKnight."

He extended a clipboard to her. "Please sign here."

Mrs. McKnight signed her name, feeling confused. She then took the bouquet from the young man's hand.

"Have a nice day." The young man turned and walked away.

Mrs. McKnight closed the door behind her and walked to the family room. Who would have flowers delivered to her? A pondering look covered her face as she sat down on the couch and placed the vase of roses on the coffee table. She carefully fingered through the roses until she saw the folded card in the center of the bouquet. Feeling anxious, Mrs. McKnight unfolded the card and began reading the message inside.

I was thinking about you today. I hope your ankle is fully recovered. It was a pleasure to serve you as your nurse. I pray that God will bless your family with peace, love, and joy. Love, Monica Whyte.

Mrs. McKnight's mind traveled back to her stay in the hospital six months ago. Suddenly, she felt like her eyes were being opened. The fact that the note had been delivered to her today, of all days, made her realize that her negative attitude was disrupting the peace from a day that was supposed to be filled with joy for her son and his bride.

On the second half of the card, it looked like Monica had written a poem. With shaking hands, Mrs. McKnight continued to read.

Red, for the blood that Jesus shed for us that day
White, the color of our souls when our sins are washed away
Yellow, like the sun God created to give us light
Black, like the sky that God's moon and starts shine in at night
Yellow, black, red, white.
Shade doesn't matter in God's sight.
All were created by Him above,
So embrace the colors of His love.

Mrs. McKnight knew right then that it had not been a coincidence that Monica had ended up being her nurse. She began to realize that she was not showing love to her son or the woman he loved by rejecting Jada because of the color of her skin. Monica had not just nursed the wound inside her ankle. Mrs. McKnight now realized that through her loving actions, Monica was nursing the pride and prejudice that was eating away at her heart. As she sat there staring at the card and vase, Mrs. McKnight's heart was convicted right at that moment.

"I'm sorry. I'm so sorry," she sobbed. As she cried, Mrs. McKnight began to feel God's presence healing her heart.

She didn't know how long she sat there crying into her hands, but when the tears would no longer fall, she wiped her face. Then she stood up and walked to the coat closet where she took out the phone book. She searched the list of names until she saw Monica Whyte. She picked up the phone to call her, but there was no answer. So she walked to her craft room instead.

Mrs. McKnight sat down at her desk and took out her personalized stationary. She constructed a heart felt letter to Monica. When she believed she had written everything she wanted to say, she reread it silently.

Dear Monica,

Thank you for your unfailing patience with me. I am truly sorry for the way I treated you as a young girl, and as my nurse. You have helped me heal in so many ways, and I would love to have the chance to share my experience with you. I look forward to the opportunity to speak with you again. May God richly bless you.

Sincerely,

Trisha McKnight

Mrs. McKnight sealed and addressed the letter and placed it on the table in her foyer. The mailman hadn't come yet, so she would put it in her mailbox on her way out. As she hurried upstairs to take a shower, she noticed that the pain in her head and ankle was completely gone.

Pete sat at the head table and watched his wife dance with her father. As he glanced toward the table where his own father was seated, he wondered how his mother was feeling at this moment. Pete was a little disappointed that she had not been able to let go of her pride and come to the wedding. With his mother not there to support him, it felt like a piece of the puzzle was missing. Having her there would have made the day complete. He still hoped that one day she would finally come to her senses. Pete let his eyes travel back to Jada, and all thoughts about his mother rolled away. He could feel the joy bubbling inside of him. He was thrilled to be married to the love of his life. Right now, it was all about him and Jada, and the new life they had just begun.

***

With Pete watching them from the head table, Jada and Charles smiled through their father daughter dance. They rocked back and forth to the voices of the Temptations singing My Girl. As Jada danced, she thought of what a great example her father had been to her. Had he not ministered to her about love and forgiveness, she would have still been bitter and not standing there the happy bride that she was. Jada glanced at her new husband and saw him grinning contentedly as he patiently sat waiting for her to return to him. The harmonic voices began to fade away, and Jada smiled at her dad as she headed back to Pete.

As Jada walked across the dance floor, the croons of Boyz II Men came bellowing through the speakers. She immediately recognized the tune. They were about to play Mama. Jada felt herself becoming instantly frustrated. She thought they had told him that there was no mother-son dance. She changed courses and headed toward the DJ.

"Ladies and gentleman," the DJ began. "I'd like to call to the dance floor Mrs. Trisha McKnight, mother of the groom, and Peter McKnight for the mother-son dance. Give them a hand ladies and gentleman."

Jada glared at the DJ. She stopped in front of him and yelled to be heard above the music. "His mother's not here!"

"What?" the DJ yelled back.

"I said 'his mother's not here!'" Jada repeated.

As the DJ stopped the music, Jada noticed that the guests were mumbling as they looked toward the other end of the dance floor. To her surprise, there stood Mrs. McKnight.

Pete and Tonya immediately got up from their seats and headed to the dance floor. Jada's parents and Mr. McKnight approached the dance floor as well. They all stopped where Jada and Mrs. McKnight now stood face to face.

Mr. McKnight gave his wife a stern look. "Trisha, what's going on? You refuse to come to the wedding, but now you show up in the middle of the reception." His statement sounded more like a question.

Pete looked at his mother firmly. "Mom, I don't want you saying anything to Jada today, unless it's an apology."

Mrs. McKnight's eyes filled with moisture as she looked at Jada and Pete. "I'm sorry."

The mouths of everyone around them were now open. Jada's eyes widened with surprise.

Mrs. McKnight looked at Jada with wet eyes. "I hope that one day you can forgive me, Jada. I'm sorry for the way I treated you." Her voice broke with emotion.

Jada stood there, shocked by what she was hearing. It was the first time she had ever heard Mrs. McKnight say her name. The sincerity in Mrs. McKnight's voice caught Jada off guard.

As she looked at Mrs. McKnight, a feeling of strength began to come over Jada. "The way you treated me did make me feel inadequate and insecure, but it's in the past. I've already forgiven you."

Overcome with emotion, Mrs. McKnight covered her face with her hands. Her shoulders shook for a moment. She then looked out at the suspicious family members who had gathered around the dance floor. All of Jada's closest family members had made a curious circle around them.

As tears streamed down her cheeks, Mrs. McKnight took a deep breath. "I judged Jada without taking the time to get to know her. I've had a lot of time to think about how I've treated her and I was wrong. I know that you all are a loving family. I can tell by the type of person that Jada is. I now know that color doesn't matter. What matters is love. With all the love that Pete and Jada have inside of them, they're going to have a great marriage, and they're going to raise wonderful kids." She focused her eyes on Dana and Charles. "I hope you can forgive me for the way I treated your daughter."

For a moment, Dana and Charles stood speechless. Dana then reached out and embraced Mrs. McKnight in a hug. Charles smiled with contentment.

Through a wet face, Mrs. McKnight smiled and turned to Jada. "I have a gift in the car that I owe you." Her face grew humble. "Do you mind if I dance with your husband first?"

Jada shook her head to indicate that she didn't mind. As Mama, by Boyz II Men, began to play again, Jada remained standing at the DJ table and watched Pete dance with his mother. Pete had never given up on his mother, and his love for his mom had encouraged Jada not to give up on her either. They had prayed and believed together that Pete's mother would have a change of heart, and now there she was. Jada let out a long sigh of relief. It had been a long journey, but they had all finally made it. They had become one family now, and Jada could feel the love in the midst.

When the song faded out, the DJ put on a slow jam and couples began to head to the dance floor. Pete and Mrs. McKnight headed back over to Jada.

"Let's have the photographer take another group picture," Pete suggested.

Jada and Pete rounded up their bridesmaids, groomsmen, and their parents. Then they headed outside at the photographer's urging to take a picture in the fiery red sunset. The new family lined themselves up in front of the Housatonic River with the sun setting behind them and flashed genuine smiles for the camera.

Before going back inside, Jada turned around and looked at the red of the sunset. In her mind, she saw God's unconditional love and Jesus' blood that washes our sins away. Jada knew that Pete had been sent to her to help her forgive and learn to love unconditionally. Jada knew that Pete's mother also understood God's unconditional love and was also ready to do her best to show that kind of love.

Jada felt Pete slip his hand around hers as they walked back into the reception hall. The sound of Intro singing their remix of Stevie Wonder's Ribbon In The Sky could be heard from the speakers. Jada followed Pete to the dance floor. She noticed that Gene and Nicole had now become dance partners. Tonya and Fernando were already staring into each other's eyes as they rocked away. From what Jada and Pete saw, there might be a few more colors in their family's ribbon of love. But for now, Pete and Jada McKnight would do.

LATER THAT NIGHT

JADA DRAINED HER VANILLA SCENTED BATH water, and quickly cleaned the tub. Then she slipped on her red and black satin and lace baby-doll lingerie outfit. This is it, she thought to herself.

She opened the bathroom door. To her surprise, she saw red rose petals trailing from the bathroom to their bedroom door. With a smile on her face, she turned the knob and slowly entered the bedroom. Rose petals were sprinkled on the hardwood floor. Red candles on crystal candlesticks were lit around the bed.

There she saw Pete, propped on one elbow, lying on their queen-sized bed. The crimson bed sheet covered only the lower half of his body. His muscular upper frame had a golden glow in the candlelight. He looked like Adam in the Garden of Eden, awaking to find his Eve.

A look of wonder filled his eyes as he stared at Jada. "Come here, Mrs. McKnight," he said.

Jada repeated the words in her head, Mrs. McKnight. Just yesterday, she would have shuddered at the sound of that name. But at that moment she felt peace and then joy sweep over her. God had done a wonderful thing at their wedding reception that night. He knitted two uniquely different families into one colorful family of love.

Jada climbed into her husband's arms, as he pulled the sheet over them and held her close. She felt Pete's hands gently caress her brown body as she looked up at his buttermilk face and into his light brown eyes. With their passions rising, their lips came together and they began to kiss one another deeply.

"I love you, doll," Pete sighed. "I'm so glad God sent me to you."

"I'm so glad you found me. I love you," Jada replied.

Surrounded by the flickering flames of candlelight, Pete and Jada ignited their own marital flame as they joined their bodies together in the ultimate expression of love.

Made in the USA
Middletown, DE
30 June 2016